Praise for Barbara Delinsky's

While My Sister Sleeps

"Fast-paced entertainment. . . . In her new family drama, Delinsky examines the roles people unconsciously play in families."
—*USA Today*

"Delinsky is interested in how the lies we tell for love can destroy us instead—and she lays out this particular deception so painstakingly that even the most honest reader will sympathize."
—*People*

"An engaging writer who knows how to interweave several stories about complex relationships and keeps her books interesting to the end. Her special talent for description gives the reader almost visual references to the surroundings she creates."
—*The Star-Ledger* (Newark, NJ)

"Delinsky treads the same domestic themes as fellow bestseller Jodi Picoult."
—*Entertainment Weekly*

"[She] may be as adept at chronicling contemporary life in New England as any writer this side of John Updike."
—*The Times Union* (Albany)

"Delinsky delves deeper into the human heart and spirit with each new novel."
—*The Cincinnati Enquirer*

BARBARA DELINSKY

While My Sister Sleeps

Barbara Delinsky is a *New York Times* bestselling author with more than thirty million copies of her books in print. She lives with her family in New England.

www.barbaradelinsky.com

WHILE MY SISTER SLEEPS

WHILE MY SISTER SLEEPS

Barbara Delinsky

ANCHOR BOOKS
A Division of Random House, Inc.
New York

FIRST ANCHOR BOOKS MASS-MARKET EDITION, OCTOBER 2009

Copyright © 2009 by Barbara Delinsky

The Library of Congress has cataloged the Doubleday edition as follows:
Delinsky, Barbara.
While my sister sleeps / Barbara Delinsky.—1st ed.
p. cm.
1. Sisters—Fiction. 2. Women runners—Fiction. 3. Marathon running—Fiction. 4. Myocardial infarction—Patients—Fiction. I. Title.
PS3554.E4427 W48 2008
813'.54—dc22 2008028457

Anchor ISBN: 978-0-307-47322-6

www.anchorbooks.com

Printed in the United States of America
10 9 8 7 6 5 4 3 2

To Andrew and Julie
forever

WHILE MY SISTER SLEEPS

chapter 1

THERE WERE DAYS WHEN MOLLY SNOW LOVED HER
sister, but this wasn't one. She had risen at dawn to be
Robin's water-bearer, only to learn that Robin had changed
her mind and decided to do her long run in the late afternoon, fully expecting Molly to accommodate her.

And why not? Robin was a world-class runner—a
marathoner with a dozen wins under her belt, incredible
stats, and a serious shot at making the Olympics. She was
used to people changing their plans to suit hers. She was the
star.

Resenting that for the millionth time, Molly said no to
late afternoon and, though Robin followed her from bedroom to bathroom and back, refused to give in. Robin could

have easily run that morning; she just wanted to have breakfast with a friend. And wouldn't Molly love to do that herself! But she couldn't, because her day was backed up with work. She had to be at Snow Hill at seven to tend to the greenhouse before customers arrived, had to do purchasing, track inventory and sales, preorder for the holiday season; and on top of her own chores, she had to cover for her parents, who were on the road. That meant handling any issues that arose and, worse, leading a management meeting—not Molly's idea of fun.

Her mother wouldn't be pleased that she had let Robin down, but Molly was feeling too put-upon to care.

The good news was that if Robin went running late in the day, she would be out when Molly got home. So, with the sun bronzing her face through the open windows, Molly mellowed as she drove back from Snow Hill. She pulled mail from the roadside box, without asking herself why her sister never did it, and swung in to crunch down the dirt drive. The roses were a soft peach, their fragrance all the more precious for the short life they had left. Beyond were the hydrangeas she had planted, turned a gorgeous blue by a touch of aluminum, a sprinkling of coffee grounds, and lots of TLC.

Pulling up under the pin oak that shaded the cottage she and Robin had rented for the past two years but were about to lose, Molly opened the back of the Jeep and began to unload. She was nearly at the house, juggling a drooping split-leaf philodendron, a basket of gourds, and a cat carrier, when her cell phone rang.

She could just hear it. *I'm sorry for yelling this morning, Molly, but where are you now? My car won't start, I'm in the middle of nowhere, and I'm beat.*

Molly was shifting burdens to free up a key when the phone rang again. A third ring came as she knelt to put her load down just inside the door. That was when guilt set in. Seconds shy of voice mail, she pulled the phone from her jeans and flipped it open.

"Where are you?" she asked, but the voice at the other end wasn't Robin's.

"Is this Molly?"

"Yes."

"I'm a nursing supervisor at Dickenson-May Memorial. There's been an accident. Your sister is in the ER. We'd like you to come."

"A car accident?" Molly asked in alarm.

"A running accident."

Molly hung her head. Another one of those. *Oh, Robin,* she thought and peered into the carrier, more worried about the little amber cat huddled inside than about her sister. Robin was a chronic daredevil. She claimed the reward was worth it, but the price? A broken arm, dislocated shoulder, ankle sprains, fasciitis, neuroma—you name it, she'd had it. This small cat, on the other hand, was an innocent victim.

"What happened?" Molly asked distractedly, making little sounds to coax the cat out.

"The doctor will explain. Do you live far?"

No, not far. But experience had taught her that she

would only have to wait for X-rays, even longer for an MRI. Reaching into the carrier, she gently drew out the cat. "I'm ten minutes away. How serious is it?"

"I can't tell you. But we do need you here."

The cat was shaking badly. She had been found locked in a shed with ten other cats. The vet guessed she was barely two.

"My sister has her phone with her," Molly tried, knowing that if she could talk directly with Robin, she would learn more. "Does she have cell reception?"

"No. I'm sorry. Your parents' number is here with yours on her shoe tag. Will you call them, or should I?"

If the nurse was holding the shoe, the shoe was off Robin's foot. A ruptured Achilles tendon? That would be bad. Worried in spite of herself, Molly said, "They're out of state." She tried humor. "I'm a big girl. I can take it. Give me a hint?"

But the nurse was immune to charm. "The doctor will explain. Will you come?"

Did she have a choice?

Resigned, Molly cradled the cat and carried it to her bedroom at the back of the cottage. After nesting it in the folds of the comforter, she put litter and food nearby, and then sat on the edge of the bed. She knew it was dumb bringing an animal here when they had to move out in a week, but her mother refused to let another cat live at the nursery, and this one needed a home. The vet had kept her for several days, but she hadn't done well with the other animals. She wasn't only malnourished; she looked like she had been at the losing end of more than one fight. Her little body was poised, as if she expected another blow.

"I won't hurt you," Molly whispered assuredly and, giving the cat space, returned to the hall. She trickled water on the philodendron—too much too soon would only drain through—then took it to the loft and set it out of direct light. It, too, needed TLC. But later.

First, a shower. It would have to be a quick one—she could put off the hospital only so long. But the greenhouse was hot in September, and after a major delivery of fall plants, she had spent much of the afternoon breaking down crates, moving pots, reorganizing displays, and sweating.

The shower cleared her mind. Back in her room to dress, though, she couldn't find the cat. Calling softly, she looked under the bed, in the open closet, behind a stack of cartons. She checked Robin's room, the small living room, even the basket of gourds—which was one more thing to pack, but it filled an aesthetic need and could easily hide a small cat.

She would have looked further, if her conscience hadn't begun to nag. Robin was in good hands at the hospital, but with their parents somewhere between Atlanta and Manchester, and with her own name first on that tag, Molly had to make tracks.

Letting her long hair curl as it dried, she put on clean jeans and a tee. Then Molly drove off with the cell in her lap, fully expecting that Robin would call. She would be resilient and sheepish—unless it truly was an Achilles rupture, which would mean surgery and weeks of no running. They were all in trouble if that was the case. An unhappy Robin was a misery, and the timing of this accident couldn't be worse. Today's fifteen-miler was a lead-up to the New York marathon. If she placed among the top ten American women there, she would be guaranteed a spot at the Olympic trials in the spring.

The phone didn't ring. Molly wasn't sure if that was good or bad, but she didn't see the point of leaving a message for her mother until she knew more. Kathryn and Robin were joined at the hip. If Robin had an ingrown toenail, Kathryn felt the pain.

It was lovely to be loved that way, Molly groused and, in the next breath, felt remorse. Robin had worked hard to get where she was. And hey, Molly was as proud of her as the rest on race day.

It just seemed like running monopolized all their lives.

Resentment to remorse and back was such a boringly endless cycle that Molly was glad to pull up at the hospital. Dickenson-May sat on a bluff overlooking the Connecticut River just north of town. The setting would have been charming if not for the reasons that brought people here.

Hurrying inside, Molly gave her name to the ER desk attendant and added, "My sister is here."

A nurse approached and gestured her to a cubicle at the end of the hall, where she fully expected to see Robin grinning at her from a gurney. What she saw, though, were doctors and machines, and what she heard wasn't her sister's embarrassed, *Oh, Molly, I did it again,* but the murmur of somber voices and the rhythmic beep of machines. Molly saw bare feet—callused, definitely Robin's—but nothing else of her sister. For the first time, she felt a qualm.

One of the doctors came over. He was a tall man who wore large, black-framed glasses. "Are you her sister?"

"Yes." Through the space he had vacated, she caught a glimpse of Robin's head—short dark hair messed as usual, but her eyes were closed, and a tube was taped over her mouth. Alarmed, Molly whispered, "What happened?"

"Your sister had a heart attack."

She recoiled. "A *what*?"

"She was found unconscious on the road by another runner. He knew enough to start CPR."

"*Unconscious*? But she came to, didn't she?" She didn't have to be unconscious. Her eyes might be closed out of sheer exhaustion. Running fifteen miles could do that.

"No, she hasn't come to yet," said the doctor. "We pulled up hospital records on her, but there's no mention of a heart problem."

"Because there isn't one," Molly said and, slipping past him, went to the bed. "Robin?" When her sister didn't reply, she eyed the tube. It wasn't the only worrisome thing.

"The tube connects to a ventilator," the doctor explained. "These wires connect to electrodes that measure her heartbeat. The cuff takes her blood pressure. The IV is for fluids and meds."

So much, so soon? Molly gave Robin's shoulder a cautious shake. "Robin? Can you hear me?"

Robin's eyelids remained flat. Her skin was colorless.

Molly grew more frightened. "Maybe she was hit by a car?" she asked the doctor, because that made more sense than Robin having a heart attack at the age of thirty-two.

"There's no other injury. When we did a chest X-ray to check on the breathing tube, we could see heart damage. Right now, the beat is normal."

"But why is she still unconscious? Is she sedated?"

"No. She hasn't regained consciousness."

"Then you're not trying hard enough," Molly decided and gave her sister's arm a frantic jiggle. "Robin? Wake up!"

A large hand stilled hers. Quietly, the doctor said, "We suspect there's brain damage. She's unresponsive. Her pupils don't react to light. She doesn't respond to voice commands. Tickle her toe, prick her leg—there's no reaction."

"She can't have brain damage," Molly said—perhaps absurdly, but the whole scene was absurd. "She's in *training*." When the doctor didn't reply, she turned to her sister again. The machines were blinking and beeping with the regularity of, yes, machines, but they were unreal. "Heart or brain—which one?"

"Both. Her heart stopped pumping. We don't know how long she was lying on the road before she was found. A healthy thirty-something might have ten minutes before the lack of oxygen would cause brain damage. Do you know what time she started her run?"

"She was planning to start around five, but I don't know whether she made it by then." *You should have known, Molly. You would have known if you'd driven her yourself.* "Where was she found?"

The doctor checked his papers. "Just past Norwich. That would put her a little more than five miles from here."

But coming or going? It made a difference if they were trying to gauge how long she had been unconscious. The location of her car would tell, but Molly didn't know where it was. "Who found her?"

"I can't give you his name, but he's likely the reason she's alive right now."

Starting to panic, Molly held her forehead. "She could wake up and be fine, right?"

The doctor hesitated seconds too long. "She could. The next day or two are crucial. Have you called your parents?"

Her parents. Nightmare. She checked her watch. They wouldn't have landed yet. "My mom will be devastated. Can't you do something before I call them?"

"We want her stabilized before we move her."

"Move her *where?*" Molly asked. She had a flash shot of the morgue. Too much *CSI.*

"The ICU. She'll be watched closely there."

Molly's imagination was stuck on the other image. "She isn't going to *die,* is she?" If Robin died, it would be

Molly's fault. If she had been there, this wouldn't have happened. If she hadn't been such a rotten sister, Robin would be back at the cottage, swigging water and recording her times.

"Let's take it step by step," the doctor said. "First, stabilization. Beyond that, it's really a question of waiting. There's no husband listed on her tag. Does she have kids?"

"No."

"Well, that's something."

"It's *not*." Molly was desperate. "You don't *understand*. I can't tell my mother Robin is lying here like this." Kathryn would blame her. Instantly. Even before she knew that it truly was Molly's fault. It had always been that way. In her mother's eyes, Molly was five years younger and ten times more troublesome than Robin.

Molly had tried to change that. She had grown up helping Kathryn in the greenhouse, taking on more responsibility as Snow Hill grew. She had worked there summers while Robin trained, and had gotten the degree in horticulture that Kathryn had sworn would stand her in good stead.

Working at Snow Hill wasn't a hardship. Molly loved plants. But she also loved pleasing her mother, which wasn't always an easy thing to do, because Molly was impulsive. She spoke without thinking, often saying things her mother didn't want to hear. And she hated pandering to Robin. That was her greatest crime of all.

Now the doctor wanted her to call Kathryn and tell her

that Robin might have *brain damage* because *she,* Molly, hadn't been there for her sister?

It was too much to ask of her, Molly decided. After all, she wasn't the only one in the family.

While the doctor waited expectantly, she pulled out her phone. "I want my brother here. He has to help."

chapter 2

CHRISTOPHER SNOW WAS AT THE KITCHEN TABLE, EATing the flank steak that his wife had grilled. Erin sat on his right and, on his left, in her high chair, was their daughter, Chloe.

"Is the steak okay?" Erin asked when he was halfway done.

"Great," he answered easily. Erin was a good cook. He never had complaints.

Helping himself to seconds, he picked out a kernel of corn from the salad and put it on the baby's tray. "Hey," he said softly, "how's my pretty girl?" When the child grinned, he melted.

"So," Erin said, "was your day okay?"

Nodding, he dug into his salad. The dressing was great, too. Homemade.

The baby struggled to pick up the corn. Christopher was intrigued by her concentration. After a time, he turned up her hand and put the slick nugget into her palm.

"How was your meeting with the Samuel people?" Erin asked.

He nodded *fine,* and ate more of his salad.

"Did they agree to your terms?" she asked, sounding impatient. When he didn't reply, she said, "Do you care?"

"Sure, I care. But they'll be a while going over the figures, so for now it's out of my hands. Why are you angry?"

"Chris, this is a major building project for Snow Hill. You spent all last night preparing your pitch. I want to know how it went."

"It went fine."

"That doesn't tell me much," she remarked. "Want to elaborate? Or maybe you just don't want me to know."

"Erin." He set down his fork. "We've talked about this. I've been working all day. I want to get away from it now."

"So do I," his wife said, "only my day revolves around an eight-month-old child. I need adult conversation. If you won't talk about work, what do we talk about?"

"Can't we just enjoy the silence?" Christopher asked. He loved his wife. One of the best parts of their relationship was that they didn't have to talk all the time. At least, that's what he thought.

But she didn't let it go. "I need stimulation."

"You don't love Chloe?"

"Of *course,* I love her. You *know* I love her. Why do you always ask me that?"

He raised his hands in bewilderment. "You just said she wasn't enough. You were the one who wanted a baby right away, Erin. You were the one who wanted to stop working."

"I was pregnant. I *had* to stop working."

He didn't know what to say. They had been the town's favorite newlyweds, both blond-haired and green-eyed (Chris would say his own eyes were hazel, but no one cared about the distinction). They had been an adorable couple.

But what was happening between them now was not so adorable. "Go back to work, then," he said, trying to please her.

"Do you want me to work?"

"If you want to."

She stared at him, those green eyes vivid. "And do what with Chloe? I don't want her in day care."

"Okay." He hated all arguments, but this was the worst. "What *do* you want?"

"I want my husband to talk to me during dinner. I want him to talk to me after dinner. I want him to discuss things with me. I don't want him to come home and just stare at the Red Sox. I want him to share his day with me."

Quietly, he said, "I'm an accountant. I work in the family business. There is nothing exciting about what I do."

"I'd call a new building project exciting. But if you hate it, quit."

"I don't hate it. I love what I do. I'm just saying that it doesn't make for great conversation. And I'm really tired tonight." And he actually did want to watch the Red Sox. He loved the team.

"Tired of me? Tired of Chloe? Tired of *marriage*? You used to talk to me, Chris. But it's like now that we're married—now that we have a baby—you can't make the effort. We're twenty-nine years old, but we sit here like we're eighty. This is not working for me."

Unsettled, he stood up and took his plate to the sink. *This is not working for me* sounded like she wanted out. He couldn't process that.

At a loss, he picked up the baby. When she put her head on his chest, he held it there. "I'm trying to give you a good life, Erin. I'm working so you don't have to. If I'm tired at night, it's because my mind has been busy all day. If I'm quiet, maybe that's just who I am."

She didn't give in. "You weren't that person before. What changed?"

"Nothing," he said carefully. "But this is life. Relationships evolve."

"This isn't just life," she fought back. "It's *us*. I can't *stand* what we're becoming."

"You're upset. Please calm down."

"Like *that'll* make things better?" she asked, seeming angrier than ever. "I talked with my mother today. Chloe and I are going to visit her."

The phone rang. Ignoring it, he asked, "For how long?"

"A couple of weeks. I need to figure things out. We have

a problem, Chris. You're not calm, you're *passive*." The phone rang again. "I ask what you think about putting Chloe in a playgroup, and you throw the question back at me. I ask if you want to invite the Bakers for dinner Saturday night, and you tell me to do it if I want. Those aren't answers," she said as another ring came. "They're evasions. Do you *feel* anything, Chris?"

Unable to respond, he reached for the phone. "Yeah."

"It's me," his sister said in a high voice. "We have a serious problem."

Turning away from his wife, he ducked his head. "Not now, Molly."

"Robin had a heart attack."

"Uh, can I call you back?"

"Chris, I need you here now! Mom and Dad don't know yet."

"Don't know what?"

"That Robin had a *heart attack*," Molly cried. "She keeled over in the middle of a run and is still unconscious. Mom and Dad haven't landed. I can't do this alone."

He stood straighter. "A heart attack?"

Erin materialized beside him. "Your dad?" she whispered, taking Chloe.

Shaking his head, he let the child go. "Robin. Oh boy. She pushed herself too far."

"Will you come?" Molly asked.

"Where are you?" He listened for a minute, then hung up the phone.

"A heart attack?" Erin asked. "*Robin*?"

"That's what Molly said. Maybe she's exaggerating. She gets wound up sometimes."

"Because she shows emotion?" Erin shot back, but then softened. "Where are your parents?"

"Flying home from Atlanta. I'd better go."

He stroked Chloe's head, and, conciliatorily, touched Erin's. She was the one on his mind as he set off. They had only been married for two years, the last third of that time with a child, and he tried to understand how dramatically her life had changed. But what about him? She asked if he felt things. He felt responsibility. Right now, he felt fear. Being quiet was part of his nature. His dad was the same way, and it worked for him.

Molly, on the other hand, tended to be highly imaginative. Robin might have suffered something, but a heart attack was pushing it. He might have talked her down over the phone, if he hadn't wanted to get out of the house. Erin needed time to cool off.

Did he feel things? He sure did. He just didn't get hysterical.

Putting on his blinker, he turned in at the hospital. He had barely parked at the Emergency entrance when Molly was running toward him, her blond hair flying and her eyes panicked.

"What's happening?" he asked, leaving the car.

"Nothing. *Nothing*. She hasn't woken up!"

He stopped walking. "Really?"

"She had a *heart* attack, Chris. They think there's brain damage."

She drew him inside, through the waiting room to a far cubicle—and there was Robin, inert as he had never seen her. He stood at the door for the longest time, looking from her body to the machines to the doctor by her side.

Finally, he approached. "I'm her brother," he said and stopped. He didn't know where to begin.

The doctor began for him, repeating some of what Molly had said and moving on. Chris listened, trying to take it in. At the doctor's urging, he talked to Robin, but she didn't respond. He followed the physician's explanation of the various machines and stood with him at the X-ray screen. Yes, he could see what the doctor was pointing out, but it was too bizarre.

He must have been looking doubtful, because the doctor said, "She's an athlete. Hypertrophic cardiomyopathy—inflammation of the heart muscle—is the leading cause of sudden death in athletes. It doesn't happen often, and the instance is even lower in women than men. But it does happen."

"Without warning?"

"Usually. In cases where there's a known family history, a screening echocardiogram may diagnose it, but many victims are asymptomatic. Once she's in the ICU, she'll have an intensivist heading her case. He'll work with a cardiologist and a neurologist."

Chris knew his parents would want the best, but how could he know who that was? Feeling inadequate, he looked at his watch. "What time do they land?" he asked Molly.

"Any minute."

"Are you going to call?"

"You are. I'm too upset."

And Chris wasn't? Did he have to be *visibly* shaking? Facing the doctor, he said, "Is this—what is she—comatose?"

"Yes, but there are different levels of coma." He pushed up black glasses with the back of his hand. "At most levels, patients make spontaneous movements. The fact that your sister hasn't suggests the highest level of coma."

"How do you measure it?" Chris asked. He didn't know what he was looking for, only knew that Molly was standing at his elbow taking in every word, and that his parents would ask the same questions. Numbers had meaning. They were a place to start.

"A CAT scan or an MRI will show if there's tissue death, but those tests will have to wait until she's more stable."

Chris glanced at Molly. "Try calling Mom and Dad."

"I can't," she whispered, looking terrified. "I was supposed to be with her. This was my fault."

"Like it wouldn't have happened if you'd been waiting five miles down the road? Be real, Molly. Call Mom and Dad."

"They won't believe me. *You* didn't."

She was right. But *he* didn't want to call. "You're better with Mom than I am. You'll know what to say."

"You're older, Chris. You're the *man*."

He took the phone from his pocket. "Men stink at things

like this. It'll be enough when she sees my caller ID." With a sharp look, he passed her the phone.

KATHRYN SNOW TURNED ON HER BLACKBERRY AS SOON as the plane landed. She hated being out of touch. Yes, the nursery was a family operation, but it was her baby. If there were problems, she wanted to know.

While the plane taxied through the darkness to the terminal, she downloaded new messages and scrolled through the list.

"Anything interesting?" her husband asked.

"A note from Chris—his meeting went well. A thank-you for the Collins' wedding shower. And a reminder from the newspaper that the article on flowering kale is due at the end of the week."

"It's all written, ready to go."

Appreciative, she smiled. Charlie was her marketing chief, a behind-the-scenes guy who had a knack for writing ad copy, press releases, and articles. In his quiet way, he invited trust. When he suggested to TV producers that Kathryn was the one to discuss fall wreaths, they believed him. He had single-handedly won her a permanent spot on the local news and a column in a home magazine.

Speaking of which, "*Grow How* is due at the end of the week," she mused. "It'll be for the January edition, which is always the toughest. Molly knows the greenhouse better than I do. I'll have her write it." She returned to the Black-Berry. "Robin didn't e-mail. I wonder how her run went.

She was worried about her knee." Accessing voice mail next, she smiled, frowned, smiled again. She finished listening just as the plane reached the jetport. Releasing her seat belt, she put the BlackBerry in her pocket and followed Charlie into the aisle. "*Voice* mail from Robin. She had to drive herself because Molly refused to help. What's wrong with that child?"

"Just refused? No excuse?"

"Who knows," Kathryn murmured, but grinned. "Good news, though. Robin got another call from the powers-that-be wanting to make sure she's set to run New York. They're counting on her for the trials next spring. The Olympics, Charlie," she mouthed, afraid to jinx it by speaking aloud. "Can you imagine?"

He lowered her suitcase from the overhead bin. Kathryn was lifting its handle when her BlackBerry jangled. Christopher's number was on the screen, but it was Molly's voice that came on saying, "It's me, Mom. Where are you?"

"We just landed. Molly, why couldn't you help Robin? This was an important run. And did you lose your phone again?"

"No. I'm with Chris at Dickenson-May. Robin had an accident."

Kathryn's smile died. "What kind of accident?"

"Oh, you know, running. Since you weren't around they called us, but she probably wants you here. Can you come by on your way home?"

"What kind of accident?" Kathryn repeated. She heard forced nonchalance. She didn't like that, or the fact that

Chris was at the hospital, too. Chris usually left crises to others.

"She fell. I can't stay on now, Mom. Come straight here. We're in the ER."

"What did she hurt?"

"Can't talk now. See you soon."

The line went dead. Kathryn looked worriedly at Charlie. "Robin had an accident. Molly wouldn't say what it was." Frightened, she handed him the BlackBerry. "You try her."

He handed the phone back. "You'll get more from her than I will."

"Then call Chris," she begged, offering the BlackBerry again.

But the line of passengers started to move, and Charlie gestured her on. She waited only until they were side by side in the jetport before saying, "Why was Chris there? Robin never calls him when there's a problem. Try him, Charlie. Please?"

Charlie held up a hand, buying time until they reached the car. The BlackBerry didn't ring again, and Kathryn told herself that was a good sign, but she couldn't relax. She was uneasy through the entire drive, imagining awful things. The instant they parked at the hospital, she was out of the car. Molly was waiting just inside the ER.

"That was a cruel phone call," Kathryn scolded. "What happened?"

"She collapsed on the road," Molly said, taking her hand.

"*Collapsed*? From heat? Dehydration?"

Molly didn't answer, just hurried her down the hall. Kathryn's fear grew with each step. Other runners collapsed, but not Robin. Physical stamina was in her genes.

She caught her breath at the cubicle door. Chris was there, too. But that couldn't be Robin, lying senseless and limp, hooked to machines—machines that were keeping her alive, the doctor said after explaining what had happened.

Kathryn was beside herself. The explanations made no sense. Nor did the X-rays. Her daughter's hand, which she clutched, was inert as only a sleeping person's hand would be.

But she didn't wake up when the doctor called her name or pinched her ear, and even Kathryn could see that her pupils didn't dilate in response to light. Kathryn figured the person doing the prodding wasn't doing it right, but she had no better luck when she tried it all herself—not when she pleaded with Robin to open her eyes, not when she begged her to squeeze her hand.

The doctor kept talking. Kathryn no longer took in each word, but the gist got through with devastating effect. She didn't realize she was crying until Charlie handed her a tissue.

When Robin's face blurred, she saw her own—the same dark hair, same brown eyes, same intensity. Two peas in a pod, they had neither the fair features, nor the laid-back approach to life of the others in the family.

Kathryn refocused. Charlie seemed desolate, Chris stupefied, and Molly was stuck to the wall. Silence from all three? Was that it? If no one else questioned the status quo, it was up to her—but hadn't it always been that way when it came to Robin?

Defiant, she faced the doctor. "Brain damage isn't an option. You don't know my daughter. She's resilient. She comes back from injuries. If this is a coma, she'll wake up. She's been a fighter since birth—since *conception*." She held Robin's hand tightly. They were in this together. "What comes next?"

"Once she's stabilized, we move her upstairs."

"What's her condition now? Wouldn't you call it stable?"

"I'd call it critical."

Kathryn couldn't handle that word. "What's in her IV?"

"Fluids, plus meds to stabilize her blood pressure and regulate the rhythm of her heart. It was erratic when she first arrived."

"Maybe she needs a pacemaker."

"Right now, the meds are working, and besides, she wouldn't be able to handle surgery."

"If the choice is between surgery and death—"

"It isn't. No one's letting her die, Mrs. Snow. We can keep her going."

"But why do you say her brain is damaged?" Kathryn challenged. "Only because she doesn't respond? If she's been traumatized by a heart attack, wouldn't that explain the lack of response? How do you test for brain damage?"

"We'll do an MRI in the morning. Right now, we don't want to move her."

"If there's damage, can it be repaired?"

"No. We can only prevent further loss."

Feeling thwarted, Kathryn turned on her husband. "Is this all they can do? We can live with a heart condition, but not brain damage. I want a second opinion. And where are the specialists? This is only the *ER,* for God's sake. These doctors may be trained to handle trauma, but if Robin has been here for three hours and hasn't been seen by a cardiologist, we need to have her moved."

She saw Molly shoot a troubled look at Charlie, but Charlie didn't say anything, and Lord knew Chris wouldn't. Frightened and alone, Kathryn turned back to the doctor. "I can't sit and wait. I want to be proactive."

"Sometimes that isn't possible," he replied. "What's crucial right now is getting her up to the ICU. The doctor there will call in specialists. This is all standard protocol."

"Standard protocol isn't *good* enough," Kathryn insisted, desperate that he understand. "There is nothing standard about Robin. Do you *know* what she does with her life?"

The eyes behind the glasses didn't blink. "Yes, I do. It's hard not to know when you live around here. Her name is in the local papers so often."

"Not only the *local* papers. That's why she has to recover from this. She works all over the country with budding track stars. We're talking teenage girls. They can't see this. They can't *begin* to think that the reward for training hard and aiming high is . . . is *this*. Okay, you may not have had a case like this before, but if that's so, just say it and we'll have her transferred."

She searched family faces for agreement, but Charlie seemed stricken, Chris was frozen, and Molly simply looked pleadingly from her father to her brother and back.

Useless. All three.

So Kathryn told the doctor, "This isn't a personal indictment. I'm just wondering whether doctors in Boston or New York would have more experience with injuries like these."

Molly touched her elbow then. Kathryn looked at her youngest in time to hear her murmur, "She needs to be in intensive care."

"Correct. I just don't know where."

"Here. Let her stay here. She's alive, Mom. They got her heart going, and it's still beating. They're doing all they can."

Kathryn arched a brow. "Do you know that for fact? Where *were* you, Molly? If you'd been with her, this wouldn't have happened."

Molly paled, but she didn't retreat. "I couldn't have prevented a heart attack."

"You could have gotten her help sooner. You have issues, Molly. You've always had issues with Robin."

"But *look*," the girl urged, glancing at the medical personnel hovering at the door. "They're waiting to take her upstairs, and we're slowing them down. Once she's there, we can talk about specialists, even about moving her; but right now, shouldn't we be giving her every possible chance?"

MOLLY FOLLOWED THE OTHERS TO THE ICU AND WATCHED the team get Robin settled. At one point she counted five doctors and three nurses in the room, as frightening as it was reassuring. Monitors were adjusted and vital signs checked, while the respirator breathed in and out. Every minute or two someone spoke loudly to Robin, but she didn't respond.

Kathryn left the bedside only when a doctor or nurse needed access. The rest of the time, she held Robin's hand, stroked her face, urged her to blink or moan.

As Molly watched from the wall, she was haunted by the knowledge that her mother was right. If Robin had started breathing sooner, there would be no brain damage. If Molly had been with her, Robin would have started breathing sooner.

But she wasn't the only one who had let Robin down. She couldn't blame her mother for being frantic back in the ER, but where was her father? He was supposed to be the calm one. What had he been *thinking* letting Kathryn go on like that? Even Chris could have spoken up.

They didn't have the guts, Molly decided, and then modified the thought. They *knew* better.

You have issues. You've always had issues with Robin. She knew her mother was upset, but Molly was feeling guilty enough to be flayed by the words. As the minutes passed and the machines beeped, she remembered occasionally deleting a phone message, buying the wrong energy bar, misplacing a favorite running hat. Each offense could be balanced with something good Molly had done, but the good was lost in the guilt.

Chris left at midnight, her father at one. Charlie had tried to get Kathryn to leave with him, to no avail. Molly suspected that her mother feared something awful would happen if she wasn't there to stand guard. Kathryn had always been protective of Robin.

Hoping her own presence might go a little way toward making up to Kathryn for what she had not done earlier that day, Molly stayed longer. By two, though, she was falling asleep in her chair. "Are you sure I can't drive you home?" she asked her mother.

Kathryn barely looked up. "I can't leave," she said and added, "Why weren't you with her, Molly?" with a speed suggesting she was brooding about just that.

"I was at Snow Hill," Molly tried to explain. "The management meeting, remember? I didn't know how long it would run. How could I commit to Robin?" There was also the issue of the cat. But putting a cat before her sister was pathetic.

Kathryn didn't ask how long the meeting had run. She didn't even ask how it had *gone*. If she was brooding, it was about Molly's negligence toward Robin, not about Snow Hill.

And Molly was guilty. That thought beat her down, before she finally broke the silence by asking, "Can I get you something, Mom? Coffee, maybe?"

"No. But you can cover for me at work."

Startled, Molly blew out a little breath. "I can't go to work with Robin like this."

"You have to. I need you there."

"Can't I do something here?"

"There's nothing to do here. There's plenty to do at Snow Hill."

"What about Dad? Or Chris?"

"No. You."

She doesn't want me around, Molly realized, her feeling of devastation growing. But she was too tired to beg for mercy, too wiped out even for tears. After asking Kathryn to call her if there was any change, she slipped out the door.

chapter 3

MOLLY'S COTTAGE FACED SOUTH, BRINGING YEAR-round sun to the loft, while the forest behind the backyard shaded the bedrooms and scented the air with pine. Molly had learned of it by accident when its owner, who was leaving New Hampshire for Florida, came to the nursery looking for a home for dozens of plants. Now the owner wanted to renovate and sell, so Molly and Robin were being kicked out.

Molly thought the vintage kitchen was just fine. She loved the weathered feel of the wide-planked floors and casement windows. Although Robin complained that the place was drafty and the rooms dark, she didn't really care where she lived. She was gone half the time—to Denver,

Atlanta, London, L.A. If she wasn't running a marathon, half marathon, or 10 K, she was leading a clinic or appearing at a charity event. Most of the cartons in the living room were Molly's. Her sister didn't have many things to pack.

Robin was happy to move. Molly was not, but she would go along, just to have Robin be her old self again.

Waiting for her mother's call, Molly slept with the phone in her hand, far from soundly. She kept jolting awake with the hollow feeling of knowing something was wrong and not remembering what it was. Too soon she'd recall, then lie awake, frightened. Without Robin getting up to ice one body part or another, the house was eerily quiet.

At six a.m., needing companionship, Molly looked for the cat. It had eaten and used the litter. But the creature was nowhere to be found, though Molly searched even harder than she had the night before. She had been wasting time then, wanting Robin to wait for *her* for a change. How petty *that* had been. Brain damage was light years worse than a torn-up ankle or knee.

Of course, Robin may have woken up by now. But who to call? Molly couldn't risk dialing her mother, didn't want to waken her father, and Chris was no use. The station at the ICU would give only an official status report. Critical condition? She didn't want to hear that.

So she watered and pruned the philodendron in the loft, picked hopeless leaves off an ill ficus, misted a recovering fern—all the while whispering sweet nothings to the plant until she ran out of sweet nothings to say, at which point she put on jeans and drove to the hospital. Preoccupied, she went straight to intensive care, hoping against hope that Robin's eyes would be open. When they weren't, her heart sank. The respirator was soughing, the machines blinking. Little had changed since she'd left the night before.

Kathryn was asleep in a chair by the bed, her head touching Robin's hand. She stirred at Molly's approach and, groggy, looked at her watch. Tiredly, she said, "I thought you'd be at the nursery by now."

Molly's eyes were on her sister. "How is she?"

"The same."

"Has she woken up at all?"

"No, but I've been talking to her," Kathryn said. "I know she hears. She isn't moving, because she's still traumatized. But we're working on that, aren't we, Robin?" She stroked Robin's face with the back of her hand. "We just need a little more time."

Molly remembered what the doctor had said about the lack of response. It wasn't a good sign. "Have they done the MRI?"

"No. The neurologist won't be here for another hour."

Grateful that her mother wasn't yelling about the wait, Molly gripped the handrail. *Wake up, Robin,* she urged and searched for movement under Robin's eyelids. Dreaming would be a good sign.

But her lids remained smooth. Either she was deeply asleep or truly comatose. *Come on, Robin,* she cried with greater force.

"Her run was going well until she fell," Kathryn remarked and brought Robin's hand to her chin. "You'll get back there, sweetie." She caught a quick breath.

Thinking she had seen something, Molly looked closer.

But Kathryn's tone was light. "Uh-oh, Robin. I almost forgot. You're supposed to meet with the Concord girls this afternoon. We'll have to postpone." As she glanced up, she tucked her hair behind her ear. "Molly, will you make that call? She's also scheduled to talk with a group of sixth graders tomorrow in Hanover. Tell them she's sick."

"Sick" was a serious understatement, Molly knew. And how not to be sick in this place—with lights blinking, machines beeping, and the rhythmic hiss of the respirator as a steady reminder that the patient couldn't breathe on her own? Between phones and alarms, it was even worse out in the hall.

Molly had had a break from it, but Kathryn had not. "You look exhausted, Mom. You need sleep."

"I'll get it."

"When?" she asked, but Kathryn didn't answer. "How about breakfast?"

"One of the nurses brought me juice. She said that the most important thing now is to talk."

"I can talk," Molly offered, desperate to help. "Why don't you take my car and go home and change? Robin and I have lots to discuss. I need to know what to do with the boxes of sneakers in her closet."

Kathryn shot her a look. "Don't touch them."

"Do you know how old some of them are?"

"Molly . . ."

Molly ignored the warning. There was normalcy in arguing. "We have to be out in a week, Mom. The sneakers can't stay where they are."

"Then pack them up and bring them home with the rest of your things. When you find another place, we'll move them there. And then, of course, there's the issue of her car, which is parked on the side of the road somewhere between here and Norwich. I'll send Chris to get that. I still can't believe you didn't drive her there."

Molly couldn't either, but that was hindsight. Right now, Robin made absolutely no show of hearing the conversation. And suddenly, for Molly to pretend that any part of this was normal didn't work. To be talking about old sneakers, when the runner was on *life support*?

Heart in her throat, she searched Robin's face. As a child, Molly had often waited for her sister to wake up, eyes glued to her face, hopes rising and falling on each breath. Molly would be grateful for *any* movement now.

"If you need help packing," Kathryn offered, "ask Joaquin. Check his schedule when you get to Snow Hill."

"I really want to stay here," Molly said.

"This isn't about what you want, Molly. It's about what'll help most. Someone has to be at Snow Hill."

"Chris will be there."

"Chris can't communicate with people. You can."

Molly felt tears spring up. "I'm a *plant* person, Mom. I communicate with *plants*. And this is my *sister* lying here. How can I work?"

"Robin would want you to work."

Robin would? Molly fought hysteria. Robin had never worked a forty-hour week in her life. She ran, she coached, she waved, she smiled—all in her own time. She had an office at the nursery and, nominally, was in charge of special events, but her active involvement was minimal. On the day of those events, she was away more often than not. She was an athlete, not a wreath maker or a bonsai specialist, as she had told Molly more than once.

But to repeat that to Kathryn now would be just as cruel as asking aloud what would happen if Robin never woke up.

SNOW HILL HAD BEEN FAMILY-OWNED SINCE ITS INCEPTION over thirty years before. Spread over forty acres of prime land on New Hampshire's border with Vermont, it was renowned for trees, shrubs, and garden supplies. But its crown jewel—with solar panels that stored summer heat for winter use, a mechanism for recycling rainwater, and computer-regulated humidity control—was a state-of-the-art greenhouse. That was Molly's domain.

Even after stopping to see Robin, she was the first to arrive at Snow Hill. The greenhouse had been Molly's childhood haven in times of stress, and though she no longer scrunched into corners or hid under benches, she found the surroundings therapeutic when she was upset. For all its technological advancement, it was still a greenhouse.

The cats greeted her with rubs and meows. Counting six, she scratched heads and bellies, then she uncoiled hoses and began watering plants. While the cats scampered, she moved from section to section, watering heavily here, lightly there. Some plants craved daily drink, others preferred to dry out. Molly catered to each.

A bench of overturned potted plants suggested that rabbits had visited during the night, likely chased off by the cats, who were effective guards, though not known for neatness. Setting the hose aside, Molly righted the plants, retamped soil, removed bruised leaves, then swept up. After spraying the last of the dirt down the drain, she resumed watering.

The sun wasn't high yet, but the greenhouse was bright. This early hour, before the heat rose, was definitely the time to water. And Molly enjoyed it as much as her plants did. When the spray glistened in oblique rays of sun and the soil grew moist and fragrant, the greenhouse was peaceful. It was predictable.

She needed that today. Pushing Robin from mind didn't work for more than a minute or two at a time. It took constant effort.

Re-coiling the hose and putting it where no customer could possibly trip, she wandered the aisles. She checked a new shipment of chrysanthemums for aphids, and carefully cut brown tips from several Boston ferns. Wandering deeper among the shade benches, she spoke softly to peperomias, syngoniums, and spathiphyllum. They weren't showy plants, certainly nothing like bromeliads, but they were steadfast and undemanding. Carefully, she checked them for moisture. The shade cloth, regulated by a computer program, would rise later to protect them from the bright light they hated, but the worst of summer's intensity was over.

Her African violets were thrilled at that. They consistently went out of flower to protest the heat, for which reason Molly carried fewer in July and August. She had just restocked and now rearranged the pots to showcase their blooms.

She picked up several tags from the floor, made note of a bench that needed mending, and, for a lingering moment, stood in the middle of what she saw as her realm. There was comfort in the warm, moist air and the rich smell of earth.

Then she saw Chris, who was never here this early. He stood under the arch separating the greenhouse from the checkout stands, and he didn't look happy.

Heart pounding, Molly approached him. "Did something happen?"

He shook his head.

"Were you at the hospital?"

"No. Dad's there. I just talked with him."

"Do they know anything more?"

"No."

"Is Mom okay?"

Chris shrugged.

A shrug didn't do it for Molly. She needed answers. She needed *reassurance*. "How could this happen?" she cried in a burst of pent-up fear. "Robin is totally healthy. She should have woken up by now, shouldn't she? I mean, it's fine for her to be unconscious for a little while, but this long? What if she doesn't wake up, Chris? What if there *is* brain damage? What if she *never* wakes up?"

He looked upset but said nothing, and just when Molly would have screamed in frustration, Tami Fitzgerald approached. Tami managed their garden products store. She was rarely in this early either, but there was purpose in her stride.

Molly wasn't in the mood for a delivery problem. Not now.

Apparently, neither was Tami. "I heard Robin was in the hospital," she said, looking concerned. "How is she?"

Actually, Molly would have preferred a delivery problem. Snow Hill people were like family. What should she tell them? Not having run this past Kathryn or Charlie, she deferred to Chris, but his face remained blank. Curious, she asked Tami, "How did you hear?"

"My brother-in-law works with the EMTs. He said something about her heart."

So much for just saying Robin was "sick."

Again, Molly waited for Chris, but he was silent. And someone needed to say something. "We don't know much more," Molly finally said. "There was some kind of heart episode. They're running tests."

"Wow. Is it serious?"

How to answer that? Too much, and Kathryn would be angry. "I just don't know. We're waiting to hear."

"Will you tell me when you do? Robin's the last person I imagine having even a cold."

"Really," Molly said in agreement and added, "I'm sure she'll be fine."

"That's good. Robin is absolutely the best. Let me know if there's anything I can do."

Molly waited only until Tami disappeared into the garden center before glaring at Chris. "*I* didn't know what to say. Couldn't you have helped?"

"You did great."

"But what if it's not true? What if she's not fine?"

He put his hands in his pockets.

"Last night?" Molly hurried on, needing to confess. "When the hospital first called? I thought it was nothing. The nurse told me to come right away, but I didn't want to have to wait for Robin, so I did things around the house for a while. She was in a coma, and I was taking a shower so I'd *feel* nice."

He looked pained but remained silent.

"She has to wake up," Molly begged. "She's the backbone of this family. What would Mom *do* if she doesn't wake up?" When Chris shrugged, she cried, "You're no help!"

"What do you want me to *say*?" he asked. "I don't *have the answers*!"

Molly checked her watch. More than an hour had passed since she'd left the hospital. "Maybe Mom does. I'm going back to the hospital."

KATHRYN STOOD BETWEEN HER HUSBAND AND THE NEUROLO-gist, studying MRI shots of a brain. The doctor said it was

Robin's, and yes, Robin had been wheeled out of intensive care and been gone the requisite amount of time. But based on what the doctor was saying about the shade and delineation of dead tissue, this film couldn't be Robin's. The damage here was profound.

Kathryn was more frightened than she had ever been in her life, and Charlie's arm around her brought little comfort. She looked to the intensivist for clarification, but he was focused on the neurologist.

We'll get another specialist, she thought. *Two specialists, two opinions.*

But there was Robin's name, clearly marked on the film. And there was all that dark area showing no flow of blood. There was nothing ambiguous about it.

The neurologist went on. Kathryn tried to listen, but it was hard to hear over the buzz in her head. Finally, he stopped speaking. It was a minute before she realized it was her turn.

"Well," she said, struggling to think. "Okay. How do we treat this?"

"We don't," the neurologist said in a compassionate voice. "Once brain tissue dies, it's gone."

Darting a look at Robin, she shushed him. The last thing Robin needed was to be told that something was gone. Softly, she said, "There has to be a way to reverse it."

"I'm afraid there isn't, Mrs. Snow. Your daughter was without oxygen for too long."

"That's because the fellow who found her waited too long before starting CPR."

"Not his fault," Charlie said softly.

The intensivist came forward. "He's considered a Good Samaritan, which means he's protected by law. Your daughter had a heart attack. That's what caused the brain damage. According to this film—"

"No film tells the whole story," Kathryn broke in. "I know Robin's with us. Maybe an MRI isn't the right test. Or maybe something was wrong with the machine." She turned pleadingly to Charlie. "We need another machine, another hospital, another something."

Kathryn had first fallen in love with Charlie for his silence. His quiet support was the perfect foil for her own louder life. He didn't have to speak to convey what he felt. His eyes were expressive. Right now, they held a rare sadness.

"Does brain damage mean brain dead?" she asked in a frightened whisper, but he didn't answer. "Brain dead means *gone,* Charlie!" When he tried to draw her close, she resisted. "Robin is *not* brain dead."

chapter 4

MOLLY WAS STUNNED. "BRAIN DEAD?" SHE ASKED from the door.

Kathryn looked at her. "Tell them, Molly. Tell them how vibrant your sister is. Tell them what she plans to do next year. Tell them about the *Olympics*."

Molly stared at her sister. Brain dead meant she would never wake up, would never breathe on her own, would never speak again. *Ever*.

Tearing up, she went to her father's side. He took her hand.

"Tell them, Molly," Kathryn begged.

"Are they sure?" Molly asked Charlie.

"The MRI shows severe brain damage."

Sharing her mother's desperation, Molly turned to the neurologist. "Can't you shock her or something?"

"No. Dead tissue can't respond."

"But what if it's not all dead? Isn't there another test?"

"An EEG," he replied. "That will show if there's any electrical activity at all in the brain."

Molly didn't have to ask what it meant if there was none. She knew her mother was thinking the same thing when Kathryn quickly said, "It's too early for that test."

But Molly needed grounds for hope. "Don't you want to know, Mom? If there is electrical activity, there's your answer."

"Robin isn't brain dead," Kathryn insisted.

"The term isn't one we take lightly, Mrs. Snow," the doctor said. "We use the Harvard criteria, which calls for a pair of EEGs taken a day apart. The patient isn't considered brain dead unless both show the total absence of electrical activity."

"We need to do this, Mom," Molly urged. "We need to know."

"Why?" Kathryn asked sharply. "So they can turn off the machines?" Disengaging herself from Charlie, she took Robin's hand and leaned close. "The New York Marathon is going to be amazing. We're staying at the Peninsula, right, sweetie?" Looking up at the doctors, she explained, "Marathoners taper their training in the week before the race. We thought we'd do some shopping."

The intensivist smiled sympathetically. "We don't have to do the EEG right now. There's time. Give it some thought."

"No EEG," Kathryn ordered, and no one argued.

Moments later, Molly was alone with her parents. Kathryn continued to talk to Robin as if she could hear. It was understandable. Robin had always been the focus of family activity. For all the times Molly had resented that, she couldn't imagine it not being so.

It was like cutting back an orchid that had once been gorgeous, and not knowing if it would ever grow again. Something beautiful once . . . now maybe dead.

Kathryn broke into her thoughts. "I really need you at Snow Hill, Molly. Please don't fight me on this."

Fine. Molly wouldn't argue. But there was bad news. "I just came from there. Tami Fitzgerald's brother-in-law is an EMT. He told her about Robin." At Kathryn's look of alarm, she added, "He didn't say much. But Tami was asking. All I said was that Robin would be fine."

"That's good."

"It won't be for long, Mom. Word'll spread. Hanover isn't a big place, and the running community is tight. And Robin has friends all over the country—all over the *world*. They'll be calling." Glancing around, she spotted the plastic bag that lay on the floor by the wall. It held Robin's clothes and fanny pack. "Is her cell phone there?"

"I have it," Kathryn said. "It's off."

Like that would solve the problem? "Her friends will leave messages. When she doesn't answer, they'll call the house. What do you want me to say?"

"Say she'll get back to them."

"Mom, these are close friends. I can't lie. Besides, they could be supportive. They could come talk to Robin."

"We can do that ourselves."

"We can't tell them it's nothing. If Robin's had a massive heart attack—"

"—it's no one's business but ours," Kathryn declared. "I don't want people looking at her strangely once she's up and around again."

Molly was incredulous. To hear her mother talk, Robin might wake up in a day or two and be fine, be *perfect*. But even mild brain damage had symptoms. Best-case scenario, she would need rehab.

Molly turned to her father. "Help me here, Dad."

"With what?" Kathryn asked, preempting Charlie.

Molly shot an encompassing look around the room. Her eyes ended up on Robin, who hadn't moved an inch. "I'm having as much trouble with this as you are."

"You're not her mother."

"She's my sister. My *idol*."

"When you were *little*," Kathryn chided. "It's been a while since then."

My fault, *my fault,* Molly wailed silently, feeling all the worse. But how to do something positive now? She appealed to her father again. "I don't know what to do, Dad. If you want me at Snow Hill fine; but we can't pretend this isn't serious. Robin is on life support."

"For now," Kathryn said with such conviction that Molly might have stayed simply to absorb her confidence.

Gently, Charlie said, "If anyone asks, sweetheart, just tell them that we're waiting for test results, but that we'd appreciate their prayers."

"Prayers?" Kathryn cried. "Like it's life or death?"

"Prayers are for all kind of things," Charlie replied and glanced up as a nurse came in.

"I'd like to do a little work here—bathing, checking tubes," the woman said. "I shouldn't be long."

Molly went out to the hall. Her parents had no sooner joined her when her mother said, "See? They wouldn't be bothering with mundane things like bathing if there was no point. I'm using the ladies' room. I'll be right back."

She had barely taken two steps, though, when she stopped. A man had approached and was staring at her. Roughly Robin's age, wearing jeans and a shirt and tie, he looked reputable enough to be on the hospital staff, but with haunted eyes and a dark shadow on his jaw, he was clearly upset.

"I'm the one who found her," he said in a tortured voice.

Molly's heart tripped. When Kathryn didn't reply, she hurried forward. "The one who found Robin on the road?" she asked eagerly. They had so few facts. His coming was a gift.

"I was running and suddenly there she was."

He seemed bewildered; Molly identified with that. "Was she conscious when you were with her? Did she move at all? *Say* anything?"

"No. Has she regained consciousness yet?"

She was about to answer—truthfully, because his eyes

begged for it—when Kathryn came to life. Shrilly, she charged, "You have *some gall* asking that after standing there paralyzed for *how* long before calling for help?"

"Mom," Molly cautioned, but her mother railed on.

"My daughter is in a *coma* because she was deprived of oxygen for too *long*! Did you not know that every *single second* counted?"

"*Mom.*"

"I started CPR as soon as I realized she had no pulse," he said quietly, "and I kept it up while I called for help."

"You started CPR," Kathryn mocked. "Do you even know how to *do* CPR? If you'd done it right, she might be *fine*."

Appalled, Molly gripped her mother's arm. "That's unfair," she protested because, family loyalties aside, she felt a link with this man. Kathryn was blaming him for something he hadn't done, and, boy, could Molly empathize. That he had revived Robin was reason enough for her to connect with him. "Did my sister make *any* sound?" she asked. "A moan, a whimper?" Either would be an argument against brain damage.

His eyes held regret. "No. No sound. While I was compressing her chest, I kept calling her name, but she didn't seem to hear. I'm sorry," he said, returning to Kathryn. "I wish I could have done more."

"So do I," Kathryn resumed her attack, "but it's too late now, so why are you here? We're trying to deal with something so horrifying you can't *begin* to understand. You shouldn't have come." She looked around. "Nurse!"

"*Mom,*" Molly shushed, horrified. She wrapped an arm around Kathryn, but felt far worse for the Good Samaritan. "My mother's upset," she told him. "I'm sure you did what you could," but he was already backing up. He had barely turned and set off down the hall when Kathryn turned her wrath on Molly.

"You're *sure* he did all he could? How do you know that? And how did he get up here?"

"He took the elevator," Charlie said from behind Molly. His voice was soft but commanding. Kathryn quieted instantly. With a single breath, she composed herself and continued on to the restroom.

As soon as she was out of earshot, Molly turned on her father, prepared to condemn Kathryn's outburst, but the sorrow on his face stopped her cold. With Kathryn so involved, it was easy to forget that Robin was Charlie's daughter, too.

Thoughts of the Good Samaritan faded, replaced by the reality of Robin. "What do we do?" Molly asked brokenly.

"Ride it out."

"About Mom. She's out of control. That guy didn't deserve that. He was only trying to help, like *I* try to help, but I'm almost afraid to speak. Everything I say is wrong."

"Your mother is upset. That's all."

Still there was a weight on Molly's chest. "It's more. She blames me."

"She just blamed that fellow, too. It's an irrational thing."

"But I blame *myself*. I keep thinking it should be me on that bed, not Robin."

He drew her close. "No. No. You're wrong."

"Robin's the good one."

"No more so than you. This was not your fault, Molly. She'd have had the heart attack whether you'd driven her or not, and no one—*least* of all Robin—would have had you crawling along in your car, keeping her in sight the whole time. At any given point, you might have been fifteen minutes away."

"Or five," Molly said, "so the damage would have been less. But if I was the one in a coma, Robin would be able to help Mom. She won't let *me* help. What do I say? How do I act?"

"Just be you."

"That's the problem. I'm me, not Robin. And if they're right about her brain," Molly went on, because her father was so much more reasonable than her mother, and the life support issue was preying on her, "this isn't about life and death. It's only about death." She choked up. "About when it happens."

"We don't know for sure," he cautioned quietly. "Miracles have been known to happen."

Charlie was a deeply religious man, a regular churchgoer, though he usually went alone, and he never complained about that. He accepted that what worked for him didn't necessarily work for his wife and his kids. For the first time in her life, Molly wished otherwise.

Charlie believed in miracles. She wanted to believe in them, too.

He pressed her cheek to his chest. His warmth, so familiar, broke her composure. Burying her face in his shirt, she cried for the sister she alternately loved and hated, but who now couldn't breathe on her own.

Murmuring softly, he held her. Molly was barely regaining control when she heard her mother's returning footsteps. Taking a quick breath, she wiped her face with her hands.

Naturally, Kathryn saw the tears. "Please don't cry, Molly. If you do, I will; but I don't want Robin seeing us upset." She pulled out her ringing cell phone and summarily turned it off. The BlackBerry followed. "I can't talk," she said with a dismissive wave. "I can't think about anything right now except making Robin better. But I would like to clean up while the nurse is with her. If you cover for me here, Molly, your father will run me home. We'll be right back. Then you can go to Snow Hill."

Molly wanted to argue, but knew the futility of it. So she glanced at her father. "Someone has to call Chris."

Charlie's eyes went past her. "No need. Here he comes."

CHRIS HAD TRIED TO WORK, BUT HIS HEART WASN'T IN IT. He kept thinking about the mess his life was in, and since he didn't know what to say to Erin, the hospital seemed the place to be. One look at his parents, though, and he had second thoughts. They were grim.

"No change?" he asked when he was close enough.

The silence answered his question.

"The MRI shows brain damage," Molly told him.

Kathryn shot her an annoyed look. "MRIs don't show everything."

"They need to do an EEG," Chris said.

"Mom wants to wait."

"Please, Molly," Kathryn said. "You're not helping."

When Molly opened her mouth to protest, Charlie intervened. "She wasn't being critical, Kathryn."

"She's rushing things."

"No. The doctors suggested the EEG. She's just updating Chris." Reaching for Kathryn's hand, he told Chris, "I'm taking your mother home. We'll be back."

Watching them leave, Chris saw no evidence that Kathryn was arguing, which made his point. His father didn't have to say much to be effective. Erin had to understand that.

"Nightmare," Molly murmured.

"Mom or Robin?"

"Both. I agree about the EEG. We need to do it, but Mom's afraid. Chris, the nurse is with Robin. If she leaves, will you go in? I'm going down for coffee. Want any?"

He shook his head. When he was alone, he leaned against the wall. And how not to think about Robin? His earliest memories in life were vague ones of her sitting him in a room and building forts around him, or dressing him up in old costumes. He couldn't have been more than three. More clearly, he remembered tagging along with her on

Halloween night. He would have been five or six then. By the time he was ten, she was taking him down black diamond ski slopes. He wasn't anywhere near a good enough skier, but Robin was—and with Robin it was all about the challenge.

"Hey," came a familiar voice.

He looked up to see Erin and felt instant relief. He wanted his wife with him now—needed her. "Where's Chloe?" he asked.

"With Mrs. Johnson. How's Robin?"

Not good, he replied with a look. "The MRI shows brain damage."

"From a *heart* attack? How could she have had a heart attack?"

Chris had passed the disbelief stage and felt a wave of anger. "She pushed herself. She was always pushing herself. If a challenge was there and someone could do it, she had to be the one. She already holds every local record and half a dozen national ones. So she wanted to win New York, but she went too far. Why did she have to set a world record? Wasn't winning enough?"

Erin put a hand on his arm and gently said, "That doesn't matter right now."

He took a steadying breath.

"How's your mom handling this?" she asked.

He made a face. *Lousy.*

"Is your dad any help?"

That revived Chris. "Yeah. He is. He doesn't have to say

a lot, but it works. I just saw that. He says two words, and she quiets down."

"They've been married more than thirty years."

He shook his head. "It isn't the time; it's the nature of their relationship."

"Chris, I'm not your mom. She and I are totally different. Besides, she's out of the house all the time. She was even when you kids were little, and I'm not criticizing that. I'm envious. She started Snow Hill back then, and look what it is now. She's an amazing woman. If I created something like that, I could live with silence at night."

"She's driven."

"By what?"

He shrugged. He couldn't figure his *wife* out, and she was less complex than Kathryn. "So," he asked, needing to know, "are you going home to visit your mom?"

"Omigod, no," Erin said quickly. "Not with Robin so sick." Her voice dropped to a whisper. "But what's happening between us isn't going away, Chris. We will have to deal sometime."

WHEN MOLLY RETURNED TO SNOW HILL, THE PARKING LOT was filled with customers' cars. Slipping inside, she took the back stairway to her office and closed the door. She shooed one cat from her chair and another from the keyboard, then sat and folded her hands.

She didn't want to be here, but her father had asked.

And besides easing her guilt, Molly wanted to help. She could fight it long and hard, but pleasing Kathryn had always been high on her list.

Right now, Kathryn wanted her to work. So, dutifully, she logged on and pulled up her calendar for the week. Today and tomorrow were for ordering, but Thursday she was supposed to follow up her mother's speech at a women's club in Lebanon with a how-to on making dish gardens. Obviously, they couldn't go. What excuse to give? Same with a pruning demonstration in Plymouth. And Friday's appearance at WMUR in Manchester? Molly hated being on TV, even with Kathryn doing the talking. Television made her eyes look too close, her nose too short, her mouth too wide. She had experimented wearing her hair back versus loose, wearing slacks versus jeans, wearing blue versus purple or green. No matter what, she paled beside Kathryn.

Neither of them would be up to doing TV on Friday so her father could cancel that one.

Her intercom buzzed. "Any news?" Tami asked.

"Not yet," Molly replied, feeling disingenuous. "We're waiting for more tests."

"Joaquin was asking. He was worried when he didn't see either of your parents' cars. They usually get here early after they've been away."

Joaquin Peña was Snow Hill's facilities man. Not only did he maintain the buildings and grounds, but because he lived on-site, he handled after-hours emergencies.

Joaquin adored Robin.

Tell him she'll be fine, Molly wanted to say, but the MRI mocked that claim. So she simply said, "Dad'll be here later," which begged the question of what to tell Joaquin or anyone else who might ask about Robin. But Charlie was good at this. Wasn't he their PR man?

Ending the call, she sorted through the requisition forms she had collected at yesterday's meeting. With fall planting season under way, Snow Hill's tree and shrub man had a list. Their functions person had booked three new weddings and two showers, and the retail store was gearing up for October's opening of the wreath room, all of which required special ordering. And then there was Liz Tocci, the in-house landscape designer and total pain in the butt, who was arguing—yet again—in favor of a supplier who carried certain elite specialty King Protea plants but who, Molly knew from experience, was overpriced and unreliable.

Molly loved King Proteas, too. As exotic flowers went, they were gorgeous. But Snow Hill was only as good as its suppliers, and this supplier had sent bad flowers once, the wrong flowers another time, and no flowers at all the third time Snow Hill had placed an order. In each instance, clients had been disappointed. No, there were other exotics Liz Tocci could use.

But how stupid was it to be worried about Liz when Robin was comatose?

Unable to spend another second thinking, Molly set to ordering for the functions. But she wasn't in a wedding mood. So she focused on Christmas. It was time to preorder.

Last year, they had sold out of poinsettias and had to rush to restock at a premium cost. She wanted plenty at wholesale this year.

How many hundreds to order—three, four? Eight-inch pots, ten-inch, twelve-inch? And how many of each size to upgrade to ceramic pots?

She struggled with the decisions, but came up short. She was about as interested in poinsettias as she was in moving. Digging up her landlord Terrance Field's phone number, she punched it in. "Hey, Mr. Field," she said when the old man picked up, "it's Molly Snow. How are you?"

"Not bad," he replied warily. "What is it now, Molly?"

"My sister's had an accident. It's pretty serious. This time I really do need an extension."

"You said that last time, too. When was that, a week ago?"

"That was a problem with the moving company, Mr. Field, and I did work it out. This is different." In the space of a breath, she realized that her argument was lame without the truth. "Robin had a heart attack."

There was a pause, then a gently chiding, "Am I truly supposed to believe that?"

"She collapsed while she was running. They say there's brain damage. She's in critical condition. Call Dickenson-May. They'll verify it."

After another pause came a sigh. "I'll take your word for it, Molly, but I'm over a barrel here. You promised to be out Monday, and my contractor is starting Tuesday. I've paid him a hefty deposit to work quickly, because if the house isn't ready for the realtor to show by the first of November, selling will be difficult. I need that money."

Molly knew his realtor. She was an old family friend. "Dorie McKay will understand," she pleaded, "and she's totally persuasive. She can work things out with the contractor. All I want is an extra week or two."

But Terrance didn't budge. "It isn't the contractor, Molly. It's me. First of December, my rent is tripling. The building is going condo. If I don't sell in Hanover, I can't buy here in Jupiter, and I can't afford the triple rent."

Molly might have begged—just *one* extra day? *two* extra days?—but one or two days wouldn't make a difference, not with Robin breathing through that god-awful respirator.

Besides, it wasn't like she couldn't do the packing. Robin wouldn't have done much anyway, and they did have a place to go. Molly just didn't want to move. Despite all the natural beauty in the area, Snow Hill being the least of it, there was a special charm to the cottage. She loved driving down the lane and parking under the oak, loved walking in and smelling aged wood. The house made her feel good. It would be nice to stay a while longer, especially with Robin's future in doubt.

One thing was for sure: Robin would be neither conducting a clinic that afternoon nor talking with sixth graders on Friday. Molly began with the Friday call, knowing that a Phys Ed teacher, who was less personally involved, would accept a cancellation more easily than a running group would. And she was right. When she explained that Robin was sick, the teacher was disappointed but understanding. The head of the running group was another story. Jenny Fiske knew Robin personally and was concerned.

When she asked what was wrong, Molly couldn't get herself to blame the flu. "She had some trouble yesterday during a long run. They're doing tests now."

"Is it her heel again?"

That would have been the recent bone spur incident. But a bone spur wouldn't keep Robin from meeting with a running group. Robin *adored* meeting with running groups. She would have gone on crutches, if need be. No, for her to cancel out on a running group would take something serious. Molly tried to come up with a possibility. Pneumonia? Stomach cramps? Migraines? Lasting for *weeks*?

Finally she just said, "It's something with her heart."

"Oh God, the enlarged heart thing. She was hoping it would go away."

Molly paused. "What do you mean?"

"I don't think she meant to tell me, but we were together last year when the news reported autopsy results on a guy who died during the Olympic marathon trials. He had an enlarged heart. It was totally tragic. I mean, he was only twenty-eight. Robin was saying how scary it was, because she has the same thing."

That was news to Molly. It would be news to her parents. But Robin told Kathryn everything. If she had known something like that and hidden it from her mother for the sake of glory, it would be awful!

"Is that the problem?" Jenny asked.

"Uh . . . uh . . ."

"Is she all *right*?"

Oh, yes, her mother would have wanted her to say. But it was a lie, possibly compounded now by Robin's lie. Angry at her sister, and at her mother, who *reveled* in the glory of parenting a world-class runner, Molly blurted out, "Actually, she's not. She hasn't regained consciousness."

"Omigod! Is she at Dickenson-May?"

"Yes."

"In the ICU?"

Starting to worry, Molly backpedaled. "Yeah, but will you kind of . . . not tell people, Jenny? We don't know where this is headed."

chapter 5

MOLLY KEPT AN EYE OUT FOR CHRIS. THE MINUTE he returned to Snow Hill, she was in his office. "Did you hear anything last year about Robin having an enlarged heart?"

He shook his head. "Who says she did?"

"Jenny Fiske. She implied Robin knew there was a problem and ignored it."

"You told her Robin had a heart problem?" he asked.

Molly grew defensive. "I had to. And anyway, it's ridiculous keeping this to ourselves when there are friends who really care."

"Mom will be pissed."

She threw a hand up. "Oh, well, what else is new? I can

never say the right thing when it comes to Mom. Lately it's Nick." She had met Nick Dukette two years earlier on the sidelines of one of Robin's races. Nick had been there as a newspaper reporter, Molly as a fan, but they started talking and hadn't stopped. Since then, he had briefly dated Robin, and though it hadn't worked out, Molly and he remained friends. Kathryn had nothing good to say about the man. "She's been after me for even meeting him for coffee. But I knew him first. So just because Robin breaks up with him, *I* have to stop being his friend? He is *not* an evil man."

"He's media."

"He was media when he was dating Robin, and Mom wasn't against him then. Wouldn't Robin have spilled more inside information than I have, or is it just that Mom thinks I'm stupidly naïve? What did I do to make her distrust me? By the way, Dad agrees with us about the EEG. If anyone can convince Mom to have it done, it's him."

"Y'think?"

"Definitely. She may be the leader, but he's smart. He doesn't have to raise his voice, and she listens."

"*Exact*ly," Chris said with uncharacteristic feeling. "He's a *quiet* force."

Molly was feeling sensitive enough about her mother to take his sudden show of passion personally. "And I'm not? Is that what you're saying? I'm *sorry,* but I can't *not* express my feelings."

"Maybe the problem is how you do it. Maybe you should lower the volume."

"But that's not me. You inherited quietness from Dad. I didn't."

"Could you be married to a guy like him?"

Molly wasn't thinking of marriage just then, but since he had asked, she answered. "In a minute. I'm like Mom. I need someone to calm me."

"Wouldn't you find it boring? Dad comes home from work and doesn't say much."

"But he's always there." She had a sudden thought. "Do you think Mom and Dad knew about the enlarged heart and kept it secret?"

Chris snorted. "Go ask."

Molly considered that for all of two seconds before saying, "I will." She wanted to be at the hospital anyway.

"SO MOLLY WILL BOX EVERYTHING UP AND TAKE CARE OF the move," Kathryn told Robin. "It's perfect that you two share a place. Molly's a great backup person for when you're away. And even now, she'll keep your friends up on what's happening until we get rid of this stupid tube—" Catching a breath, she came out of her chair.

Charlie was quickly by her side.

"Did you see that?" Kathryn asked excitedly. "Her other hand. It moved."

"Are you sure? There's a lot of tape on that hand."

Kathryn's heart raced. "Did you do that, Robin? If you did, I want you to do it again."

She stared at the hand.

"Come on, sweetie," she ordered. "I know it's hard, but you're used to hard stuff. Think what it's like at that twenty-first mile when you hit the wall and feel dizzy and weak, and you're sure you can't finish. But you always do. You always manage to dredge up a little more strength." The respirator breathed in, breathed out, but not a finger moved. "Do it now, Robin," she begged. "Let me know you can hear me speak." She waited, then tried, "Think of the games you play. When you run, you imagine that long, smooth stride. Imagine it now, sweetie. Imagine the pleasure you get from *moving*."

Nothing happened.

Brokenly, she whispered, "Am I missing it, Charlie?"

"If you are, I am, too."

Discouraged, she sank back into the chair and brought Robin's hand to her mouth. Her fingers were limp and cool. "I know I saw something," she breathed against them, wanting only to keep them warm.

"You're exhausted," Charlie said.

She looked at him sharply. "Are you saying I *imagined* it? Maybe your problem is that you don't *want* to see it as much as I do."

There was a pause, then a quiet, "Low blow."

Kathryn had known that the instant the words left her mouth. With his warm hazel eyes, shoulders that were broader in theory than fact, and a loyalty like none she had seen in any other person before or since, Charlie had been there for her from the start. The fact that she could accuse him of less showed how stressed she was.

Stressed? She wasn't stressed. She was *devastated*. Seeing Robin like this was *killing* her, and that was even before she thought of the long-term meaning. This wasn't just a setback. It was a *catastrophe*.

Charlie understood. She could see it on his face, but that didn't excuse what she'd said. Slipping an arm around his waist, she buried her face in his chest. "I'm sorry. You did not deserve that."

He cupped her head. "I can take it. But Molly can't. She's trying, Kath. None of us expected this." His hand lowered to massage her neck at just the spot where she needed it most.

Kathryn looked up, haunted. "Did I push Robin too far?"

He smiled sadly. "You didn't have to push. She pushed herself."

"But I've always egged her on."

"Not egged. Encouraged."

"If I hadn't, maybe she wouldn't have pushed so hard."

"And never run a marathon in record time? Never traveled the country inspiring others? Never eyed the Olympics?"

He was right. Robin lived life to the fullest. But that knowledge didn't ease Kathryn's fear. "What are we going to do?"

"Ask for an EEG."

Her panic shot up. "What if it shows no activity?"

"What if it doesn't?"

Charlie was the face of quiet confidence. Always. And

she loved him for it. But this was too soon. "I can't take the risk. Not yet."

"Okay," he said gently. "Then what about friends? They can't get through to you, so they're calling me. We need to tell them the truth."

"We don't know the truth."

He chided her with a sad smile. "You aren't asking to have her transferred, which tells me that you accept the MRI results."

How not to, when the pictures were so clear? "Okay," she conceded. "Let's tell them there are irregularities. That's the truth. We don't have to tell them everything, do we? I can't bear having the world think the worst."

"These are friends, Kath. They want to talk to you. They want to help."

But Kathryn didn't want sympathy. She wasn't the type to talk for the sake of talking; she couldn't *bear* the thought of giving progress reports to friend after friend, especially when there was no progress to report. And what were friends supposed to *do*?

No. No calls. Kathryn didn't want people saying things that she wasn't ready to hear. "I can't talk with them yet. I just can't. Handle this for me, Charlie?"

MOLLY STRUCK OUT AT THE HOSPITAL. SHOWING NO IM-provement at all, Robin lay pale and still, a cruel parody of the active person she had been, and Kathryn was appalled at the mention of an enlarged heart. "Absolutely untrue," she declared. "Robin would have told me if she had a serious problem."

Molly kept her voice low. She had never thought of her brother as being particularly insightful when it came to human nature, but she wasn't doing real well herself. What better time to test his theory than with something as difficult as this? "You might have stopped her from running. What if she didn't want that?"

"Robin may be daring, but she isn't stupid, and she certainly isn't self-destructive. Why in the world would you believe a stranger over your sister?"

"Because I can't ask my sister," Molly said softly still. "I'm just trying to make sense of this, Mom. Did the doctors mention an enlarged heart?"

Confused, Kathryn looked at Charlie, who said, "Yes. We assumed it was something new."

"Did anyone in your family have an enlarged heart?"

Charlie shook his head and deferred to Kathryn, who said, "I have no idea. I never heard of anything, but doctors didn't know as much in my parents' or grandparents' day. Besides, it's the kind of thing a person wouldn't know unless he had symptoms."

"Did Robin have symptoms?"

"Molly. You're assuming it's true. *Please*. And why does it even matter? This is water over the dam. Robin had a heart attack. It's a *fait accompli*."

"For her maybe, but what about for Chris and me? Shouldn't we know whether we're at risk?" Realizing how selfish that sounded, she added, "If Robin knew she was at risk, she never should have run so hard. She never should have run *alone*."

"She always ran alone."

"Most runners train in groups. If she had a heart condition, shouldn't she have made sure there were other people around just in case?"

"You were supposed to be around."

Molly might have argued, but her mother was right. Somberly, she said, "Yes. I'll have to live with that. Always."

Kathryn seemed taken aback by the admission, but only briefly. "Besides, there *was* someone else there." The Good Samaritan.

"He didn't have to come see us, Mom," Molly said, still cringing at her mother's outburst. "That took courage."

"It was guilt. He wants to be absolved."

"He was *concerned*," Molly argued, deciding that Chris's theory wasn't worth beans. Loud voice, soft voice—she just couldn't get through. *"He* wasn't the one who put her here. If we're talking cause and effect, what *doctor* would have let Robin run marathons if he knew she had this condition?"

"Like a doctor could control what she did? Please, Molly. You were the first one defending doctors last night. Why the change?"

"I don't want my sister to die!" Molly cried, eyes filling with tears because Robin was lying there, *totally* unresponsive. "When we were kids," she said brokenly, focusing on her sister, "I'd be on her bed, moving closer and closer, imagining that I would wake her up with just the power of my eyes, and she'd lie perfectly still until I got really close. Then she'd bolt up and scare me to death." She took a shaky breath and looked at her mother. "I'm sorry. I feel helpless. I want to know why this happened."

"Anger doesn't help," Kathryn said quietly.

Neither does denial, Molly thought. "Can't we do the EEG?" she asked. "Just to know?"

But Kathryn was still hung up on the enlarged heart issue. "Robin wouldn't lie to me about something as important as a heart condition. She shared everything with me."

Let it pass, Molly told herself, but the remark was just too outrageous. "Did she tell you she got drunk with her friends the night after she ran Duluth?"

Kathryn stared. "Robin doesn't drink."

"Robin does. I've driven her home afterward."

"And you *let* her drink?" Kathryn asked, shifting the blame. "And why didn't she tell *me* about Duluth?"

"Because you're her *mother,* and you *hate* drinking." Molly took pity because Kathryn looked truly distraught. "Oh Mom, I wouldn't have said anything if you hadn't been so adamant that Robin wouldn't lie. Duluth was a blip. No harm came of it. I'm sure that if you'd asked her outright whether she'd ever been drunk, she'd have told you. But she didn't want to disappoint you. She swore me to secrecy."

"You should have honored that."

Molly hung her head. She couldn't win. Discouraged, she

looked at Kathryn again. "All I'm saying is that Robin didn't tell you everything. She was human, like the rest of us."

"*Was* human? Past tense?"

Charlie held up a hand. At the same time, from the door came a gentle, "Excuse me?" It was the nurse. "We have people gathering in the lounge down the hall. They say they're Robin's friends."

Kathryn's eyes went wide. "How do they know she's here?"

"I told Jenny Fiske," Molly said. Her mother was already angry; a little more couldn't make it worse.

Kathryn sagged. "Oh, Molly."

"It's okay," Charlie said. "Jenny's a friend. Molly did what she felt was best."

"Robin would want Jenny to know," Molly tried. She was actually sure about this. "She's always been right out there with her friends. I think she'd want Jenny here. And she'd want that EEG, too. She liked knowing the score— *likes* knowing the score, *likes* knowing what she's up against. I mean, think of the way she studies the competition before every major race. She wants to psych it all out— who'll run how on a given course, whether they'll break early, how they'll take hills, when they'll fade. She's a strategizer. But she can't strategize for *this* race unless she knows what's going on."

When Kathryn continued to stare at her, Molly figured she had pushed as far as she could. And Jenny was in the lounge. The last thing Molly wanted was to have to be the one to talk with her. Plus she was worried about the nurse's reference to friends, plural.

Feeling responsible, she set off to do damage control.

KATHRYN WONDERED IF MOLLY WAS RIGHT. ROBIN MIGHT want to know what she faced. The problem was that Kathryn didn't. She wanted to see improvement first, which was why Molly's spreading the word wasn't good. "Why did she have to tell Jenny?"

Charlie drew up a chair. "Because we put her in an untenable position. How can she talk with a friend of Robin's and not tell her Robin is sick? Really, Kath, there's nothing wrong with what she's done. What happened to Robin isn't a disgrace. It's a medical crisis. We could use people's prayers."

This time, Kathryn didn't argue about prayers. She had begun saying a few herself. Doctors had been in and out all morning examining Robin, and they never actually denied Kathryn hope, simply gave her little to hold onto. Same with the respiratory therapist, who checked by every hour and refused to say whether he saw any change in Robin's breathing. And the nurses? As compassionate as they were, repeatedly testing Robin's responsiveness, they were cautious in answering Kathryn's questions. Once too often she had been told that patients didn't come back from the kind of brain damage Robin had suffered.

Charlie took her hand. "Molly's right, y'know. Not knowing is the worst."

Kathryn knew where he was headed. "You want the EEG."

"I don't want *any* of this," he said in a burst so rare that it carried more weight. "But we can't go back," he added sadly. "The Robin we knew is gone."

Kathryn's eyes teared as she looked at her daughter again. Robin had been an active infant, an energetic toddler, an irrepressible child. "I can't accept that," she whispered.

"You may have to. Think of Robin. How can we know what to do for her if we don't know the extent of the damage?"

It was a variation of Molly's argument. And it did hold some merit.

"You love Robin to bits," Charlie went on. "You always have. No one would question that."

"I wanted so much for her."

"She's *had* so much," he urged. "She's lived more in her thirty-two years than many people ever do, and you were the force behind it."

"I'm all she has."

"No. She has me. She has Molly and Chris. She has more friends than any of us. And we love her. Yes, Molly too. Molly's had to live in her shadow, not always a fun place to be, but she does adore her sister. She covers for Robin a lot."

"Do you believe her about Duluth?" Kathryn asked in a moment's doubt.

"How can I not? You set yourself up for that one, my

love. No daughter tells her mother everything, especially when she knows it'll disappoint."

"I wouldn't have been disappointed if Robin had told me she had an enlarged heart. Worried, yes."

"You'd have discouraged her from running."

"Probably."

"What if she didn't want that? What if she wanted to take the chance? She's an adult, Kathryn. This is her life."

Is? Kathryn thought. *Or was?* She had criticized Molly for using the past tense, but if Charlie was right, and the Robin they knew was gone, everything changed.

She had always thought she knew Robin through and through, and that what *she* wanted, Robin would want. If that wasn't so, and if Robin couldn't express her wishes now, how could Kathryn know what to do?

This wasn't the time for a crisis in confidence, but Kathryn suffered one nonetheless. It had been a long time since the last such crisis. She was rusty at it.

Crises in confidence had been the norm when she was growing up, something of a family tradition. Her father, George Webber, was a lumberjack. Then a carpenter. Then a bricklayer. Then a gardener. At the first sign of discouragement in one field, he moved on to the next. Same with her mother, Marjorie, who ran a little cottage industry—first knitting sweaters, then sewing tote bags, then weaving Vermont's equivalent of the Nantucket basket. Everything she produced was beautiful—or so Kathryn thought. When business was brisk, Marjorie agreed; but at the first sign of a lull, she moved on.

Kathryn learned from her parents. She raced for the town swim team until she realized she would always be second tier, at which point she turned to violin. When she couldn't get beyond second seat in junior high, she turned to acting. When she couldn't get beyond chorus in the high school musical, she turned to art.

That was when she met Natalie Boyce. Head of the high school art department, Natalie was a free spirit prone to wearing wild clothing and speaking her thoughts. Kathryn was mesmerized by her confidence and no match for her resolve, neither of which she saw much of at home. At Natalie's suggestion, she started with watercolor. She immersed herself in the basics of brush control, palette, texture, and wash, and she thrived on Natalie's encouragement. Natalie loved her use of line and shape and saw a natural feel for space in her work—but timidity in her use of color. Kathryn tried to be bolder, but her life was more muted tones than vibrant ones. So she switched from watercolor to clay.

Natalie was having none of that. They talked. They argued. Their discussions went beyond art to life itself.

Kathryn returned to watercolor. She worked at it doggedly through her last two years in high school. When she applied to art school, the strength of her portfolio was her use of color. But it wasn't until she left her parents' home that she was able to articulate what she had learned.

Her parents were loving people who wanted to provide for their family—wanted it so badly that they went from one thing to the next in an endless search for a smash hit. What they didn't understand was that smash hits didn't just happen but took talent, focus, and hard work.

chapter 6

$\mathcal{T}$HE FRIENDS IN THE LOUNGE WERE RUNNERS, CLUS-
tered at a small table in a knot of denim, spandex, and
backpacks. Molly recognized them as Dartmouth graduate
students with whom Robin often worked out. They had no
connection to Jenny Fiske.

Had she known that, she wouldn't have rushed out. But
it was too late. She was surrounded before she could retreat.

"My cousin was in the ER last night with her little boy,"
one explained. "How's Robin?"

"Uh, we're not sure," Molly managed.

"I ran with her three days ago and she was fine," said another.

And a third, "We talked in the bookstore just yesterday."

"I heard it from Nick Dukette," put in a fourth.

"Nick?"

"Newspaper Nick. He saw it on the police blotter this morning, and he knows I know Robin. He said she's in critical condition."

Molly was taken aback. Nick claimed they were good friends; but if that was so, he should have called her first. Granted, she had her cell phone on vibrate and had been distracted enough to miss it.

Pulling the phone out now, she scrolled down. Okay. There it was. A missed call from Nick. No message.

Nick was a reporter for the state's largest paper. On general assignment when Molly first met him, he had since been named to head the local news desk; but with his strength in sniffing out a story, he was a shoo-in for investigative editor at the next change in command. Like Robin, he had star written all over him. And he was hungry for it. He had piercing blue eyes that could either drill or charm, and he used them well. Had he been a lawyer, he would have chased ambulances; he was that addicted to breaking news.

Molly admired his doggedness, but there was a downside. What Nick knew, the world might soon know.

Kathryn would be horrified and would surely blame Molly. She had to talk with him.

But first these runners. Denying Robin's official condition was absurd. The question was how much more to say, and the key was saying it quietly. The lounge wasn't empty. A woman and her daughter dozed on one sofa, a family huddled on another.

Molly leaned into the group. "The official status still is critical condition," she said, because anyone calling the hospital would hear that. "We're waiting for follow-up tests."

"Was she hit by a car?"

"No. It's an internal thing."

"Internal, like *organs*?"

Molly gave a quick nod.

"Will she be okay?"

"We hope so."

There was a moment's silence, then a quiet barrage.

"Is there anything we can do?"

"Can we make calls?"

"Does she need anything?"

"Positive thoughts," Molly said and was momentarily startled when one of the women she didn't know gave her a hug. She was even more surprised to miss the warmth when the woman pulled back. Unable to speak, she waved her thanks and, cell phone in hand, made for the door.

Waiting just outside in the hall, standing half a head taller than Molly, was the Good Samaritan. His tie was loose, collar unbuttoned. He was visibly relieved when she stopped. With the earlier scene rushing back, how could she not? Her first thought was to apologize for her mother's abominable behavior, but he spoke first.

"How is she?"

Molly scrunched up her nose and shook her head.

He made a defeated sound. "I knew it was bad. She was clammy and cold. It was terrifying. As soon as the paramedics took over, I left." He seemed tormented. "I just freaked out. Her name was right there on her shoe tag, and after I read it, I recognized her face. She's every runner's idol, and there I was, trying to get her to breathe. It didn't help, did it."

Molly hesitated, then shook her head.

"Brain dead?" he whispered.

She lifted a shoulder—couldn't quite deny it to this man, who clearly connected the dots.

He seemed to deflate. "I keep thinking that if I'd been doing a faster pace, I'd've gotten there sooner."

Molly hugged herself. "If you'd been on a different road, you'd never have found her at all."

"I should have stayed, maybe gone in the ambulance; but she didn't know me, so it wasn't like I was a friend going with a friend."

"I'm her *sister*," Molly blurted out, "and I was supposed to have been tracking that run, only I had other things to do. Know how guilty I feel?"

He didn't blink. "Yes. I do. The minute the EMTs took over, I turned around and ran home so I could shower and go back to school and try to convince parents that I'm a good, caring person who's well qualified to teach their kids. As if I could really focus on work."

Oh boy, did Molly agree. Sitting in her office had been a joke. She couldn't work while her sister was on life support.

Nick was working, though, and she did need to reach him. Gesturing toward Robin's room, she said, "I have to make a call." She set off, stopped, turned back. She was really glad he returned. "Thank you."

"I didn't do enough."

"She wasn't breathing. You did what you could. She's alive now because of you." When he still looked haunted, she smiled. "Forget what my mom said. She needs to blame someone for this. One day, she'll thank you herself."

She continued on this time, past Robin's room to a spot by a window where her cell phone had four bars. "It's me," she said when Nick picked up.

There were several seconds of newsroom buzz, then a passionate, "Geez, Molly, I've been trying you all day. Why'd you take so long returning my call?"

"It's been a little hectic, Nick."

"How is she?"

"She's holding on."

"What does that mean? Is she awake? Talking? Moving around? Is she breathing on her own? Has she been stabilized?"

Molly could feel those prodding blue eyes. She wasn't sure she liked being on this side of the notepad. "They'll run more tests later."

"*Was* it a heart attack?"

"They're trying to figure out exactly what's going on."

"But the initial problem—definitely the heart? Has she had heart trouble before? Is it a structural problem, like a valve or a hole? Can they fix it?"

Molly was growing uneasy. "Is this for an article?"

"Molly," he protested, sounding hurt. "It's for *me*. I used to date Robin. Plus, her sister is my *friend*."

Molly was duly chastised. "I'm sorry. You just sound so

reporter-like." And there was the issue of Andrea Welker and a bad drug test, something Robin had told him in confidence that had shown up in the paper. Nick swore he had gotten the information from a separate source, but neither Robin nor Kathryn fully bought that. *Don't believe what he says,* Robin had told Molly once too often, and lest she forget, Kathryn repeated the warning often. But Molly liked Nick. He was interesting, and he was going places. That he liked Molly enough to *want* to be her friend even after her sister had shafted him was flattering.

"No, *I'm* sorry," he said now, conciliatory. "If you'd called me last night, we wouldn't be having this conversation. When you didn't return my call this morning, I started calling other people. It's an occupational hazard."

"That's what frightens me. Nick, I need your help. Can you keep this out of the paper?"

There was a short pause, then a surprised, "How can I do that? It's news."

"You have clout there. You can get them to hold off. The more people hear, the more they call us, and we just can't talk until we know more."

"What do you know now?"

Molly had been hoping for a promise. Disappointed, she didn't reply.

"Are we friends?" he asked quietly. "Friends trust one another."

Friends also call more than one measly time before calling other people, Molly thought. Of course, she was hyper-sensitive.

But she wasn't stupid. "The point is my family needs privacy," she explained. "And honestly, there isn't much to tell. Robin did have a heart event, but all her vital signs are good." It wasn't exactly a lie.

"Is a heart 'event' the same as a heart 'attack'?"

"They're just words to me right now. I'm pretty shaken. We all are. I've told you as much as we know for sure." Not exactly a lie, either.

"Okay. That's okay. Will you call me when you learn anything more?"

She said she would, but ended the call feeling uncomfortable. It was a minute before she put her finger on it. For all his questions, he hadn't asked how *she* was doing with all this. Friends who claimed they were good buddies did that.

Telling herself that it was a simple oversight—that he knew she was upset, so had no need to ask—she closed her phone and went back up the hall. She was nearly at Robin's door when her father emerged. He was taking his own phone from his pocket. "Your mom agreed to the EEG. Want to stay with her while I give Chris a call?"

THE EEG WASN'T DONE UNTIL EARLY EVENING TO ACCOM-modate the neurologist, who wanted to be present to interpret the results. The machine was brought into Robin's room. Since quiet was required for the truest reading, Kathryn was the only family member allowed to stay.

She was grateful that the nurses sensed her need to be there, but if she had been hoping to bring Robin luck, it didn't work. She cheered silently. She repeated every motivational thought that had goaded Robin on in the past. She counted on her brain waves connecting to Robin's.

But the news wasn't good. After an hour of the machine's pen scratching on paper, Kathryn could see it herself—one flat line after the next over twelve different readings.

What could the neurologist say? Crying quietly, Kathryn couldn't think to ask new questions, and after he left, the nurse lingered, focusing not on Robin but on her, which almost felt worse. *Did she want to talk with social services?* No. *Perhaps a minister?* No.

I want that second test, Kathryn finally managed to say. The nurse nodded and replied, *It's a process,* which didn't help at all. Kathryn didn't want a process. She wanted her daughter.

For the longest time after the nurse left, Kathryn stood holding Robin's hand, studying her face, trying to square what the test said with the daughter who had done cartwheels at the age of three. Charlie was behind her, with Chris and Erin nearby. Molly was back by the wall. No one spoke, and that didn't help either. It wasn't fair, *none* of it— not their silence, not her pain, not Robin's fate.

Furious, she turned on her family. "You all wanted this done. Are we able to help Robin more now?"

Charlie looked crushed. Chris clutched Erin's hand. Molly was in tears.

"I *said* it was too soon," Kathryn argued, starting to cry again herself. Charlie gave her a tissue and held her until she regained composure. "Some patients need more time. The doctor said that. I'm going to keep talking to her. She hears me. I know she does." Determined, she returned to Robin. "And I know how to give pep talks, don't I. So here's a really, really important one." She bent down, spoke low. "Are you listening, Robin? I need you to *listen*. We've faced tough fields before. You've competed against some of the best runners in the world and come out ahead. That's what we'll do this time. We'll surprise them all. We're going to *win*."

Molly materialized at her side. "Mom?" she asked in a very young voice.

Kathryn softened at the sound. Molly wasn't often vulnerable. It was a throwback, a reminder of what Charlie had said. "What, honey?"

"Maybe we should tell Nana."

Kathryn should have been hurting enough to be immune to more pain, but there it was. Squeezing her eyes shut, she fought hysteria. She wasn't sure how much a person was expected to bear all at once, but she was reaching her limit.

Opening her eyes, she said, "Nana isn't herself."

"She has lucid times."

"She can't remember our names, much less take in something we tell her. She isn't the Nana you knew, Molly.

Besides," she returned to Robin with a last glimmer of hope, "it would be cruel to tell a woman her age something we don't know for sure. This was only the first EEG. There's a reason they require two. I don't care what the doctors say; I'm not believing a thing until the second is done."

OF THE DISAGREEMENTS MOLLY HAD WITH HER MOTHER, with one the least and ten the worst, their dispute over her grandmother ranked an eight. That was one of the reasons she went from the hospital to the nursing home. Visiting hours were over by the time she arrived, but the staff was used to her coming and going. She smiled at the woman at the front desk and was quickly waved on. After running up the stairs to the third floor, though, she faltered.

"Is she alone?" she asked at the nurse's station. She didn't mind that her grandmother had a boyfriend. The staff said that they didn't actually have sex, but Molly wasn't taking any chances.

The nurse smiled. "Thomas is in his room by himself. He has a cold."

Grateful, Molly slipped into a room halfway down the hall, closed the door and turned to the figure in the chair. Marjorie Webber was seventy-eight. She had been diagnosed with Alzheimer's five years before, and for the first two of those years had been cared for by her husband. Then his health declined, and hers spiraled to the point where she needed round-the-clock attention. Putting her in a nursing home had been the only option.

To be fair, Molly knew Kathryn had agonized over the decision. They had all agreed that moving Marjorie in with Charlie and her was impractical, what with so many stairs. Besides, Marjorie needed constant watching, and Kathryn was rarely home. A dedicated facility seemed their best hope for maximizing safety and care. They had looked at many before choosing this one. Housed in a large Victorian with multiple wings adapted for the purpose, this nursing home exuded warmth the others lacked. Part of its appeal was its closeness to the Snows' home.

Kathryn had taken her father to visit often, and after George died, went by herself. Then Marjorie met Thomas, and Kathryn flipped out. No matter that George was dead, she took her mother's having a boyfriend as a personal affront and stopped visiting. Kathryn reasoned that her mother didn't know whether she came or not, and Molly had no proof either way. She herself had always adored her grandmother. Even in her diminished state, Marjorie gave Molly comfort.

This evening was no exception. Her room was filled with reminders of the past—framed family photos, a tote Marjorie had sewn that was now brimming with yarn, a woven basket in which Molly had put small pots of pothos, foliage begonia, and ivy. In the midst of these soothing mementos, Marjorie looked totally sweet and, in a cruel twist, more like a woman ten years her junior. Her hair was gray but remained thick, styled in a bob much like Kathryn's. Always a pastel person, she wore a pink robe, and she was reading a book—such a familiar activity for a long-time reader that Molly could pretend she was mentally there.

"Nana," she whispered, hunkering down by the chair.

Marjorie looked up from her book and studied her quizzically. And here was another cruel twist: Though they had been warned she would lose facial expressions, she hadn't yet. She appeared to be totally aware, which made some of her behavior seem even worse.

"It's Molly," she said before Marjorie could call her something else. Yes, she understood what Kathryn felt when that happened. Marjorie didn't do it deliberately, but it was still sad to hear. "What're you reading?"

Marjorie looked at her book and brightened. "It's *Little Women*," she said. "My granddaughters loved this book. Do you have any children?"

Molly felt a lump of emotion at not being recognized as one of those granddaughters. Swallowing it, she shook her head.

"Well, you will, a pretty girl like you." Closing the book, Marjorie smoothed the cover. It was not *Little Women* at all, but a book of knitting witticisms Molly had brought the week before, hoping that the pictures would ring a bell. Once, her grandmother had been an amazing knitter. Occasionally, she could still do the stitches. Other times she blankly studied the needles.

Now she turned to Molly. "Do I know you?"

She should. There were pictures on the nightstand and the dresser, others framed and grouped on the wall. Some had been taken on holidays, some on vacations. All were meant to jog the memory.

"I'm Molly, and I miss you, Nana."

Marjorie smiled. "My granddaughters used to call me Nana—you know, like the big furry goat that takes care of the children in *Peter Pan*. There were actually three goats, and they wanted to go over the bridge to the meadow." She lowered her voice. "But a troll owned that bridge."

"Robin is sick, Nana." *Brain dead.* Allowing herself to think the word here with her grandmother, Molly felt sick herself.

"Robin?" There was a frown. "I know a Robin. Her mother named her that because of the expression."

"What expression?"

"You know," Marjorie said with a hint of pique. "The *expression*—about the early bird getting the grease."

Molly didn't correct her. "How does that relate to Robin?"

"A Robin is a bird. They come early."

They go early, too, Molly thought and was suddenly grateful that her grandmother had lost touch with reality. She wouldn't have to think the phrase *brain dead,* wouldn't have to feel the pain of knowing what was happening to Robin. She didn't even feel pain at her own condition, though it hadn't always been that way. At the beginning, Nana had known what was happening. Her behavior had become erratic, but she was aware enough when she was first diagnosed to be upset. In some regards, the speed of her illness's progression was a blessing. She had attended her husband's funeral without fully understanding who had died.

Seventy-eight wasn't old for a woman in excellent physical condition. Had it not been for her mind, she could live to be a hundred. She might yet do that. It would be cruel if Nana were to live so many clueless years, Molly decided—though nowhere near as cruel as what was happening to Robin at thirty-two.

Molly wondered if Robin had known what was happening to her out there on the road. The thought that her sister might have felt a pain in her chest, sensed what it was, and realized that she was all alone gave Molly a chill. Worse, though, was the shutdown that might have followed—lights snapped off, everything black. *Brain dead.* It was too much.

Needing her grandmother's kind heart, she said, "I'm such a bad person. I blew my sister off, and now she's dying."

Marjorie tipped her head. "You remind me of someone."

"My fault, Nana, and it wasn't only Monday. There have been times when I deliberately missed her races. Sometimes I actually hoped she would *lose.* So is this my wish coming true?"

Marjorie seemed pensive. Finally, curiously, she asked, "Have we met?"

"And with Nick," Molly went on, "I *like* annoying her by staying friends with him. If I was a loyal sister, I'd let it go. So I'm not loyal, and Mom'll never forgive me, even though I bust my butt at the nursery. I mean, I love my work. But I like knowing that it's something Mom likes, too."

Marjorie tipped her head. She was listening.

"So is it all about Mom?" Molly asked. "Am I her daughter and nothing else? My friends can't believe I went right back into the family business. They think I should go somewhere else, and there are times when I want to. I've interviewed at other places, Nana. I had an offer from a *huge* nursery outside of Boston—just last *week*—but I said no. I love Snow Hill. Mom is so smart." Marjorie had started to frown, so Molly added, "Don't tell her about the job offer. She'll kill me if she knows. I was disloyal to even consider it. So here I am, worrying about her again. Is it all about Mom? Who am *I*?"

"Well . . . well . . . I'm not sure," Marjorie said.

Molly knew it was ridiculous to be discussing identity with a woman who had lost her own, but the words wouldn't stop. "I'm one person one minute and another person another. I love my sister, I hate my sister. I love my mother, I hate my mother. I love Snow Hill, I hate Snow Hill. Who *am* I?"

Marjorie looked upset. "Have we met?"

"Nana, it's me, Molly," she pleaded, "and I don't know how to help Mom. I need you to tell me what to do."

Marjorie's frown deepened. "Don't you know?"

"I always say the wrong thing."

"But you *have* to speak," Marjorie cried in distress, and added, "I should know you."

"You do," Molly whispered and laid her cheek on her grandmother's knee. It was a minute before Marjorie's hand touched Molly's head and another before it began stroking her hair, but the familiarity of it was comforting. *Brain dead* briefly lost its edge. For that short time, Molly was back in a place where life's woes could be solved by a caress.

Then the stroking stopped, and Molly looked up. Her grandmother's eyes were on the door, her face lit with pleasure.

Thomas was there, his nose red, his white hair disheveled, his robe crookedly tied.

"Why hello," Marjorie said, sounding mystified but pleased. "Do I know you?"

He didn't reply. From what Molly had been told, he rarely spoke. It was anyone's guess whether Thomas had deliberately left his room to come here, or whether the draw was subconscious. But the distress Molly had heard in her grandmother moments before was gone. For that reason alone, Molly thought Kathryn should be grateful for Thomas.

Marjorie had paid her dues in life. She had been devoted and hardworking, and she certainly hadn't asked for this disease. Yet Alzheimer's had taken her identity, had wiped clean a slate of nearly eighty years. If she could still have moments of pleasure, how was that bad? She was trapped in an unfamiliar world, but it was one in which husbands didn't die, daughters didn't stop visiting, and granddaughters didn't end up on life support. A tiny part of Molly envied her that.

chapter 7

MOLLY AGONIZED OVER WHETHER TO TELL NICK about the EEG. As she drove back from seeing her grandmother, she vacillated, repeatedly opening and closing her phone before finally admitting the truth. Yes, she trusted him . . . but not entirely. *Brain dead* was ominous, and Nick was the press.

He was also something of a local celebrity—man on the scene, most eligible bachelor, possessor of the most amazing blue eyes—and he valued her friendship. Robin claimed he was using Molly, but for what? Molly and Nick had been friends before he and Robin ever dated. Molly had *introduced* them.

But she did respect her mother's need for privacy. So she kept her phone off.

Focusing on Robin, she returned to Dickenson-May. She had barely reached the front door, though, when the half-light of the hospital sign showed a man on a bench. It was the Good Samaritan. The tie was gone, the shirttails loose. His elbows were on his knees, but when he spotted her, he sat straighter, eyes questioning.

She smiled sadly. "Not good."

He sagged. "I'm sorry."

Recalling her mother's scathing words all too clearly, Molly wondered if Kathryn knew he was here. "Have you been upstairs?"

"Only long enough to see that you weren't around. Your mom doesn't need me upsetting her. I had to talk with someone else anyway."

"Here at the hospital?"

"Yes. A friend of a friend. I need information on anorexia. One of my students has a problem."

Finding anorexia preferable to brain death, Molly joined him on the bench. "What age do you teach?"

"Eighth grade. That's thirteen- and fourteen-year-olds." When she winced, he drawled, "Yeah. It's a difficult age. They're the oldest in middle school, so they're cocky. There's a lot of bullying, and not only of younger kids. They bully each other. The girls are fully developed and precocious. They're social. They dress provocatively. Half of the boys have hit puberty, half haven't. The ones who haven't are vulnerable."

"Who is anorexic?"

"One of my girls. She's a dancer who's really talented and the sweetest kid you'd ever want to meet. She isn't into the social scene because she spends every free minute at ballet school. If she's hit puberty, you'd never know it. She's a rail."

"Her parents must see it."

He looked doubtful. "You'd think. But they're over-achievers themselves. Mom's a lawyer, Dad's an educator. I doubt they want to see this."

"Have you talked with them?"

"No. There's a catch. Her father is the school superintendent—my boss. He takes pride in his kids. They always get great grades and win all the local awards. He won't like my pointing out a flaw."

"Anorexia isn't a flaw," Molly argued. "It's an illness."

"In his daughter, it would be a flaw and one that would reflect on his wife and him, which makes it a sensitive issue to raise."

"But you're concerned." She could see it in his eyes.

"Yes, but am I sticking my nose where it doesn't belong? They have to know something's wrong. Other people must have mentioned it. I'm just her history teacher."

"Maybe you care more than the others."

"Maybe I'm just more rash. A couple of years ago—different city, different school—I reported a cheating incident. It was pretty blatant. I really had no choice. But the student was the son of friends of my parents. There's still a rift between our families. My parents haven't forgiven me for it."

"But if this girl is in physical danger . . ."

"That's where I'm torn," he said. "Being a good guy can backfire. Like with your sister. If she's brain dead, I didn't save her at all. I only prolonged the agony."

"You had no way of knowing which way it would go. You can't fault yourself for that."

"Do your parents agree?" he asked and went on before Molly could come up with a diplomatic response. "Sometimes a person is damned either way. Is it better to err on the side of commission or omission?"

Molly didn't know. She was torn herself. She might have driven Robin out for her run and been sitting with drinking water five minutes down the road, waiting, listening to the radio while Robin's brain tissue died.

"The difference," she said, "is that you tried. Your intentions were good. You acted because you cared."

"But there's an irony here. I became a teacher to stay out of the fray. My family is in publishing, high-profile, definitely A-list. They get recognition for everything they do, good or bad, so I've seen the underside of the spotlight. The pain isn't worth it. I'm the youngest of their kids and have always been the least visible. I like it that way."

Molly totally identified. She was the youngest and least visible, too. "Very comfortable."

"Cheating, anorexia, heart issues—I don't go looking to interfere."

They were kindred spirits in this, making Molly like him all the more. *He* would understand her reluctance to be the family spokesperson.

But who else could do it? The circumstances were dire. "Keeping a low profile isn't always possible."

"My dad says that. He equates being proactive with being courageous, and I agree to some extent. That's probably why I confronted my boss about his daughter." His eyes drifted toward the parking lot, then suddenly returned. "I'm sorry. I'm going on about me, when you're the one who's in crisis."

She smiled. "It's nice to think about something else. Besides, there are parallels. Do we act, or don't we? Do we know we did our best, or do we die of regret?"

"Do we die, period?" he remarked somberly. "That haunts me. Look at your sister. Do any of us ever know when something like this might happen to us?" He snorted. "Pretty selfish thinking."

"But it's real," Molly said. "Mortality, I mean." She guessed he was in his early thirties and figured he was as new to this as she was. "Do you have a will?" she asked bluntly.

He seemed unfazed. "No wife, no family, no need."

"Robin had no need either."

"That's what I mean. We don't expect this."

"But now it's happened," Molly said, voicing her own concerns, "so we have to *do* things. But how do we find out what a person wants when she can't talk, can't *think*?"

"Did your sister have a living will?"

"Like a do-not-resuscitate order? Not to my knowledge."

"No health-care proxy?"

Molly shook her head. "I'd criticize her for that, only I don't have them either. Is it arrogance? Complacency?"

"Fear. We don't want to think it can happen to us."

Well, now she knew it could. She shared that knowledge with this stranger.

"Do you have a name?" she asked on impulse and immediately began to hedge. "You don't have to give it to me. I won't tell my parents." Especially not her mother. Though Kathryn was no longer hysterical, she still believed that the Good Samaritan had done too little too late. "I was just wondering. For me."

"It's David," he said. "David Harris. I have a phone number, too." He took a card from his pocket, wrote on its back, and gave it to Molly. "That's my cell. Don't feel like you have to call. I'll keep checking here to find out how your sister is doing. But if there's anything I can do, or if you just want to talk . . ."

Molly didn't know if she would, but it was nice to be asked. Pocketing the card, she rose. "I think you should also tell your student's father that you're *worried* about her. Omission feels worse here. If you look the other way and something bad happens, you'll always wonder." At least, that was what Molly felt. She should have been waiting for Robin on that road, rather than watering plants at home.

NEEDING TO REDEEM HERSELF, SHE WENT TO ROBIN'S room. "Any change?" she asked.

Kathryn shook her head. "I didn't think you'd be back tonight."

"I'm not sure I can sleep."

"You'll sleep."

Molly might have argued. Funny thing about the term *brain dead*. It jangled the nerves even when you weren't thinking about it.

But she hadn't come to argue. "What can I do, Mom? Tell me. I really want to help."

Kathryn smiled sadly. "Not much to do right now. She's sleeping calmly."

"Can I stay here while you get some sleep yourself?"

"No thanks, sweetheart."

"Are you sure?"

Kathryn nodded. "I am."

GRATEFUL AT LEAST THAT KATHRYN HADN'T YELLED AT HER, Molly took the elevator to the ground floor. The parking lot had thinned out, but she was distracted, and it was dark. When a man straightened from leaning against her car, she jumped a mile.

"Nick! I didn't see you. Why are you sneaking around out here?"

"I'm not sneaking around," he replied calmly. "I'm waiting for you. You wouldn't tell me much on the phone. What's going on, Molly? And who's that guy you were talking to before?"

"Before?"

"Before you went inside. You were sitting over on that bench by the hospital sign."

Nick had been here a while. That said something for friendship. But David was a kindred soul, and she felt protective. "He's just someone I've seen around."

"Around the hospital?"

"Come and go enough, and you see the same faces."

"He looks familiar. What's his name?"

She felt guilty not trusting Nick. A first name couldn't hurt. "David."

"David what?"

"I don't know," she lied. "When you see someone over and over like that, you nod, you smile, you ask about who they're visiting. You don't get personal. There's no point in exchanging last names."

"Did he ask about Robin?"

"Yes. He's polite."

"Did you tell him more than you told me?"

She hung her head, then raised it. "Oh Nick, there's nothing to tell."

"Big understatement. Let's start with, is Robin going to be okay?"

"I don't know. We're waiting for more tests."

"Did she have a history of heart problems?"

"No," Molly said before realizing that by confirming a heart problem, she had fallen into his trap. Annoyed that he was setting them, she added, "Do you?"

"I'm not in the ICU at Dickenson-May. What's the prognosis?"

She needed comfort, not questions—a word of encouragement, maybe something he had gotten from one of his sources that would ease the sense of total loss she felt. But he just stood there, obviously angry that she wouldn't give him the details he wanted.

"I'm really tired," she said quietly.

"Does that mean it's bad?"

"It means, that today has been a long day."

"People are asking me, Molly, and I don't know what to say. They're imagining the worst, and I can't deny it. Help me out here, Moll."

"For the paper?" the devil in her asked.

He was quiet, then impatient. "You have the power to stop unfounded talk. Robin would want that."

He struck a nerve. "How do you know what Robin would want?" Molly asked sharply. Her mother didn't know. Her father didn't know. Chris didn't know. *She* didn't know. And Nick thought *he* did?

There was a pause, then his gentle, "This isn't like you. What happened to the friend I rely on for straight talk?"

The reality of life and death is weighing on her, Molly thought but couldn't say aloud.

"This can't be good," Nick decided in her silence. "Are we talking a massive heart attack?"

She rubbed her forehead, then dropped her hand. "It's pretty serious."

"Does that mean she won't recover? Is there permanent damage? Can it be fixed?"

The dark might have muted the force of his eyes, but

Molly still began to squirm. "Don't interrogate me, Nick. You're putting me on the spot."

"Because you're hiding how bad it is?"

"Because my mother doesn't trust you. She would be furious if she knew we were talking."

"I just want to know."

"So do *we*. But we don't. Not yet. We just don't *know* the bottom line."

She pulled out her keys, but he didn't give up. "Come on, Moll," he coaxed. "The doctors must be telling you more. They either give you hope, or they don't. Hey, I work with these guys. I have a list of names to call when I want a quote from an expert. I'd guess some of the ones treating Robin are on my list; but I haven't called, *precisely* out of respect for your mother. But you're not helping. Yeah, I know the first few days are crucial, but there's mild damage and not-so-mild damage. Which is it?"

"*I'm* not helping?" Molly cried, mystified. "Helping who, Nick? What about your supporting *me*? What about your trying to understand what my family is going through right now? This isn't a walk in the park. We've been blindsided, and your questions aren't helping."

He was oblivious to her point. "Is part of the shock because Robin is who she is? She's made a name for herself doing twenty-six-mile runs. Will she ever run again?"

"I don't *know*."

"What does she say?"

"*Nothing*."

For a minute, the only sound was a hum of crickets in

the distant wood. Then came a quick-fire, "She's not talk-ing? She's sedated? Unconscious? In a *coma*?"

"She's brain dead!" Molly cried in a burst of despair. Her eyes filled. "Okay? Is that what you want to hear?"

Nick went very still. He didn't speak.

"And now I've betrayed her again." Horrified, Molly clutched his arm. "Do not put this in the paper, Nick. I *beg* you. I'm very emotional, not a credible source right now. It's been a scary day, and the fact is, they are . . . doing . . . tests. We won't have any definitive answers for another twenty-four hours."

"Brain dead?" he repeated, seeming stunned and so un-aware of Molly that her hand was yanked free when he turned. Silently, he walked off.

"Please, Nick?" she called across the dark parking lot, but he didn't answer. Hugging herself, she watched him disappear into his sleek black car. The engine turned over. As he headed toward the street, he drove slowly, and she wondered if he was already on the phone.

She considered going inside and telling her mother about Nick. First, though, she needed to do something good, and for that, she had to go home.

THE WORDS *BRAIN DEAD* HAUNTED HER ALL THE WAY HOME. SHE didn't understand how Robin could be *brain dead,* which meant that by the time she got home, in addition to being frightened she was bewildered. Brain death was a perma-nent thing. It would impact all their lives.

The house was dark, but familiar and comfort-filled. And here was another source of angst. The clock was ticking. She had only five more days here.

Unable to deal with that, she turned on a light and went straight to the phone. Moving was forgotten in the raft of messages from Robin's friends. Molly recognized one name after another on the caller ID. Most were runners, a few were calling from as far as Europe, proof of the closeness of the running community. How had Robin explained it? *You bond when you run. It's like a therapy session. There's no eye contact. Confession becomes safe.*

Molly wondered whether, if that was true, Robin had told others about her enlarged heart. More pertinent, Molly wondered whether, in some philosophic moment, Robin might have said what she would want done if she were ever disabled.

But how embarrassing was that, having to ask Robin's friends what her own family didn't know?

Nick hadn't known anything about the enlarged heart. That was something, at least.

Molly needed information, such as what Robin had known and when. How else could she make sense of what had happened?

As she headed for the den, she heard a scrabbling on the wood floor. Glancing down the hall, she saw the wisp of an amber tail disappear into her room.

The cat. She had forgotten. Conscience-stricken, she followed it, but it had hidden again. Talking softly so it would hear at least, she saw to its litter and water. Thinking to keep it company for a few minutes, she sat on the floor with her head on the seat of the armchair and closed her eyes.

When she opened them again, an hour had passed. Startled, she pushed herself up and spotted the cat sitting in the hall, staring at her from the farthest possible point where it could still see her. Suddenly desperate to touch something warm and alive, she crouched down and held out a hand. "Come here, kitty," she cooed. "It's okay. I won't hurt you." The cat didn't budge. Nor did it run away until she crawled toward it on all fours. Then in a flash it was gone.

Desolate, she sat on her heels, thinking first of the cat, then of Robin. She was trying to decide whether to chase the cat or go back to the hospital when her stomach growled. She went to the kitchen. One look around, though, and she felt an old annoyance. Robin was a slob.

Guiltily, she took back the thought. Robin wasn't there to defend herself. This was absolutely not the time for mean thoughts.

But Robin *was* a slob. The kitchen was exactly as she had left it when she had gone for yesterday's run. Used tea bags were on the counter beside dirty mugs. A half-empty energy drink stood beside an open bag of granola, the crumbs of which lay next to the wrappers of three energy bars. Two unopened bars spilled from their box, which Molly had returned *so often* to a cabinet that held another ten such boxes.

Robin was a health nut. Molly didn't miss the irony of that.

Kathryn might have wanted things left as they were. But

that was morbid. And Molly was the one who lived here. She always cleaned up after Robin. So she did it now.

When her stomach growled again, she opened the fridge. There were more energy drinks, along with tofu and yogurt. There was also a chocolate cake, definitely Molly's contribution to the food supply. She pulled it out, intent on having a piece, only to realize she wasn't in the mood. Chocolate cakes—or cupcakes with frosting and sprinkles, or glittery butter cookies—were the most fun to eat while Robin watched in disapproval. If Robin wasn't there, what was the point?

Molly pushed the cake down the disposal. Thus purged, she heated a turkey frank, wrapped it in pita, drizzled it with mustard, and downed it in two seconds flat. Craving something warm to drink, she took an envelope of hot chocolate from her side of the cabinet. Like the cake, though, it lacked appeal. So she brewed a cup of Robin's ginseng tea and carried it into the den.

It was a small room, just big enough for bookshelves and a desk. Molly had already packed the books that had been on her own shelves, but Robin's were still full. The top one held a neat lineup of sneakers, one pair more worn than the next. The shelf beneath held a random arrangement of books, and, on the lowest shelf, carelessly placed accordion files bulging with papers.

Sitting on the floor, she opened one. It was stuffed with term papers, tests, and class notes from a decade before. Replacing that file, she took another. This one was jammed with race entry forms, speeches Robin had given, and newspaper clippings of her own wins, the wins of her friends, and articles on every aspect of running. There were even several running magazines crammed in. Nothing was chronologically arranged.

She had to open more files before she found bills—electricity, gas, rental. Robin had lived in two other apartments before they moved here together. Molly found leases for two of the three. She found credit card bills, dental bills and, yes, medical bills referencing Robin's endless little mechanical problems; but none mentioned her heart. Molly was thinking that Jenny Fiske had to be wrong, perhaps had mistaken something Robin had said, when she found an envelope from Robin's primary care physician. It was tucked a little too neatly at the very back of the file. Molly might have missed it if she hadn't put the folder on her lap to stuff the bills back inside.

"Dear Robin," the doctor wrote, "I'd like to reiterate your cardiologist's optimism. As frightening as a cardiomegaly diagnosis can be, since you've been asymptomatic, the prognosis is good. You're one of the lucky ones who are alerted by a hereditary condition. If your father hadn't told you about the problem, you might have ignored symptoms down the road. Forewarned is forearmed. The cardiologist has discussed medication with you. Your running shouldn't be affected, but it is crucial that you see one of us immediately if you experience any of the symptoms we've mentioned. If all is well, I'll see you at your regularly scheduled appointment."

The letter was dated eighteen months earlier. But it

made no sense to Molly. Charlie had denied a history of heart problems. Either he was lying, or Robin was.

Dropping the letter, she scrambled up and went into the bathroom. Having always ceded the medicine chest to Robin's running remedies, she had no idea what was inside. Looking now, she found over-the-counter products, and a single bottle of prescription painkillers. Not surprisingly, it was barely used. Robin hated taking anything but vitamins.

Rushing to the kitchen, Molly searched her sister's stash of vitamins, thinking she might keep a bottle of heart medication there to pretend it was just another healthy thing to take each day, but each bottle Molly found appeared to be nothing but vitamins. Back down the hall, she rummaged through the nightstand by Robin's bed, then through her dresser drawers. No pills.

Of course, discussing medication with a doctor didn't necessarily lead to taking it, especially where Robin was concerned.

Temporarily at a standstill, Molly returned to the den. After putting the bills back, she put the file back on its shelf. She reread the doctor's letter before returning it to its envelope. The woman practiced out of Concord. Molly could contact her.

Right, Molly. If the goal was helping her mother, calling either Charlie or Robin a liar wouldn't help. Besides, the heart damage was done.

Molly didn't understand how she couldn't have known. Even if Robin planned to keep it from her, wouldn't something have accidentally slipped out? She racked her brain, trying to recover even the smallest mention. Yes, Robin had been more worried lately about being with people who were sick, but that was understandable. The stakes were higher than ever in the races she had entered.

Frustrated, Molly tucked the letter in her pocket and turned on the computer. Here was something she could definitely do. So many notes of concern on both her and Robin's e-mail accounts, sweet notes from people who cared—all deserved an answer. She sent simple ones to acknowledge the kindness of the sender, but gave little medical detail. She sent similar notes to some of those who had left phone messages.

When she finished, it was after one. Wide awake, with that letter sitting in her pocket like a hot stone, she went into Robin's room. It was as messy as always. Here, too, Kathryn might have wanted things left alone. But Molly had been cleaning up after Robin since they had moved in together, and Robin never seemed to mind. She liked being pampered. Neatening the room was something she would want. It was the least Molly could do.

Finding penance in it, she carefully made Robin's bed, hung up a nightshirt, pushed dirty clothes into the laundry bag on the back of the door. She put away two fanny packs, took the book that was open facedown on the bed and closed it, using the cover flap as a marker. It was a book on self-motivation. Opening it again to the page Robin had been reading, Molly suddenly heard her sister's voice, deeper than her own and with a resonance born of passion. *Training is the tough part. Not everyone can do it. When you do that long run, with no water stations, no TV crews, no crowds cheering you on, it's hard. But that's the point. The long run helps develop the mental toughness you need to run a marathon. It's during the long run that you learn how to cope.*

Realizing that Robin might be on her last long run now, Molly grew weepy; but along with tears came a glimmer of hope. If anyone had mental toughness, Robin did. If anyone could pull through, she could.

Believe in yourself, Robin always told running groups, *and you'll make it happen.*

Drying her eyes, Molly grabbed a large canvas bag and began filling it. There was the picture of Robin wearing the laurel wreath in Boston, and a framed article that had appeared in *People.* There was the running book she had coauthored and, from the corkboard, handwritten letters of adoration from would-be runners. There was the hat she had worn running London and the singlet and shorts she had broken in for New York. There was her lucky wristband. And her favorite running shoes. And her journal.

Molly dug the journal from the closet, which was a total disaster. Narrow but deep, her closet was packed full of everything Robin didn't want to look at day to day. Robin claimed mice lived at the back. Molly hated mice—which was one reason she loved the Snow Hill cats and might be good reason to have a cat where she lived—but even aside from that, this closet would be the pits to pack. CDs were tossed in with a tangle of headset cords, MP3 players, and multiple generations of iPods. Tee shirts with race names were strewn about, along with plaques, rolled photos, and other memorabilia. And there were more diaries, dating back to Robin's childhood. *My Book,* Robin called each, and Molly had long since read every one, hoping in vain for a dramatic divulgence of her sister's darkest secrets. By the time Robin reached high school, she called them journals and filled them with reports on the races she had run. Once she graduated from college, she stopped writing.

Molly took the very last journal. It was only about races. But running defined Robin. If these things helped make her hospital room more personal, if some hidden vibe could spark her back to consciousness, they should be there.

CHRIS COULDN'T SLEEP. HE DIDN'T UNDERSTAND HOW A person could be alive one minute and dead the next. The fact that Robin's heart was beating was a technicality. The damage was done. Robin was gone.

He knew things like that happened. He remembered 9/11. He remembered Virginia Tech. He just hadn't personally known anyone who had died like that.

Erin's voice came quietly through the dark. "I wish I'd known Robin better. I kept thinking there'd be a time when she wouldn't be running so much, maybe even when she'd have a baby and we'd have more in common." Her voice turned his way. "Do you think tomorrow's test will be any different?"

"No."

"What'll your Mom do?"

He had no idea. They had never faced anything catastrophic before.

"The machines could keep Robin alive forever," Erin said. "Would the hospital allow that?"

"If the insurance pays."

"Does it?"

"I can't go there yet, Erin."

"How can you not?" she asked. "Your sister's about to be declared brain dead."

He might have snapped if she hadn't sounded so upset herself. She also happened to be right. Today—tomorrow—they would face a decision. Insurance might pay. But if Robin's brain was dead, what was the point?

Climbing out of bed, he went down the hall to Chloe's room. In the pale yellow haze of a butterfly night-light, he looked at her. She was lying on her back, her hands up by her head, her mouth nursing an imagined bottle. Even asleep, she was sweet.

He couldn't think of life without her, but it hadn't always been that way. He hadn't been ready for kids and had gone along with Erin only because she wanted one so badly. He had been hoping that getting pregnant would take a while, but two months was all it took; and even then, he didn't focus on having a child. It wasn't until the sonogram showed something resembling a human being that it hit him. A subsequent sonogram increased the feeling, and then, when Erin got big and the baby started to move under his hand, he was completely won over. He adored Chloe the instant she was born.

"I'm sorry," Erin said from the door. "I didn't mean to make things worse. Are you okay?"

He nodded.

She came to stand beside him. After a minute, she reached into the crib and smoothed the baby's blond hair. "I can't imagine . . ."

"Me either."

"I didn't know what to say to your mom."

"What's there to say? There's no solution."

"Maybe it isn't about solutions. Maybe it's about helping Kathryn."

Chris felt an anger come from nowhere. "Maybe Robin should have thought of that. How could she have kept racing if she knew she had a heart problem? She should have thought about what we'd go through, what *Mom* would go through if something happened to her. But Robin was into Robin. It was always about her."

"We were the ones who put her on a pedestal."

"Not me," Chris declared.

"Well, I did. I thought she was amazing. I was totally intimidated."

"Most people are."

"I feel closer to Molly."

"Molly's more human."

"That's unkind."

"It's realistic."

"Robin is brain dead."

"I know that, Erin. She's my sister. Don't you think I'm hurting, too?"

Erin faced him in the dark. "Maybe if we talked it out—"

"Look, this is a tough time for me."

"The nurse mentioned social services. Maybe we should be talking to them."

"I'm not talking to strangers."

"They're trained in things like this. They know what we're facing."

"They can't cure Robin."

"This isn't about Robin anymore."

One part of Chris knew that. But he couldn't focus on what Erin wanted. "It'll be about Robin until her heart stops. Give her that much, okay?"

chapter 8

KATHRYN USED A PULL-OUT BED IN ROBIN'S ROOM but slept sporadically. Nurses came and went, and the equipment beeped and hissed. Rarely did an hour pass without an alarm ringing somewhere in the unit.

By dawn, she gave up on sleep. This was race day. She didn't care if Robin came in last, as long as she placed. The clock was ticking. The second EEG would be done tonight. One tiny blip. That was all they needed to redouble their efforts. Just one.

As soon as Charlie spelled her, she drove home to shower and change. She couldn't hide exhaustion, but when she returned to the hospital, at least she felt fresh. She was wearing her favorite blazer and slacks, perhaps overkill for a hospital room, but appearance mattered. If she looked like a somebody in the eyes of the hospital staff, Robin would benefit.

Charlie, bless him, didn't need to dress up. With gorgeous, so-blond-as-to-be-nearly-white hair, a straight back, and confident hazel eyes, he was distinguished even in an open-collar shirt and slacks. But he was feeling the strain. As she entered the room he looked up unguarded. He was suffering, too, she realized, and she wrapped her arms around him. She lingered there for her own benefit, gearing up for what came next, but found it didn't help. When she finally looked at Robin, she was hit in the gut.

She actually needed a minute to catch her breath. Then the words came out in a bewildered rush. "Why Robin? Why this? Why now? And why *us*? We did everything right raising Robin. Body, mind, heart—we nourished it all. She didn't want for *anything*."

"We were blessed to be able to do those things, Kath. Not all parents can. Are they any less worthy?"

"No, but this is unfair. Robin is so close. She's on the . . . the cusp of greatness. What kind of God would take that away?"

"One who has something better in mind."

"Like what?" Kathryn demanded. When Charlie didn't reply, she goaded, "You and my mother. Things happen for a reason. Tell me. I want to know what good can come of this."

Quietly, he said, "We can't see it now. But we will."

"*When*? Before the test? After the test? Next week? Next month?"

He drew her in and held her until she let the anger go in a sorrowful sigh. That was when she saw the vases on the windowsill. One held yellow roses, one green hydrangea, one a field mix of lavender and blue. "Who?"

"Robin's friends. The flower shop downstairs delivered them. We're just starting to get plant orders at Snow Hill. The calls are coming from New York and L.A."

"How many arrangements will the nurses allow?" Kathryn asked. As surprisingly liberal as the hospital's policy was regarding family involvement, this was still the ICU.

"As many as we want," Charlie replied.

She met his gaze. The implication was clear. "It's about us now, not Robin." When he didn't argue, she left his side and went to the bed. Staying positive was getting harder, but she dug deep inside and produced a bright, "Good morning, Robin!"

MOLLY WAS UP AT DAWN, PUTTING HER TOTE IN THE CAR and driving to Snow Hill. Her plants needed watering, and, yes, one of her staff could have done it. But the greenhouse fortified her. Strapping an apron around her waist, she worked her way from section to section. As the moisture added to the rich smell of earth, she grew calmer. Robin swore by aromatherapy. This was Molly's own brand.

Had she not been under its lingering effect, she might have been more upset when she took a break and saw the newspaper. Mention of Robin had won a spot totally separate from the police blotter. The piece wasn't long, but it was under Nick's byline. Even beyond personal disappointment, this created problems.

Unable to dwell on them, she headed for the hospital. Her parents were there when she reached Robin's room, but a respiratory therapist was working with the breathing tube. Crossing to the window, Molly read the notes on the flowers until he left. Then she turned back.

Her mother was as attractive as ever. Her brown hair had a healthy shine, her cheeks a subtle blush. Her slacks were neat, her blazer trendy. But her eyes were filled with fear, which had the effect of aging her ten years.

Unsettled, Molly spoke gently. "These flowers are just the start. Robin has *the* best friends. I swear, half of them would hop on a plane and be here this afternoon if we gave the word. The e-mail just doesn't stop. I've told everyone that we're taking it one day at a time." She paused, but knew it had to be said. "I've also told them that it doesn't look good."

"Molly—" Kathryn started.

"Silence doesn't work," Molly reasoned. She kept her voice soft, but if she was being forced into the role of spokesperson, she did have a say. "Take these flowers. They're from people I didn't talk with—Susie Hobbs, the San Diego running club. Robin's friends are calling each other, leaving messages, playing phone tag, and the story keeps getting wilder. If we want them to spread the truth, we have to give them the truth."

Sensing her parents were listening, she pulled the morning paper from her tote. It was already folded with

Nick's piece on top. She passed it to her father—who may or may not have had a heart defect. In her entire memory, he had been quiet and well-paced. She had assumed it was just his personality. Now she wondered if the discipline was deliberate.

Kathryn read the paper over his shoulder. Then, staring at Molly with reproach, she sank into a chair by the bed.

Molly was quickly defensive. "There was no avoiding it, Mom."

"Nick is your friend. Couldn't you keep this from happening?"

"The paper would have printed something with or without him. This is news."

"And he couldn't make them wait? Of course he could have, but he didn't want to. He is ruthless. He is also fixated on your sister. He's using you to get news of her."

"No, Mom. We carry on whole conversations that have nothing to *do* with her."

"Now? No, I didn't think so. How much are you telling him?"

"*Nothing*. Can't you tell from this article? I refuse to talk, and he can't get past the hospital's privacy laws, so he's printing gossip. But maybe we're taking the wrong tactic. We should use him to get out what *we* want in print."

Kathryn glanced at Charlie, who raised an eyebrow, acknowledging the point.

Emboldened, Molly said, "Same with Snow Hill. We have to tell our employees something. Right now, they're just speculating. Tami came in early again today—"

"You were there?" Kathryn asked in surprise. "Dressed up like that?"

Molly was wearing a belted blouse and short skirt. "This isn't dressed up."

"You usually wear jeans."

"This is cooler. Besides, maybe I need to look authoritative if you want me to be your stand-in. Tami says rumors are flying. They range from Robin needing a transplant to something being wrong with you or Dad. I focused her on Robin by telling her about the coma; but if you want me to say something else, you need to tell me what."

Neither of her parents spoke. And Molly didn't have the heart to badger. She understood why they couldn't deal with this. She didn't want to deal with it either.

But here was Robin, silent and inert. Discouraged, Molly studied her sister. "It's ridiculous to sugarcoat this. Even if she wakes up, her life will be changed." Of course, she was daring her mother to argue.

But Kathryn simply said, "I know. I just can't go there yet."

The admission helped. This was progress.

Charlie gave Kathryn's shoulder a squeeze and left the room. Molly's first instinct was to follow to ask about his heart, but she sensed a softening in her mother and wanted to take advantage of it.

"I'm sorry, Mom. I wish it was me in that bed."

"I wish it was *me*," Kathryn replied.

"But then, who would run Snow Hill?" Molly countered, only half in jest.

"You. What's in the bag?"

"I can't run Snow Hill. I was only joking about the skirt."

"Of course you can run Snow Hill. You know it better than anyone else. What's in the bag?"

Loath to argue, Molly hoisted the tote to the bed. "The nurses said to personalize the room, so I brought things from home."

"They haven't repeated it," Kathryn told her with a frightened look. "Not since yesterday morning. That worries me."

What worried her, Molly knew, was that the nurses had started thinking of Robin as beyond help; but that was where mothers and sisters came in. She began taking things from the tote. "We personalized Nana's room to help spark memories. If it works for her, it can work for Robin."

"It doesn't work for Nana."

"It does. She told me yesterday that you have a daughter named Robin."

Kathryn sat back. "Oh Molly. You told her about this."

"She didn't take in the bad part. Really, Mom, I didn't upset her. But I needed to talk with someone, and she needed a guest."

Kathryn shot her a skeptical look.

"Besides," Molly went on, "we don't know that it doesn't work." Without looking at Kathryn again, she set up picture frames and tacked letters to the bulletin board. She laid

Robin's book on the bed stand, set her London hat on the ventilator, hung her sneakers from the IV pole.

She hesitated when it came to the wristband, looking for an appropriate spot, but there was only one. Carefully, she eased it over Robin's limp fingers and adjusted it on her wrist.

She was crying by then, but there was still the journal. Taking it from the tote, she hid behind it. "I'm sorry . . . I know you don't want crying . . . but how not to . . . with Robin lying here . . . and it's like every one of her motivational mantras is useless . . . and this journal is so *old* it doesn't *begin* to capture what she is now . . . so what *good* is it?"

Kathryn's arms came around her, and the comfort wasn't too different from the comfort Marjorie had unwittingly given. What was happening to Robin was shocking and new, but Kathryn's arms brought comfort from the past. Slowly Molly stopped crying.

"I'm sorry," Kathryn finally said, sounding none too steady herself. "This is hard on you, and I haven't been able to help. There are times when I feel . . . stuck in the moment."

"Like Robin."

"Maybe."

Molly wiped her eyes. "It's the waiting. You hope and you hope, and nothing happens, and now there's this second test."

"I may ask them to postpone it."

Molly caught her breath. "No, Mom. Don't do that. We need to know."

"I'm not ready."

"We need to *know*."

Kathryn looked away.

"It's the *waiting* that's so bad," Molly repeated. "How do we get through that?"

Kathryn was quiet. Then, in a measured way that said her brain knew the answer even if her heart did not, she declared, "We do our jobs."

MOLLY WANTED TO ASK HER FATHER ABOUT HIS HEART, but hated to leave Kathryn alone. So she waited for Charlie to return, but then couldn't raise the issue with her mother sitting there. Thwarted, she left them together and went down to the lounge. Chris and Erin were nursing coffee at a table.

She pulled up a chair and murmured, "Nightmare."

"You've already said that," Chris remarked. "So, do you think she'll wake up?"

"Science would say no, but I've had plants I thought were stone dead—I mean, so dried up and shriveled that I cut them off just shy of the root—and they've come back."

Chris stared at her as if she was an imbecile. "Robin isn't a plant."

"Okay." Molly smiled, putting the onus on him. "*You* tell us something positive."

He studied his coffee cup.

"You look nice," Erin said, leaning around to look. "You have great legs. You should wear skirts more."

"Maybe you can catch a doctor," Chris put in.

Molly bristled. "You are sick. So I'm wearing a skirt. I don't need to look like I've been digging in dirt all the time."

"That is what you do."

"Chris," Erin protested.

Molly could fight her own battles. "What's *with* you?" she asked her brother.

He frowned. "I'm upset about Robin."

"And I'm *not*?" she cried. Struck by her own shrillness, she lowered her voice. "Let's not argue right now. I'm still hung up on the heart thing, Chris. Robin told her doctor that her father had a problem."

Chris recoiled. "Her father? How do you know that?"

"I found a letter. Why would she say Dad had a problem if he didn't?"

"Better to blame someone else," he said, unkind but true.

"Have you told your father about the letter?" Erin asked.

"I haven't had a chance. I wanted to stay with Mom. I worry about her."

"What can we do?"

"To quote her, 'We do our jobs.' "

"Uh-huh," Chris said acidly. "While Robin is on life support."

"Snow Hill doesn't stop," Molly reasoned. "I'm already doing my own work, and I'll cover for Mom. Someone has to cover for Dad."

"I lost most of yesterday," he said, "so I'm behind on payroll and bills, and quarterly estimates are due in a week."

"I'm moving in five days," Molly countered calmly, "but that doesn't mean I can let the garden club in Lebanon think Mom is still giving her speech. I'll talk with the people who need answers outside Snow Hill. You talk with people inside."

Chris waved a hand *no*.

"Okay," she tried. "I'll talk with people inside. You talk with people outside."

The look on his face said he found that thought even more distasteful.

"I know you don't want to, Chris. But we're all doing things we don't want to do."

He turned the cup in his hands.

"Please," Molly appealed, but he remained silent. "Fine." She pushed herself up. "I'll do it myself."

"SHE'S RIGHT," ERIN SAID AS SOON AS MOLLY WAS GONE. "Everyone here is having to do things they don't want to do."

But Chris was angry. "Do I need Molly telling me what to do?"

"It isn't her fault. She's only the messenger."

"She's used to filling in for Mom. I'm not used to filling in for Dad. He can't do my work, and I can't do his."

"No one's asking you to design a media campaign, just to make a few phone calls."

"I'm not a PR person."

"Did I know how to change a diaper before Chloe was born? I learned fast, because it had to be done. And if we're talking about doing things we don't *want* to do, do you think I like cleaning up when she throws up? I don't. But I have to. This is about doing what has to be done even when you're uncomfortable doing it."

"Erin, I can't be at Snow Hill right now," he stated. It seemed perfectly obvious why.

"It's a way to help your family. It wouldn't take much time. Molly's already doing a lot, and she's right about moving. Now she has to move herself *and* Robin."

Chris snorted. "No one's evicting her."

"That's not the point. Her landlord needs her out, so she's trying to cooperate." She grasped his arm. "Snow Hill is a family business. If you can't *pinch-hit* for your family in a time of crisis, what good are you?"

But he was in crisis, too. "Do we have to discuss this now?"

"Now's when it counts. You either step up to the plate, or you don't."

He sighed. "Baseball isn't your thing."

"But it's yours, and if there's no other way I can get through, I'll give it a shot. What's happening now is big league. We've never gone through anything so stressful."

Chris wondered what planet *she* had been on. "Planning a wedding wasn't stressful? Or buying a house? Or having a baby?"

"Those things are different. This is something we didn't ask for and don't want, and it's making me nervous about the future. What if something happens to me? Can you take over with the baby? You may not want to, but someone would have to."

"Nothing's happening to you."

"Like nothing was happening to Robin? Doesn't this *shake* you, Chris? I mean, we don't even have a will."

He stared at her. "I am *not* drawing up a will right now."

"But doesn't what's happening here make you think?" she cried. "And this is exactly what I'm saying. I don't want to be having this conversation. It's messy and uncomfortable, and I'm not good at confrontation, so I'm probably doing it wrong. But you're hanging back when it comes to your family—and yes, when it comes to me, too. You let other people do the dirty work by default."

"I change diapers," he argued.

"I'm not *talking* about changing diapers. I'm talking about taking responsibility, not just sitting back and letting everyone else do things so you don't have to. I'm talking about *joining the team,* Chris. You can't hit a home run while you're sitting in the dugout!" Softly she added, "You might have gotten away with it in your family if this hadn't happened to Robin. But you chose to marry me, and on that day something changed. Life isn't only about you anymore."

"This is about you?"

"It's about us right now—us as we're part of your family. It's about Chloe, whose aunt and grandparents are in there and can't be at Snow Hill. They need *help*."

MOLLY WASN'T IN THE MOOD ANY MORE THAN CHRIS WAS, BUT she was determined to do her job. She had to finish the ordering she hadn't done yesterday, had to cancel Kathryn's appointments, had to write the article for *Grow How*.

She also had to pack. When to do that? She couldn't imagine what would happen if the second EEG was bad—did not want to even *think* that worst-case-scenario word. But she had barely started to work when Joaquin Peña appeared at her door. His normally olive skin was pale.

"Your brother just said Miss Robin is dead."

Molly was livid. "She is not. She is on life support."

"But will she be dead soon?"

Chris might be. Molly could have killed him right then. Leaving the desk, she put an arm around Joaquin's shoulder. "It's bad. Not good at all."

He teared up. *"Por qué?"*

"I don't know."

"How is your mother?"

"Very, very upset."

"What can I do?"

"What you always do, Joaquin. Take care of things here so my parents don't have to worry. If there are any problems, call me. Okay?"

He nodded, touched her cheek, and went to the door.

Erin was there. She let Joaquin pass, then gave Molly a look. "My husband wasn't very subtle."

Molly let out a breath. She just didn't have the strength to fight. "Maybe he was right," she said. "What are we hiding?" Besides, Nick knew Robin was brain dead. His next article might announce it publicly. It struck her that the Snow Hill staff deserved better.

Glancing past Erin, she saw Deirdre Blake. Deirdre was as close as Kathryn came to having a personal assistant. A part-timer, though, she hadn't been in the day before.

She looked frightened. "I saw today's paper, but no one can tell me much. How is Robin?"

Molly swallowed. "Not good. It's a process."

"Her heart?"

"For starters."

"Will she recover?"

Molly exchanged glances with Erin, then said, "Y'know, I think Erin and I need to work on a statement. Maybe you could give us a little while. We'll come up with something, then you can get it out to everyone, okay?"

As soon as she was gone, Molly leaned the door closed and turned expectantly to Erin. "What do we say?"

"Don't you want Chris in here?"

Molly didn't. "Not if you're willing to help."

"I'm willing, but he might be better."

Molly made a face giving her opinion of *that,* then pulled up a blank screen on her computer and began to type. It took only five minutes. There wasn't much to say.

Erin worked over her shoulder, suggesting a word here, a thought here. "What you told Joaquin about taking care of things at Snow Hill so that your parents don't have to worry—that was good. I think you should include that."

Molly did. When they were both satisfied, she e-mailed the finished product to Deirdre.

"What else can I do?" Erin asked. "Chloe's with a sitter. I have time."

She seemed sincere, and Molly welcomed the help. Gesturing her into Charlie's office, she set her up with his Rolodex and a list of calls. "Start with WMUR. Explain that there's a family illness, so we have to cancel Friday's show. It's probably good that you're the one calling. You can just go with the party line and plead ignorance as to the details."

Erin lifted the phone, at which point Molly returned to her office to check her e-mail. Friends had definitely seen the paper. Their notes were sympathetic to a fault. On the chance that Terrance Field would be more sympathetic now that he'd had a chance to consider it, she called him.

And yes, he was more understanding than he had been the day before. "I did hear about your sister," he said. "It's frightening in one so young. I even called my landlord after you and I talked. But the news here isn't good, Molly. He said he was about to call me. He has someone willing to rent my place at the higher rent. He wants me out a month earlier. I do have a lease, so I don't think he can force me out. My attorney is attending to his mother-in-law over in Sarasota, but when he gets back . . ."

He went on for a minute, but Molly heard little of it. She made a final plea, then let him go and, needing a distraction, focused on an e-mail that had just come in from a supplier asking about the poinsettia order. Yesterday, she hadn't been able to come up with a figure. Now she quickly did. She shot him the number in a reply, then pulled up an actual order form and filled it out. Same with an order of garden supplies.

Scrolling farther, she stopped abruptly at an order confirmation. It was from the supplier she refused to deal with. She read the body of the e-mail and began a slow burn.

Leaning into the phone, she buzzed Liz Tocci. "It's Molly," she said politely enough. "Could you come to my office for a minute?"

Liz said she was on the phone with a client. Molly said it couldn't wait. Maybe she was wrong, since Kathryn put a premium on customer relations, but Molly had a lot on her plate. Her time was worth something. And her sister was dying.

Liz was a confident woman just shy of forty, though Molly had had to piece that together. Liz guarded her age, alternately projecting experience and exuding youth. This day she was an even mix. Blond hair swinging as coolly as someone young and naïve, she strode into the room wearing the silk blouse and slacks of someone who was an authority on design. She looked duly concerned. "I am *so* sorry to hear about Robin. How is she?"

"She's the same. But we need to talk about King Proteas."

Liz seemed puzzled. "Right now? You should be thinking about Robin, not this."

A tiny light went off, goading Molly. "You ordered from Maskin Brothers. I said we wouldn't do that, and I'm the one who does the ordering."

"You were at the hospital. I thought this would help."

"I was also here twice yesterday. And no, this doesn't help. Maskin Brothers is off-limits."

"That doesn't make sense, Molly," Liz said in a chiding way. "I worked with the Maskins for years before I came here, and I've had no problem at all. They have gorgeous King Proteas."

"Snow Hill has lost customers because of the Maskins."

"Maybe the problem is on this end."

"Me, you mean?"

"Or whoever did the ordering when you had trouble."

"Me," Molly said, starting to simmer. "I told you this at the meeting on Monday. Snow Hill doesn't work with the Maskins. They're asking for a deposit on the order. No deposit, no order."

"Your mother wouldn't approve," Liz said with a reproach that only riled Molly more.

"I think she would. She runs a tight ship."

"I've had more experience in this business than you have, Molly," Liz reminded her. "And let's be honest. Your specialty is plants, not cut flowers. I'm trying to build the interior design side of Snow Hill."

Molly smiled. Pulling rank wasn't something she wanted to do, but Liz had been a problem for months. When someone was as condescending as she was, there was only one way to deal. In a cool, Kathryn-like voice, she said, "Okay, let's *be* honest. I do the ordering. I decide who our vendors will be, because—bottom line—I own the business." She looked at her watch. "You have, oh, thirty seconds to come to terms with that. Think you can?"

"You don't own the business. Your mother does."

Molly said nothing, simply looked at her watch.

"There is nothing wrong with this supplier, Molly. Do you know how many other plant nurseries use them? Joe Francis in Concord doesn't have trouble with them. Nor does Manchester Landscaping. Our butting heads over this is ridiculous. I'm good for Snow Hill. I bring in work."

And more headaches than that, Molly thought. She didn't even wait out the last five seconds. "You're fired."

Liz looked startled. "Your mother won't stand for that."

"If she has to choose between the two of us, she will."

Liz stared. "Not a good move on your part. You need my goodwill."

"Well, we disagree about that, too. Snow Hill's reputation goes a long way in the goodwill department. If you'd like to tell people how bad I am, be my guest. You've only lived in this area for two years. People here have known me all my life. Besides, I might be worried if I were looking for a job, but I'm not. You're the one doing that."

Liz stood for another minute, then turned to the door.

She paused briefly when she saw Erin. "Chris's wife, right? I'm glad you're here. Molly isn't thinking straight. Want to try quieting her down?" She glanced at Molly. "I'll be in my office."

"Not for long," Molly informed her and buzzed Deirdre. "Would you ask Joaquin to meet Ms. Tocci at her office and take her to her car?"

Liz made a face. "Well, *that's* overkill."

But Molly had reached a boil. "My specialty may be plants, but while I was studying horticulture, I also took some business courses. I know how things work." She walked out of the office and, with Liz following, went down the hall, around a corner and down the stairs. She retrieved the Rolodex from Liz's desk. "Your contract says that everything you use for your work here is the property of Snow Hill. Feel free to take your purse, though."

Liz might have argued had not Joaquin appeared. Molly waited until they had gone before leaving the office and closing the door. Back at her own desk, she buzzed Deirdre again. "I want the lock on Liz's office changed. Will you ask Joaquin for me, please?"

Straightening, Molly took a deep breath and looked at Erin. "What . . . a . . . *bitch.*"

Erin was grinning. "Molly, that was great! Good for you!"

Molly pulled out her hair clasp, regathered her hair, and put the clasp back in. As quickly as that, her bravado crumbled. "What did I just do? I have no authority to fire someone."

"Of course, you do. You're acting in your mom's place while she's with Robin. This *is* your business."

"It's Mom's business," Molly argued because Liz had been right about that. "She hired Liz herself. She'll be furious."

But Erin was still grinning. "You're Kathryn's proxy. You looked like her. You *sounded* like her. That was amazing."

"I'm supposed to be helping her."

"You did. I drop by here enough to see Liz ordering people around. They roll their eyes behind her back."

"But now we have no designer."

"There must be others you can hire; and in the meantime, why not use Greg Duncan? You rave about what he does for you in the greenhouse. Listen," Erin said, "Liz moved up here to build her name in the area. She was using Snow Hill. Greg is loyal in ways she would never be."

"But he doesn't have the cachet of Liz Tocci. She's right; she did bring in work," Molly admitted, but the little light that had gone off in her mind earlier started to blink now. "The thing that's so bad about what she did is the timing. She figured I'd be looking the other way because of Robin. She exploited that."

"Which is exactly why your mom will support you."

"Mom wouldn't have lost her temper. Neither would Robin. She's a good loser. Okay, so this isn't a race. But I did lose. Liz snuck an order past me."

"She bypassed company policy. You do the ordering. Besides, you have a right to be short-tempered. These aren't ordinary times. Give yourself that much, Molly. Don't you think that's why Chris came down hard on you earlier? He needed an outlet. So did you."

Molly wondered if anything was happening at the hospital.

"Anyway," Erin went on, "the reason I came in here is that your dad just got a call from the paper. Do you know anything about an article on flowering kale?"

"It's on his computer." Molly gestured her back into Charlie's office and pulled it up. "Do they want it faxed or e-mailed?"

"E-mailed. I'll take care of it. Also, the sales department at *New Hampshire Magazine* wants to confirm Snow Hill's ad in the winter issues."

"Confirm them," Molly said, satisfied that they were helping with this at least. They? Erin. Molly had always liked her, but had never before seen her as a resource. Thinking how wrong she had been, she gave Erin a hug. "Thank you. My brother is very lucky."

Erin grunted. "He doesn't think so right now, so I wouldn't remind him if I were you. He's not in the best of moods."

"It's the waiting," Molly said. Smiling sadly at Erin, she returned to her office. It was so true. Waiting was the worst. Glancing at the clock every few minutes, she finished the immediate ordering, then tried calling Charlie on his cell, but it was off. She cancelled Kathryn's appointments. Ten minutes gone. She studied several recent issues of *Grow How,* debating what to write for the January issue, but her mind wouldn't focus.

Finally she went to the greenhouse. She was stopped along the way by Snow Hill people expressing concern about Robin, and she had an easier time talking now. Such a difference from Liz in their sincerity, she thought more than once.

The greenhouse had its share of customers, but Molly knew every corner. She settled onto a bench behind a palm where, if she sat very still, she wouldn't be seen.

But she could see out. One customer was filling her wagon with shade plants; another trailed back and forth between those and the gloxinia on the far wall. The latter were beauties, their velvet blossoms vibrant shades of pink and much more eye-catching. Still, Molly preferred the shade plants. Though lacking the splash of a flower, they had longevity. At least most shade plants did and, in that sense, were seriously undervalued. She loved it when they got attention.

Wagons rattled off toward the cash register, leaving the aisles momentarily quiet. Distant little bursts came from sprinklers in the shrub yard and, from farther away, the rumble of the backhoe lifting a burlap-based tree. Here in the greenhouse, though, it was quiet.

Molly loved these moments. Not so Robin. Robin was an action person. She wanted movement.

But Molly saw movement in the plants as the sun's arc shifted. She saw movement in the change of the seasons and the corresponding life cycle of her plants. Robin was a nominal New Englander, charting the seasons from forsythia to roses, fall leaves to snow. The changes Molly saw went well beyond that.

No, Robin wouldn't have lost her temper with Liz. Maybe, though, that was because she didn't love Snow Hill the way Molly did.

chapter 9

EVEN TWELVE HOURS AFTER SEEING MOLLY, NICK
Dukette was numb. He had known from the start that
Robin's condition was serious. His police contact had told
him as much. But he had expected some kind of fix, like
surgery or medication. *He* didn't care if Robin had to give
up running. It might work to his benefit. If she couldn't
run, she wouldn't travel as much, which would only en-
hance the appeal of a local guy.

Not that he planned to be local for long. He wasn't making the same mistake his parents had. They were brilliant
and totally unknown—Henry Dukette a novelist, Denise
Dukette a poet. Each time Nick read their work, he wondered how the world could not stand up and take notice.

Yet Henry had had to work for the highway department to support his family, and he had never complained. He said that seeing people around town was where he got his ideas. Nick didn't see the point of getting ideas if they had nowhere to go.

He vowed to change that once he had a name for himself. Newspaper work was one step removed from book publishing, and book publishing was all about who you knew. In time, he would get his parents' work read.

It wasn't about money. His older brother had made it big on Wall Street and even after taking care of his own family, had plenty to spare for Henry and Denise. He had bought them a condo not far from the state college in Plymouth, where Denise taught poetry, and had invested enough in their name to allow them to live comfortably on the interest. But Henry wouldn't hear of retiring. He claimed he was too young, that he liked being out and about. Nick wanted him out and about promoting a book, which was what would happen if Nick had his say.

First, though, good-bye New Hampshire—and he was getting closer. Once he was in charge of investigative news, he would have access to a higher level of contacts, which would open new doors. That was all he needed. He knew how to say things people wanted to hear. He also knew how to write a story—had already been recognized on a national level for a series on the presidential primary. The future looked bright.

Robin was to be part of that. Given her local stardom, he had been half in love with her even before they'd met. And after? They were amazing together. The fact that she was looking to compete globally didn't discourage him. She was approaching the height of her career. Once she had Olympic gold in hand, she would scale back. She was a family girl at heart. He guessed that as long as he stayed close, he was in the running.

But now this. He didn't know how much to believe of what Molly said. As contacts went, she wasn't the most reliable. She had said it herself. She was too emotionally involved.

So was he, in this instance. But he was also a professional. He knew how to get information. Right now, that demanded legwork.

Pushing aside the paralysis that had stilled him for much of the last twelve hours, he left his cubicle, pausing only when the editor-in-chief called his name from across the city room. "Where you headed?"

"The hospital. I'm following up on the Robin Snow story."

"The O'Neal indictment is at two."

Nick wasn't about to forget. Thanks to his own exposé on Donald O'Neal, the state was finally looking at election fraud. Nick had given them their case. "I'll be there," he called back and, touching the holster on his hip to make sure his phone was there, he left.

He didn't see Molly's car in the hospital lot, which was good. She was in a rough spot. He needed to get his information elsewhere.

Starting in the cafeteria, he homed in on the chief of cardiology, but the man wasn't being charmed. Nor was the hospital's top neurologist, though he had cooperated with Nick in the past. "Confidentiality," he'd murmured this time.

"Word I got was that she's brain dead," Nick said in his most confidential tone. "An exaggeration?"

The doctor eyed him askance. "Who'd you hear that from?"

Nick shot a suggestive look at the crowded cafeteria. Divide and conquer often worked. Suggest that one person had talked, and another would talk. "Should I believe it?"

"Even if I knew, which I don't," said the stoic neurologist, "I wouldn't confirm or deny."

"I heard they're discussing organ transplants." Of course, he hadn't heard that. All he needed was an inadvertent "Not yet" for confirmation.

But the doctor shot him a knowing look, held up a hand, and walked off, leaving Nick to seek out his favorite nurse-informant. Fifteen years his senior, she had loved him since he had written a favorable piece on her husband's business the year before.

She claimed she knew nothing, and though he asked question after question, he couldn't trip her up. When he asked if she could try to get information, she expressed her regret.

Thinking that they were all too good to be believed, he took the elevator to the ICU. Unable to get into the unit itself, he went to the lounge. He didn't recognize anyone there. Confident that would change if he waited long enough, he sank into the sofa. He was thinking that Molly had to be wrong—that Robin wasn't brain dead at all, simply unconscious—when he realized that a young girl and her mother, seated on an abutting sofa, were talking about Robin.

Elbows on his knees, he asked a casual, "Robin Snow?"

The girl nodded. She looked to be in her early teens.

"Are you family friends?" he asked the mother.

"No, but Robin was the reason Kaitlyn took up running."

"She spoke at my school," the girl explained. "And when I wrote to her afterward, she answered. I have a doctor's appointment this afternoon. Mom let me leave school early to come here."

"What's the latest on her?" Nick asked the mother.

"All they'll say is that she's in critical condition. Do you know more?"

"Nah," he said. He was thinking that striking out here was his punishment for using Molly—when he saw Charlie Snow in the hall. Without a word, he took off in pursuit. He caught up at the elevator. The man was lost in thought.

"Mr. Snow?" Charlie looked up. "How is she?"

"Oh. Nick. Hello."

"Is it as bad as Molly says?"

"What did Molly say?"

"That she's still unconscious." Molly had said more, of course, but Nick couldn't get himself to repeat it. He was starting to feel bad about Molly. He had put her on the spot.

"That's about it," Charlie confirmed. "We're waiting it out."

Nick had a dozen questions, but didn't ask a one. The elevator came, and before he knew it, he was alone. He stood there for the longest time, wondering what was wrong. He could ask anyone anything—*what are you feeling?* he had asked a mother watching divers search the river for the body of her son. That was how reporters got answers. Squeamish reporters got nothing.

He wasn't squeamish with the Snows, but maybe he was too close. Hell, he was almost family. At least, that was how he saw himself.

Discouraged, he took the next elevator down and returned to the city room to follow up on half a dozen small stories; but if he had hoped to distract himself, he was mistaken in that, too. He kept thinking of the last time he had seen Robin. She was having dinner with friends at a local restaurant and looked fabulous.

Call Molly, he told himself. *Let her say it isn't true.* But Molly had issues with her sister, and his putting her in a bind only made them worse.

He could return to the hospital just to hang out. If Molly saw him there and they started to talk, she might innocently pass something on. Alternately, he might bump into the guy she'd been talking with. David. The one who looked familiar. Nick wondered if *he* knew anything more about Robin's condition.

Feeling hollowed out, he leaned back and pressed his eyes. David, who looked familiar. David.

Trying to place him, he opened his eyes and rifled through printouts of recent stories, piled on his desk. He thumbed through a pile of photos. He sat back again. He had gone to a local bar after dropping Molly home Sunday night. He might have seen the guy there.

A face appeared over the front wall of his cubicle. "You want me with you at the courthouse?"

Nick glanced at his watch. In the process of looking back at Adam Pickens, his preferred photographer, his eye had to clear what he called his "idol wall." Here were photos of Rupert Murdoch, Bernard Ridder, and William Randolph Hearst. There were also pictures of Bob Woodward and Carl Bernstein, but another photo caught Nick's eye. It was of Oliver Harris, owner of the nation's third largest newspaper chain, several sports teams, and a cable network.

Molly's David looked exactly like that guy.

Leaning forward, Nick quickly googled Oliver Harris. After wading through several business-related entries, he found a write-up of Harris's family. The man was married to Joan, and had four children, three of whom worked for the corporation. The fourth and youngest was named David.

Possibly a coincidence. Neither David nor Harris were unusual names. But then there was the physical resemblance.

He googled David Harris, but got many pages of different David Harrises. Narrowing his search, he typed in "son of Oliver." Seconds later, he had what he wanted.

Smug, he sat back. The idea that Oliver Harris's son taught nearby was a windfall. The guy didn't know it yet, but he was about to meet his new best friend. Well, *almost* about to meet his new best friend. It would take some finesse. That was where Molly came in.

Leaning forward again, he pulled up her e-mail address, but there was Robin's, right under it in his address book, and the thought of Robin twisted his gut. So he wrote his note to Robin. It wasn't long. None of the notes he sent her were. He just wanted her to know that she had reason to recover.

Feeling profoundly sad, he sent it off. Then he pulled up Molly's address and simply said, "After I left you last night, I tried to kill the piece on Robin, but they'd already gone to press. I won't tell anyone what you told me, and there won't be anything else until you give the okay. You can trust me on that. I'm still shocked about Robin, but it must be even worse for you. Can I do anything to help?"

DAVID HARRIS DIDN'T HAVE TO READ FROM A TEXT. SITTING on a corner of his desk, he faced his eighth graders. "Fourscore and seven years ago our fathers brought forth upon this continent a new nation ..."

He recited the entire address, all two minutes worth, and was gratified that his students were listening. "Think about the words," he told them and repeated the address. He slowed at the parts that had always touched him the most, culminating with, "... we here highly resolve that these dead shall not have died in vain ..."

Of the subjects in American history that he taught, the Civil War was his favorite. He had visited every major battle site, knew that 620,000 deaths made the Civil War the country's bloodiest and that 200,000 boys under the age of sixteen had fought in the ranks over the course of those four years. He also knew that Ulysses S. Grant had been an alcoholic before rising to become the Union's top general, and that the Confederacy's Stonewall Jackson died of complications from a wound inflicted by one of his own men. Of many points of Civil War trivia, he particularly liked these two. They offered lessons about the precariousness of life and the sweetness of redemption.

David identified with both. *Life can turn on a dime,* his father always said. *The direction you head in when it does makes all the difference.* Oliver Harris took pride in what he had done following those turn-on-a-dime moments in his life. The long list of his successes cancelled out the few failures he'd had.

David didn't have a list to hide behind. He was only thirty-one. Everything he did showed.

He was thinking about that as he laid the groundwork for the Confederate States of America, talking of secession, Lincoln's inauguration, and the shots fired on Fort Sumter; but his eye kept returning to Alexis Ackerman. With her dark hair pulled back starkly and her layered tees snug, she looked bony and even more pale than usual.

Too soon, the bell rang. He barely had time to mention the assignment before he was drowned out by the rustle of backpacks and the shuffle of students leaving the room. He was turning back to his desk when he heard several gasps.

Alexis was on the floor by her desk, clinging to the chair.

He hurried down the aisle. "You all go on," he urged the others and hunkered down by her side.

"I don't know what happened," she said in a wispy breath. "My legs just didn't work."

"Are you dizzy?"

"No. I didn't faint. I'm okay now." Though her face had no color, she pushed herself up.

He stood to give her space, but when he said, "I'll walk you to the nurse's office," her eyes grew large, haunting her thin face.

"No, I'm fine. Really. I just need lunch." She gathered her things.

He guessed she would go straight to the salad bar and help herself to lettuce. "You've lost more weight, Alexis."

"No, I'm holding steady."

"Steady at what?" he asked.

"I just look thinner in these clothes," she said without answering the question. Floating past him, she made for the door. She looked back with an apologetic smile. "I'm really fine, Mr. Harris. Really. That was just a weird whatever." Turning away, she dissolved into the hall.

David needed lunch, too; but rather than head for the cafeteria, he went outside, down the front steps of the middle school, and across the street to the administration building. The superintendent had an office on the second floor. He was on the phone when David arrived, but the door was open. He gestured for David to wait.

Having been seen, there was no retreat. Otherwise, David might have lost his nerve. He didn't have the best of records where going out on a limb was concerned. Things seemed to backfire or, at the very least, cause more angst than good for those involved. It was fine for his father to pontificate about life turning on a dime, but the events on which Oliver's life turned were business-related. Rarely did they have to do with character, and certainly not with life and death as had been the case on the Norwich road Monday night. Molly was right; David couldn't *not* have revived Robin. But what good had it done?

And now here was Alexis. Her parents had eyes.

But parents saw what they wanted to see. His own brother had been addicted to their mother's painkillers before a math teacher called him on it, and only because *he* knew the signs. It was handled quietly. That brother, now forty-two, was slated to take over as publisher when Oliver retired. As attentive a mother as Joan Harris had been, she had never explained why she didn't notice her painkillers disappearing.

"Come on in, David," Wayne Ackerman called from his desk and, when David went to close the door, said, "Leave it. Our A/C is on the fritz. The more air circulating, the better. What can I do for you?"

Wayne was a plain man with a penchant for dramatically dark shirts and ties. His office, done in dark woods, was crowded with family pictures in chocolate brown frames. Wayne and his wife had five children; their faces were everywhere in his office, just as they were all over town. But Wayne's warmth didn't stop with family. He prided himself on knowing every teacher in his system.

Granted, as school systems went, this one wasn't large. But he was a master at making the personal connection. David had been to his office many times.

This was the first time he had come of his own accord. Committed, he sat and quickly said, "I'm worried about Alexis."

"My Alexis?"

"She just had an episode in my class. She didn't faint, but her legs gave way. I wanted to take her to see the nurse, but she refused. I'm worried, Dr. Ackerman. She's painfully thin."

"She's a dancer," Wayne said. "Dancers are always thin." He brightened. "Have you seen her dance? She's being primed as a soloist."

"I haven't seen her myself, but I hear she's incredible. I just worry. Dancers often have eating disorders."

Wayne dismissed that with a wave. "Her ballet teacher would tell us if she saw a problem."

"Even if severe thinness is part of the culture? I talked with someone last night—"

"About my daughter?" Wayne cut in.

"No. About the general symptoms of anorexia. I've seen many of them in Alexis."

"Today, David. Did it occur to you that she might have the flu?"

"This wasn't the flu."

"Do you know that for sure?"

"No," David conceded. "But I'm worried, Dr. Ackerman. I had Alexis in class last year, too. She was thin then, but the change over the summer is frightening. Now she's even thinner. Her voice is weaker. She doesn't hang out with classmates. She sits alone in the lunchroom."

"She studies through lunch," Wayne explained, "so that she can spend the rest of the day at the studio. She's very focused. I don't see anything wrong with that, David, and if you're saying she doesn't have friends, you're wrong. Her friends are dancers. They come from all over the state to dance at the academy. She sees them every afternoon." He frowned. "Are other teachers talking about this?"

"I don't know. I haven't raised the subject with them."

"Good. Please don't. My daughter's health is our business, not yours," he stated, and his good humor went downhill from there. "I don't like the idea that a young teacher with no kids thinks he knows about mine. I've raised five children and done a damn good job. My kids don't do drugs. They don't drive drunk. My sons respect women, and my daughter has a future ahead of her. I don't want rumors starting because one teacher thinks he sees something to worry about."

His phone rang. Putting a hand on it, he stared at David expectantly.

Dismissed, David left the office, went down the stairs and out into the sun, but he took no pleasure in the glory of the day. He stood on the sidewalk with his hands on his hips, disappointed in himself for botching his case. He had made the grand gesture . . . for what?

Oliver could make the grand gesture and end up with a prestigious newspaper to add to the group. His siblings could make the grand gesture and earn a promotion. Even his mother made the grand gesture and, yeah, it was often a charitable one, but it worked. She got accolades for everything she did.

David didn't want accolades. He hated the limelight. But he loved teaching, especially at the middle school level where the kids were vulnerable and in personal flux, and the wrong turn could echo for years. *Life can turn on a dime. The direction you head in when it does makes all the difference.* David knew that. But when he tried to do something good, it came out wrong.

And here was a perfect example. Wayne Ackerman came up from behind and passed him by without a word. Watching him go, David wondered whether Alexis would get help and, if so, whether he would be here next year to see it.

chapter 10

MOLLY TOOK HER LAPTOP TO THE HOSPITAL. NICK'S article continued to reverberate, with e-mail coming in fast. She figured that if she answered it from there, it would be as if Robin were involved. If nothing else, it would help pass the time.

Kathryn was sitting at Robin's bedside. She had her elbows on the bed and was holding Robin's hand to her own neck.

"Hey," Molly said gently. She didn't ask about change. Nothing was different except the curve of her mother's back. Kathryn's spirit was starting to drain. "More flowers?" she asked as a diversion and read the cards.

"Getting a little out of hand," Kathryn murmured.

"Would you like me to clear some out? We can have them taken to the children's floor."

"Pretty soon. For now, this is fine. Plants are my friends. They make this all feel less strange."

"Really," Molly said in agreement. "I just came from the greenhouse. Same thing. A comfort."

Kathryn let out a long breath.

Molly thought she looked more pale, and had the sudden vision of *Kathryn* having a heart attack. "Are you okay?"

"No. I'm dying inside. There's this sense of injustice. Like I'm the mother of someone sentenced to die, only I don't know what Robin did that was so bad."

"Nothing bad, Mom. She inspired everyone. Half the people in the lounge are here to show support. They just love her. They'd tell you that themselves," she coaxed, but Kathryn gave a short, can't-go-there head shake. "What about e-mail?" Molly tried. "You'd feel good reading them."

"Like rough drafts of a eulogy?" Kathryn asked and shot a helpless look at the ceiling.

"It's about doing something to pass the time," Molly said. "I just came from work." When Kathryn simply stared silently at Robin's face, Molly gave her an update on Snow Hill. She didn't mention Liz.

Kathryn gave little sign of taking anything in. So Molly drew up a chair, opened the laptop, and pulled up her e-mail. More notes had come even in the short time since she last checked. "Here's one from Ann Currier. Do you remember? She was—"

"Your fifth grade teacher."

"Dearest Molly, I'm horrified to read about your sister. She's in my prayers." Molly shot back a quick thank-you and pulled up the next. "This is from Teddy Frye. Robin dated him in college."

"Please don't read it."

"He lives in Utah. How did he find out?"

"Your friend Nick."

Molly felt a tug inside. Her friend Nick hadn't called. Not to apologize for the piece in the paper, not to see how she was doing. A true friend would have offered to help. Molly would have liked to tell Kathryn he had done that.

Discouraged, she turned back to the laptop and answered several more notes. She didn't read any others aloud. Kathryn seemed to prefer listening to the sough of the machines. She wasn't even talking with Robin, though whether that was because she was tired, realistic, or depressed, Molly didn't know. But the longer her silence went on, the more frightening it was.

So Molly did say, "I fired Liz."

Kathryn didn't react.

"Did you hear?"

Kathryn looked at her and raised a questioning brow.

"I fired Liz. I told her at the meeting on Monday that we wouldn't work with the Maskins. She waited until we were distracted with this, then went ahead and submitted the order herself."

"She did that?"

"Yes. I can't work with her, Mom. I'm sorry. I know she's

good, but there have been other instances where she badgers me until she gets what she wants, and Snow Hill suffers."

Kathryn returned to Robin.

"I'll call her and apologize if you want."

"No. It's fine."

"Greg Duncan can fill in until we hire someone else, and he wouldn't be a bad person to take over anyway. He's really artistic and totally loyal."

"Molly. It's fine."

"The timing stinks. But that's why what she did was inexcusable. I'm sorry. I lost my temper. She was making me feel like a little kid who didn't know a whole lot." She stopped talking. Her mother wasn't listening. Molly waited, but finally returned to her e-mail.

And there it was—a note from Nick. Reading it, she felt a huge relief. "He tried to kill the piece, Mom."

"Who?"

"Nick. They'd already gone to press, but he says there won't be anything else unless we ask for it. His heart's in the right place, really it is."

Kathryn looked doubtful. "Oh, Molly. I don't know. If he's so great, where is he?"

"He knows you don't like him."

"It isn't that I don't like him. I simply question his motives. He is seriously driven."

"Yes, because his parents weren't, and they paid a price. He wants to be successful."

Kathryn gave a confirming nod. "Seriously driven. He'll use you as long as you have something to offer."

"He doesn't use me. Nick and I were friends long before he ever met Robin."

"Like he didn't know who Robin was before that?"

Molly couldn't believe they were rehashing this now, but she couldn't end the argument. Her friendship with Nick involved her own self-worth. "You're saying he deliberately befriended me to get to her. But if that's so, why is he still my friend?"

"More to the point, if he *likes* you so much, why aren't you a couple?"

"Because that's the way your generation thinks, not mine. We have friends of both sexes."

"Maybe. But he uses you to stay close to Robin."

"They *broke up,* Mom."

"Your sister did the breaking up," Kathryn pointed out quietly. "If he had his druthers, they'd still be together. His attraction to her bordered on obsession. Robin found it stifling."

"She broke up with him because of Andrea Welker."

"That was the catalyst. But the other was a real problem, and your friendship with him doesn't help. He needs a clean break. He can't get over Robin, as long as he's hanging around you."

Feeling just ornery enough to change the subject, Molly pulled the note about Robin's heart from her pocket. Kathryn frowned at the envelope, looked away from it and removed the letter. Something in her face changed as she read it. She read it more slowly a second time, and even more slowly a third. Then she set it down and looked at Molly with a dismay that put Molly to shame.

"I found it in her files," she said meekly. "It was tucked in with her bills."

"Why were you going through her bills?"

"I'm supposed to be packing us up to move next week, and there are all these big file folders with papers bulging out." She tried changing the subject again. "How can I move on Monday? I can't think of packing."

Kathryn gave no sign of hearing. She was studying the letter. "Was this anywhere special?"

"No, just tucked in with bills. I called Terrance Field again. He heard about Robin from other people, so he knows I'm not making it up. But he still says he needs his contractor in on Tuesday."

"People in *Florida* are talking?"

"Actually," Molly backtracked, "he just said that he heard. He could have read it online. Or he could have called the hospital to check out my story."

Kathryn stared for a minute, then refocused on the letter. "Was there anything else with this—medical records or anything?"

"No," Molly said and, because her mother persisted, asked, "So, does Dad have a heart problem?" She was putting Kathryn on the spot—who to call a liar, Charlie or Robin? But Kathryn was the one who wasn't letting it go.

Molly expected her to deny it. All she said was, "Dad takes good care of himself."

"Meaning he does have an enlarged heart, but it's under

control?" Molly was suddenly frightened. She didn't want anything happening to her father either! "He denied it yesterday. Why the secret?"

One of the machines began to ring.

Molly's heart lurched, but Kathryn remained calm. "It's the ventilator. It happens a lot. They'll be in."

She had barely finished speaking when the nurse arrived. She adjusted the machine, checked Robin, talked quietly with Kathryn for a minute—*no change, everything looks fine, she's hanging in there*—then left.

Molly became as quiet as Kathryn. The waiting was torture. She sat for a few minutes here, then in the lounge. She took the elevator to the ground floor and idled through the gift shop. She returned to the room and sat with Charlie while Kathryn used the restroom, but she didn't ask about his heart. It didn't seem to matter.

Three o'clock became four, and then five. Chris came from work but didn't talk about Snow Hill, and neither Charlie nor Kathryn asked. Their minds were on Robin.

So was Molly's, which was why she opened her laptop again and this time logged on to Robin's e-mail account. There were fewer messages today than yesterday; friends were realizing that Robin couldn't answer. With a slimmer in-box, though, the list was easily viewed. Nick's name jumped out.

"Hey, babe," he wrote, "I'm hearing things I don't like. Where's that determination? Where's that GRIT? Miracles don't just happen—we have to MAKE them happen. I'm counting on you recovering. It isn't only your life, it's mine too. Remember our plans? I love you. Duke."

Heart pounding, Molly read it again. And again. She wanted to think that the note was simply a good friend cheering Robin on—except that to hear Robin tell it, Nick was neither good nor a friend, in which case *Remember our plans?* was delusional. And then there was that *I love you* at the end. Obsessive, as Kathryn claimed?

She skimmed back over e-mail Robin had received prior to Monday. Finding nothing from Nick, she went back one week, then a second. And there it was.

"Hey. Last weekend's race wasn't a big one, but you did well. You keep getting better and better. I really miss you, babe. Remember how we used to talk after each race? I talk to myself now—not much fun. Sometimes I talk with your sister, but that makes it worse. She doesn't like talking about you, so what's the point? I still don't know what went wrong with us. Are you sure we can't work it out?"

What's the point? Molly should have closed the computer before more harm was done, but a morbid curiosity drove her on. She found a note sent five weeks ago. "Have you thought about what I said, babe? I know your family is a problem. That's why it would be better if we moved away. Your parents will come around. They just need time." And another sent two weeks prior to that. "You're killing me, Robin. Here's a thought. I don't need to wait to move up the ladder here. I can do it anywhere. So where would you most like to live? Name it, and we'll go."

Molly felt like a fool. Her mother was right—Nick was using her. And why did she care? Friends came and went. But she had believed him. She had believed *in* him. She had felt better about herself, thinking that a person like Nick valued her friendship.

She didn't tell anyone what she had read, didn't speak at all. Nor could she eat when Chris brought pizza from the shop down the street. She left the room quietly when the neurologist came to do the EEG. And when Kathryn emerged in tears, Molly cried for Robin.

KATHRYN'S TEARS DIDN'T LAST LONG. SHE WAS ANGRY again—at the neurologist for the results of his test, at Charlie for urging her to have it done, at Molly for causing trouble at Snow Hill, at Chris for doing nothing. She let each of them know it when they returned to the room. In the process, she exhausted herself.

Charlie took her hand. "Let's go home, sweetheart."

But Kathryn felt a sudden, almost childlike fear. "I can't leave her alone."

"I'll stay," Molly offered.

"You don't understand. I'm her mother."

"I'm her sister. I love her, too. She'll be okay, Mom. I'll make sure nothing happens."

Her voice was convincing. And Kathryn was just tired enough to give in.

MOLLY WAITED UNTIL SHE AND ROBIN WERE ALONE. THEN she put her head down, touching her sister's arm, and wept.

She tried to imagine a life without Robin and came up short. Robin might be a self-centered slob who overshadowed Molly in everything. But she never went anywhere without bringing something back that was just right for Molly.

It's not the gift, her grandmother used to say. *It's the thought.* For the first time, Molly understood.

In time her tears dried and she sat quietly. She remembered the strength Robin had always shown, and tried to absorb what little bits might still exist.

Then she let out a defeated sigh. "Oh, Robin," she said sadly. "You were right. How could I not see the truth about Nick?" His ongoing curiosity about Robin should have been a tip-off.

Molly hadn't seen the truth, because she hadn't wanted to see. That said, she wasn't stupid. She knew who was calling the instant her phone rang—knew that a higher force was at work because whereas her phone usually showed only one bar in this room, it now had three—and knew that this was her chance to recoup some of her self-respect.

"Hey," she said in a friendly enough way.

"Hey, yourself. Did you get my e-mail?"

"Sure did. It was sweet."

"Where are you? You sound nasal. Are you getting a cold?"

"No cold." Lots of tears, but he didn't have to know that. "It's probably the reception."

"You're at the hospital?"

"Yes. With Robin."

"Can I come?"

"Not a good idea."

"Why not? You're upset."

Molly wanted to scream. But Robin would appreciate this. Talking for her sister's benefit as much as her own, she said clearly, "It's the whole thing with Andrea Welker. My parents don't trust you."

"I told you. I won't report another thing without your say-so. That's a *promise*."

"Oh, Nick," Molly said sadly, "it's more than the paper. They think you're using me to be near Robin."

"That is ridiculous. Robin and I broke up. There was nothing there, Molly. You and I were friends before and after. Let me come over, and I'll explain to your mom."

Molly might have started crying again, if he hadn't been playing so perfectly into her hand. She had never been a devious person. But she had never felt so hurt.

"Really, Nick. Not a good idea right now. I actually think there's a little improvement. So if you come over and Robin senses it, she could be upset."

"Improvement? You said she was brain dead. What do you mean, improvement?"

"There may be some movement," Molly said. Devious? Try evil, but just then, she didn't care. "It's hard to tell what's voluntary and what isn't. I've started reading notes aloud to her—you know, notes from friends, e-mail they've sent her. Some of them are really good—like this one I just read." She knew the words by heart. *"Where's that grit?* you asked. *Miracles don't just happen—we have to make them happen. I'm counting on you recovering. It isn't only your life, it's mine, too.* I mean," Molly said tartly, "what girl wouldn't be moved by a love letter like that?"

In the silence that followed, she made a face and nodded at Robin. Oh, he got it. She waited, wondering how he would handle *that*.

Finally, with a dismissive laugh, he said, "Okay, Moll. You've cornered me. But you're jumping to the wrong conclusion. Don't you think I wrote that deliberately to give Robin reason for hope? Look, she was in love with me. If something like that wakes her up, isn't it worth the lie?"

"The question becomes, who's lying. See, Robin says she didn't love you. She's said that from the start. She kept telling me you were using me, only I didn't believe her. I would have if she'd shown me this e-mail. She was protecting me, Nick. She didn't want me to read what you wrote her three weeks ago about how talking with me made things worse because I wouldn't talk about her. She wasn't sick then, Nick. No need to try to wake her up. So why did you say that? And the little love note you sent her *seven* weeks ago, the one where you said you'd move to wherever she wanted to live? No, Nick. If anyone's lying, I think we know who."

Molly was about to say something rude, but thought better of it. She had made her point with dignity. "One last thing," she added. "I've said all of this in front of Robin. She looks satisfied." Quietly, she ended the call.

KATHRYN BARELY SLEPT, BUT WHEN CHARLIE SUGGESTED a sleeping pill, she refused. To escape the pain felt like desertion.

She made it until three in the morning before returning to the hospital. Molly was asleep, but not on the pull-out bed. She had climbed up with her sister and lay with her back against the bedrail and her face against Robin's shoulder.

Kathryn sat quietly in the chair. Molly needed comfort, and Robin could give it. Kathryn couldn't. She didn't have the strength.

When a nurse came to check on Robin, Molly stirred. She looked up in confusion, staring blearily at the nurse, then at Kathryn. Quickly, she pushed herself up. "I didn't mean to fall asleep," she said to Kathryn, but it was the nurse who answered.

"Don't get up," she said. "Your sister is fine."

Your sister is fine. The words echoed through Kathryn's stupor until Molly broke in.

"You should have stayed home, Mom. You need sleep." She was sitting cross-legged by Robin's knee. The nurse was gone.

"I need to be here." Kathryn tried to explain. "I know they say nothing's happening in her mind"—she held up a hand—"and I do accept that, Molly. But I'm still her mother. That will never, ever end. Robin is my daughter. As long as her heart continues to beat . . ."

Molly inched her way to the foot of the bed and slid off. Sinking to the floor by Kathryn's chair, she leaned against her leg. Kathryn rested a hand on her head, but found no comfort in the gesture. It was lost in grief. Like Molly's question. *What happens now?* Or was it Kathryn's question?

She knew the short-term answer. There would be a meeting with Robin's team that morning.

The long-term answer was more troubling.

THE MEETING WAS HELD IN A CONFERENCE ROOM. The intensivist and neurologist were there along with two of Robin's nurses and a social worker. The neurologist sat at the head of the table. On his left were his colleagues, on his right four Snows.

It wasn't that Kathryn felt hostility. The doctors were kind people who were doing a difficult job the best way they could. Their voices were gentle, their eyes sympathetic. But she knew she wouldn't like what they said, which made them the enemy.

Numbness was a shield. Taking refuge in it, she caught only general threads of the conversation. The neurologist laid out the EEG strips and summed up what he saw. The intensivist added the results of his own empirical tests. The nurses talked of their repeated efforts to elicit a response from Robin. The social worker listened.

Kathryn definitely caught the bottom line. There was no hope that Robin would recover. With her brain devoid of activity, she would never again respond or wake up. The respirator might keep air moving in and out of her lungs, which would keep her heart pumping and her blood circulating; but without that, her body would shut down.

There was no treatment for brain death. In accordance with hospital policy, Robin would be transferred to a regular room. If the family so chose, she might go to a long-term care facility. If not, the hospital would continue to provide medical care. This point was reiterated often and by each member of the team. Robin could be kept alive indefinitely.

The intensivist described what would be done to prevent dehydration and starvation. He talked of the surgical insertion of a feeding tube and emphasized that since Robin felt no pain, pain control was unnecessary. He deferred to the social worker for a discussion of the emotional issues involved in long-term care, but it was the intensivist who raised the possibility of ending life support.

Kathryn tuned in here, her heart beating double-time. The rest had been warm-up. This was the point of the exercise.

She waited only until the hospital team had left the room before looking from Charlie to Molly to Chris. "The answer is no," she told them all. "We are not ending life support. I'm not ready to let her go." When none of them spoke, she looked at Charlie. "They imply that Robin is only a body, but she's still my child. This is happening too fast. I can't think."

"You need time," Charlie said.

CHRIS LEFT THE CONFERENCE ROOM. WHILE THE OTHERS returned to Robin, he got coffee in the lounge, but he tossed it out before he drank much. Erin was home with Chloe. He wanted to hang out with his wife and daughter awhile.

He was waiting at the elevator when the social worker joined him. She had a round face and a headful of curly hair. "How's your mom?"

Stubborn, was his first thought, but he took his cue from Charlie. "She needs time."

"That's understandable. End of life issues are tough. How about you? Where do you stand?"

He eyed the elevator pad. "The tests are clear. Time won't change that."

"It won't change the tests. It might change your mother's feelings. Do you have kids?"

"A daughter."

"Can you think of her and try to imagine what your mom feels?"

"Not really. I'm a guy. It's different."

The elevator arrived. They stepped on and rode down in silence, but when Chris would have nodded a good-bye, she said, "Can I buy you a cup of coffee? There's a quiet part of the patio where we could talk."

He had already tried coffee. It hadn't helped. But he hadn't tried talking. This woman seemed to understand Kathryn. He wondered if she might understand him, too. He could use an ally at this point.

Moments later, they were crossing the patio. The sun was warm, but well-placed lindens offered shade. Beyond the trees were the bluffs, beneath the bluffs the river, across the river another state. Chris loved a good view—before Chloe, he and Erin had often climbed local peaks—but today he was oblivious.

The social worker chose a table away from the rest. "Were you close to your sister?" she asked as soon as they were seated.

He nodded. "We're a tight family."

"But you and Robin—were the two of you close?"

"We were when we were kids. Then we got our own interests. But you can't be a Snow without being involved in Robin's life. Her running is everything."

"You don't sound bitter."

"Why should I be? It's exciting."

"Do you ever envy her the attention she gets?"

"No. I'm support staff." And happy enough to be that. Support staff felt less pressure. He liked going to work, coming home, seeing Erin and the baby, watching the Sox. He didn't have to make decisions like his parents or work weekends like Molly. If he had wanted to be a CEO, he wouldn't have become a CPA. Enough said.

"Support staff is important," the social worker acknowledged.

"I'm the numbers guy for Snow Hill."

"Is that why you agree with the test results?"

Chris shrugged his assent. "It isn't like there was only one test. Don't you trust them?"

"I do. But it's like I said before. Tests don't give the whole picture. They don't take emotions into account."

"If you believe the test," Chris argued, "Robin has no emotions."

"Your parents do."

But he parted ways with his parents on that. "How can they let her live like this? It's no existence."

"It may be the only one your mom can handle right now."

He lifted his cup, then put it down without drinking. "She isn't the only one affected. It's like with Robin's running. Everyone is involved."

"This is different. It's a process."

He considered that. "When does it end?"

"When your mother accepts that Robin is gone."

"So we all just stand around and wait for weeks— months—*years?*" He had done his homework. Terri Schiavo was kept alive for fifteen years. He couldn't imagine his parents doing that to Robin.

"Like I say, it's a process."

Chris sat back. "I vote for organ donation, but Mom won't hear of it."

"It's a tough concept to grasp when a loved one's heart is still beating."

"Then why did they mention it at the meeting?"

"Because it's an option. And for some people trying to decide what to do, it's a help. Donor families often feel that good can come from bad. I take it none of you know how Robin felt about this?"

Chris shrugged. "Not me. But hell, I'm just a guy."

"Hold on now," the social worker said with a smile. "You said that before. Is it an excuse?"

"For what?"

"Not getting involved? Guys have emotions. Don't you love your wife?"

"Yes." The phone in his pocket rang.

"And your child?"

Nodding, he pulled out the cell, looked at the panel, and felt a nagging worry. He had known this was coming and was not in the mood.

"Work call," he told the social worker dismissively and was about to repocket the phone when she rose.

"Answer it," she said, reaching into her purse. "That's how you can help your family most right now. Here's my card. Call anytime." She left before he could tell her that his family didn't need counseling.

Frustrated, he opened his phone. "Why are you calling on this line?"

"Because you're not at work," said Liz Tocci, "and right now I don't feel welcome calling Snow Hill. Do you know that your sister fired me?"

"Liz, this is a bad time."

"I'm still fired. That means I'm out of work."

Turning his back on the hospital, Chris faced the bluffs,

but the view held no escape from Liz. He hung his head. "Do you *know* what's going on here?"

"Yes. Robin is on life support, and it's a bad time, but I wasn't the one who asked for this. Your sister went berserk, just flew off the handle over a petty issue. I was counting on at least one more year at Snow Hill. I don't have enough of a following yet to go out on my own, and finding a new job is hard when you've been fired from the last. The more people learn about this, the worse it is for my career."

"Tell them you quit."

"I didn't quit. I was fired. That wasn't part of the deal when I agreed to come."

"What deal?" Chris asked, annoyed. "I introduced you to my mother. Any arrangement you had was with her."

"Oh, come on. We both know I was coming for you."

He was silent for a minute. "I didn't know it, Liz."

"Excuse me? What about those lunches? What about our *phone* calls?"

"They were always work-related."

"Don't be dense, Chris."

Chris might be. But he wasn't stupid. "The only thing going on was in your mind. I'm married."

"To a very sweet young thing who will bore you to tears. I can be patient on that. This business with Molly is something else. Talk to your parents. I want to be reinstated."

"Liz," he said pedantically, "my parents are with my sister, who is dying. I will not talk with them about this."

"Do you want them to know about us?"

"*What* us? There *is* no us. We were together when I was in college. That was eight years ago."

"I have pictures," she taunted.

"That's old news."

"Nuh-uh. These pictures are new. There's one from last year's Christmas party and another from the Snow Hill booth at the Concord design conference. We look pretty chummy. Combine that with an eight-year-old picture, and your wife might be upset. Your mother, too. You never told her about our relationship, did you?"

No, Chris hadn't. He was a guy—and that was *not* an excuse. Guys didn't call their mothers each time they slept with a woman, particularly when the mother in question was straight-laced and the woman in question was ten years his senior. Kathryn would never have understood the attraction. Frankly, Chris didn't either just then.

"Are you trying to blackmail me?" he asked.

"It won't come to that. I know you'll do the right thing."

MOLLY STAYED WITH HER PARENTS IN ROBIN'S ROOM, but conversation was sparse. Nurses came and went. The respiratory therapist stopped by. Charlie filled out paperwork regarding Robin's continued care. Kathryn sat silent, holding Robin's hand tightly. And there Robin lay in a pale, beautiful mockery of life.

Given the choice, Molly would rather have been at the greenhouse or with her grandmother. Either place held the promise of comfort—but how selfish was that? There was no comfort for Kathryn and certainly none for Robin.

When Charlie suggested lunch, she went gladly. It was something to do, and she was desperate to talk. They settled at a table in the cafeteria, Charlie with a grilled chicken salad, Molly with a cheeseburger.

She stared at the burger for a minute, then sat back and said, "Robin would be sitting here with a salad like yours, telling me how many grams of fat are in this burger. I've always loved cheeseburgers. Can I really eat this now?"

"Are you hungry?" her father asked with perfect logic.

She had thought she was, but something about the burger bothered her. It might have been the size, though it wasn't as big as some. It wasn't the smell, which was really good, or the sheer appeal of comfort food. The problem, she realized, was her guilt. Robin could have none of this. Even if they inserted a tube straight to her stomach, she couldn't enjoy food.

But Molly was hungry. Leaving the table, she returned with a fork and knife. She took off the top half of the bun and cut into the burger. This was better.

"If you're worried about gaining weight," Charlie said as he worked on his salad, "don't be. Did it ever occur to you that Robin was jealous?"

"Of me?" Molly asked.

"You've always been able to eat what you want without gaining weight. That's the kind of thing other women hate you for."

"Robin never gained weight."

"Because she ran. And because when she wasn't loading

up on carbs for a race, she ate salads." He eyed the burger. "Cholesterol's another story, but you don't have to worry about that yet."

"Robin thought she didn't either."

"Her problem wasn't cholesterol. It was being an extreme athlete. That would tax even the best of hearts."

"Does that mean that you may have a bad heart," Molly asked, "but since you're not an extreme athlete, it never became a problem?"

"My heart's fine."

"Why do you eat salads?" She had never thought twice about it. Now she wondered if there was a reason.

"I like salads."

"That's all?" When he gave her a strange look, she said, "Robin told her doctor that her father had an enlarged heart. I found a letter. It was right there in black-and-white. Why would she say it if it wasn't true?"

Charlie frowned. He gave a small head shake, lifted his soda but studied the straw for a minute before sipping.

"That's the thing," Molly said sadly. "We just don't know. She isn't here to tell us why she said what she did. And she can't tell us what she wants." She picked at the burger for a minute, then set the fork down. "What are we supposed to do, Dad? How does a family make a decision like this? How do they even *begin* to approach it? Mom's right. To hear the doctors tell it, what's up there in that room is just a body, a shell with nothing inside."

"Nothing intelligent," Charlie corrected. He was no longer eating either.

"Do you believe that?"

"I trust the doctors when they say her brain no longer functions."

"Do you believe that there's absolutely no chance of recovery?"

At one time he had talked of miracles. Now, he said quietly, "I believe they're right about that."

"Then what's upstairs is just a body."

"There's still a heart beating," he cautioned.

"Would it beat if the machines were turned off?" She saw the answer on his face, and could almost understand why Kathryn was so stubborn. She wasn't clinging to hope, but to her child's last remnant of life.

"What about her soul?" Molly asked.

"It's in heaven."

"Already?" He nodded. "Not hovering here still? How can we feel it, Dad? How do we know what to do if Robin doesn't give us a hint?"

Charlie took her hand. "Robin is in a good place. From this point on, we have to do what's best for us."

"We know what Mom wants," Molly said, remembering Kathryn's hand holding Robin's. "What do you want?"

"What Mom wants."

She might have predicted that answer, but it wasn't what she wanted to hear. "Do you agree with her?"

"It doesn't matter. I want what she wants."

"Chris wants to turn everything off."

"What do you want?"

"What Robin wants."

He smiled sadly. "If only we knew."

That was the challenge. Molly grew pensive. "Would Robin want to be lying up there for months? She does love being the center of attention, but there's no winning this, and she hates to lose. Remember Virginia Beach? She was the best female runner in the field until the organizers lured in three better contestants a week before the race. Robin withdrew rather than lose."

"It was a political decision," Charlie explained. "She needed a win at that point."

Molly understood that. "But take what she did then and apply it to now."

"No comparison. This is life and death. There's nothing political about it."

"Maybe not, but Robin has pride. This is the woman who pays two hundred dollars for Luciano to cut her hair before every major race."

"She does that for luck."

"She does it for looks," Molly insisted, "and I would, too, if I had hair like hers and a perfectly shaped scalp."

"What's wrong with your scalp?"

"I don't know since I can't see it through all this hair, but that's not my point. Robin does care about how she looks. Would she want the world seeing her like this?"

"It's just us, sweetie," he said quietly. "I take it you want her off life support."

"I want what *she* wants."

Charlie looked past her, and suddenly Nick was standing there. Not only hadn't Molly seen him coming, but she was astonished that he would show up after their phone conversation last night. In a split second, she was livid.

He looked nervous. That gave her some satisfaction. Actually, he was grossly pale. When he shot her an uneasy glance, she steeled herself. But he turned to Charlie. "Mr. Snow? I'm sorry—I want you to know how sorry I am about Robin. This just isn't what anyone expected. I hope my article didn't make things worse. I'll make sure there aren't any others. I know privacy is important right now, but if there's anything I can do, anything at all to help, I'd like to do it."

Molly wondered what he was up to.

"Thank you for offering," Charlie said politely—and why not? He didn't know what a *snake* Nick was.

"I'd like to see her—just to talk," Nick went on. "Would that be possible?"

"No," Molly snapped before Charlie could reply. Calmer in the next breath, she shook her head. "Not possible."

"Not for the paper. For me."

Molly smiled. "Not possible."

Nick appealed to Charlie again. "She and I were connected. I can't explain it."

Charlie looked confused.

"My parents are going through hell," Molly said. "This doesn't help."

Nick gave her a beseeching look before leaving.

"What was *that* about?" Charlie asked.

Such a loaded question—Molly might have laughed if it

weren't so tragic. Smile gone now, she said with conviction, "I may not know whether Robin would want to spend years on life support, but I do know that she would not want that man here." Rising, she took her tray and walked off toward the trash.

CHRIS NEVER QUITE GOT HOME. AFTER DRIVING FOR AN hour, he ended up back at the hospital and went looking for Molly. He caught her in the lobby and drew her into a quiet corner.

"We have a problem," he said in a low voice. "Liz is threatening to make trouble. What's the story? Is her firing a done deal?"

Molly looked angry, not a good sign. "Yes," she said. "Did she actually call you to complain?"

"She's out of work, so she's concerned," he explained, trying to be casual. "Is there any chance of her being reinstated?"

"Absolutely none."

"Does Mom agree with that?"

"She will," Molly warned. "If Liz is reinstated, I'm outta here. Mom won't want that."

Chris was feeling squeezed. His sister was putting him in a bad position. "You've made this personal. That's no way to run a business."

"This is a family business. We can run it whatever way we want. What's she threatening?"

He looked away in disgust. "Oh, stupid stuff, but she has a big mouth."

"That's why I fired her."

"I wish you'd checked with me first. She and I go back a ways, so I feel responsible. I was the one who introduced her to Mom."

"And Mom liked her. We both did. That must have gone to her head, because she's become impossible. A prima donna? *Big* time. No one is shedding tears that she's gone."

"Maybe we should offer severance," he tried.

"Maybe we should threaten to sue," Molly countered. "What she did was one step shy of fraud."

"That's pushing it."

"She took advantage of a family *tragedy*, Chris. It doesn't get much worse than that."

"Okay," he conceded, "her timing was bad."

"It still is. She calls you to complain about money, when your sister's *life* is about to end?"

"That's Mom's decision to make, not mine."

"But you're family, so you're involved. How can Liz expect you to deal with her pettiness right now?"

"She doesn't see this as petty," Chris reasoned. And yes, he was involved. The social worker was right about that. He felt a hard tug at the thought of Robin. That was one reason he wanted this settled. Looking for a compromise, he said, "What if we let Liz work at Snow Hill just until she finds something else?"

"Do that," Molly warned again, "and she'll spend the time duplicating her Rolodex, stealing our vendors, and bad-mouthing us to any customer who'll listen. Am I wrong?"

Sadly, no. Liz was not an easy person when she felt she had been crossed. That was one of the reasons Chris had broken up with her. And he had never looked back.

The problem was what he should do now.

chapter 12

WITHIN FIVE MINUTES OF THE START OF THURSDAY'S class, David knew something was bothering Alexis Ackerman. She refused to look at him. When he tried to engage her in the discussion, she shrugged and looked back at her book. He might have challenged another student—*Have you read the assignment? Would you like to share your thoughts?*—but Alexis was too vulnerable. He couldn't push her, especially when feeling as guilty as he did.

The bell rang, but she didn't move. When the room cleared, he walked to her desk. "Are you all right?"

"What did you say to my father?" she asked angrily.

Guilty? No point denying it. "I said I was worried about you."

"Did you call me anorexic?"

"No. But I did tell him that you collapsed."

She grew plaintive. "I didn't collapse. My legs just felt funny. I wish you hadn't talked with him, Mr. Harris. He was angry at me."

For showing *weakness*? David wanted to ask. For having a problem? Oh boy, could he empathize. He had grown up in a family where performance mattered. His heart broke for Alexis.

"I'm sorry," he said. "But you do worry me."

"I am totally fine," she insisted, gathering her books. "I eat plenty of food. *More* than enough. And I'm no thinner than the others. You just don't know what dancing's like."

"I guess I don't," he said, stepping back.

She made it out of the chair and all the way to the door this time before crumbling. By the time he reached her, she was opening her eyes. She raised her head when he knelt, but dropped it back to the floor. "I feel weird," she whispered.

He pushed the books off her. Holding a hand to keep her from moving, he reached for the wall phone. He had barely finished his call when she tried to get up again. She made it to an elbow before falling down.

"I'm okay, I'm okay," she breathed.

Frightened, David sat on his heels. He wanted to comfort her by taking her hand, but that was a no-no. Sexual harrassment? He hated it. What about basic human warmth?

Left with no option but a soothing voice, he said, "The nurse will be right here."

"Oh no," she wailed feebly, "not the nurse. She'll tell my father." When she tried to roll away, David did hold her shoulder as a matter of safety. He couldn't have her standing up. "You don't understand." Her eyes were dark and woeful. "I'm a good dancer. There is nothing wrong. Maybe I overdid yesterday. Or maybe it's school. Wearing me out."

"It wouldn't hurt to be checked out," he suggested.

"It *would*. They'll take forever. I can't miss practice."

"All right, Alexis," said the nurse, swooping in and taking over.

But when David stood back, Alexis almost seemed to panic. "Don't leave, Mr. Harris," she begged him. "You can tell them. I was fine in class. Wasn't I? Then something hit me. Maybe the flu?" she asked the nurse, but the woman was taking her pulse.

"Weak," she said worriedly. "You're going to the hospital."

"Nooo—"

"Your dad is in Concord, your mom is in court. I left messages. One of them will meet us at Dickenson-May." Looking at David as the EMTs arrived, she muttered under her breath, "A disaster waiting to happen."

David went in the ambulance. He had lunch period anyway, and nothing scheduled for the afternoon except monitoring a study hall, which a sub could do. Not that he was eager to run into Wayne Ackerman at the hospital, but when the nurse started to climb in, Alexis pointed at David. "*You*. Please." He might have come up with an excuse had it not been for Robin Snow. He regretted having sent her off alone. If there had been any brain activity during that ride, he should have been there. Yes, it was a matter of basic human warmth.

With two EMTs flanking the girl during the ride, he sat by her feet. He smiled reassuringly when she looked his way, though her eyes were closed most of the time. When his phone vibrated, he pulled it out, checked the panel, put it back. He didn't know a Dukette, Nicholas. The man had tried earlier, but left no message.

When the ambulance pulled up at Dickenson-May, David was the first one out; but with the eyes of a frightened child, Alexis checked to make sure he was there, so he walked alongside as they wheeled her in. Filling in for her parents, neither of whom had arrived, he told the doctor what had happened yesterday and today.

Then he sat in the waiting room. There were only two other patients; Dickenson-May was known for its efficiency. As relieved as he was that Alexis was getting help, he worried that he had overreacted. If it was only the flu, he was in trouble. Well, *more* trouble than he already was in. Wayne Ackerman wouldn't be pleased.

The doctor emerged from Alexis's cubicle and approached him. "Parents not here yet?"

"No. How is she?"

The man gave a look that said more than his words. "You were right to worry. She needs to be admitted."

"How do you treat her?"

"We feed her intravenously while we run more tests. If the parents prefer a private clinic—"

"Alexis Ackerman?" came a loud voice.

Alexis's mother wore power suits and exuded authority. David had met her at numerous school events, most recently at the open house on Monday night. She had sat in his classroom listening to him talk for ten minutes. Yet she made no sign of recognizing him when the doctor beckoned her over.

Dropping back, he went outside. He was scanning the parking lot to see if Alexis's father had come—the superintendent drove a dark blue BMW 335i with the top down—when he saw Molly Snow. She was just leaving the hospital.

Something inside him warmed. He liked Molly. Even in dark moments, she had a touch of brightness.

But just now she did seem grim. *Let her be,* a tiny voice said. *She's dealing with a family crisis, and you remind her of the worst.* He jogged over anyway. "Molly?" he called when he was close enough.

She looked up and refocused. "Hey, David."

"How's Robin?"

She lifted a shoulder. "The ICU can't do anything more. They've just moved her to a regular room. The respirator is all that's keeping her alive."

A bad day all around. He had been hoping for a miracle. "I'm sorry."

"Me, too. My parents are faced with an awful decision. All of us, really. But my mother is the one who'll say when."

David felt partly responsible. "It might have been better if I hadn't found her."

Molly cleared her throat. "Well, that is one of the things my mother has said in the last few hours. She's depressed."

"She has a right."

"But the ICU has other patients in bad shape. Some will be handicapped for life. For Robin, that would have been devastating. So maybe this is a blessing—not that my mother wants to hear that. She didn't want it to happen at all."

A telltale purr came from the parking lot as Wayne Ackerman cruised in. Parking the convertible, he was out in a flash and trotting toward the emergency room. There was a moment of clear recognition when his eyes touched David, but he didn't wave.

Molly watched him pass. "Do you know him?"

"That," David said, "is my boss."

She gasped. "The one whose daughter has a problem?"

"Uh-huh." He told her what had happened.

"Good for you for speaking up," Molly said. "If someone had told us about Robin's condition before this happened, she might be okay. Did Ackerman really tell you to mind your own business?"

"That was the gist of it. But I'm not sorry about today. Based on what my doctor friend said Tuesday night, she's showing signs of malnutrition; and, if that's so, shame on her parents. 'Course, I could still lose my job. Each time Dr. Ackerman looks at me he sees the guy who was right about his kid when he wasn't—like I know a secret that they don't want anyone else to know. It'll be interesting to see what he and his wife do. I'm guessing they'll whisk Alexis off to a private clinic in Massachusetts and tell the world she's with a ballet guru in St. Petersburg." He snorted. "My class. Both times. Why was that?"

"Because she trusts you."

"Oh, no. She thinks I betrayed her by going to her dad." But she had wanted him in the ambulance. That was something.

"You did the right thing," Molly said.

And that was something. But he was embarrassed. Molly was in the midst of her own crisis. "You were headed somewhere." He took a step back. "I should let you go."

She smiled sadly—she did that often, he realized, and guessed she was a chronic smiler who was simply now very sad. "I'm going home," she said. "I have to pack. I'm moving Tuesday." Her eyes filled. "*We're* moving Tuesday. I rent a place with my sister. We have to be out before the wrecker comes. We were moving back to our parents' place until we found something else." Again that sad smile. "Irony, of course. Going home. For Robin, forever." Her voice cracked. She pressed a hand to her mouth and lowered her eyes.

He touched her shoulder. "I'm sorry."

She nodded and sniffled.

He didn't have a tissue. But he did have strong arms. "Want some help with the packing?"

She brushed the heel of her hand against her nose. He was thinking that she didn't have a tissue either, which made her an unusual woman, when she looked at him with a sudden ferocity. "Not out of pity," she declared. "I've been covering for Robin for years and can do it now. If you're feeling guilt about her, I don't want your help. I've had it with men who do things with me because of their feelings for her."

"Whoa." David held up his hands. "I have no feelings for her. I don't know her."

As suddenly as it had come, her ferocity left. "No. You don't."

"Helping you pack would be therapeutic for me. It'll balance out all the times lately when I've felt useless."

"Don't you have to work?"

"No more today. Where do you live?"

She paused. "Are you *sure*?"

"Very," he said.

He must have looked earnest enough because she said, "I'll give you a ride," and set off for her car.

MOLLY FELT THE SAME LIFT SHE ALWAYS DID WHEN SHE turned in at the cottage; but with only four nights left, the pleasure was bittersweet. That was one of the reasons she had taken David up on his offer. His presence would be a diversion that might keep her from dwelling on this place that she loved. But there was also the issue of discipline. If David was there to help, she couldn't put it off.

"It really is an adorable house," she said, defending it as she unlocked the door and led him inside. "I know it doesn't look like much with all these cartons, but before this, it was very sweet. I've tried to find another place like it, but nothing comes close." Dropping her keys and the mail, she opened several windows. "My grandmother always said things happen for a reason. Maybe the reason I haven't found another place is because this was destined to happen to Robin, and her stuff would have to go home anyway." She cocked her head, listened. "I have a cat. I don't hear it."

"What's its name?"

"No name yet. I just got her." She shot him a guilty look. "Monday. I was taking my time settling her in while Robin was fading away at the ER."

"Would it have made a difference if you'd reached the hospital sooner?"

"No. Still . . ."

"Maybe you have to let that go," he said kindly. "Like I have to let go of the fact that if I'd been running faster, I'd have gotten there sooner and saved her."

"You did save her," Molly said.

"For what?"

Well, there was a reason. There had to be. "I'll let you know," she said and set off for the kitchen. "This cat may be another of Nana's destined happenings. Robin wasn't wild about cats. The problem is that my mother isn't either, but this one'll have to come home with me—unless you want her?" she asked hopefully. David was a gentle person. She had sensed that from the first. "Do you have pets?"

He shook his head. "My condo has a no-pet clause. I grew up with dogs, though."

"Where?" Molly asked, opening the fridge.

"Washington."

She had good Washington memories. "Robin loved the Marine Corps Marathon. We had the best times on those weekends. Do you want a cold drink? I have plain water, fruit water, energy water, or soda." She didn't offer the Scooby-Doo chocolate milk box. Too embarrassing.

"Soda, thanks," he said.

She took out two Diet Cokes. "But I'm talking about DC. Are you from the District or the state?"

"The District. Everyone else in my family is still there. I'm the black sheep."

"That makes two of us. Why you? Because they're in publishing and you teach?"

"It's more than that. They're newspaper people. I'm not."

"And better for it," she declared, thinking of Nick, then realized what she'd said. "Oh, gosh. I'm sorry. I didn't mean to imply that there's something wrong with your family."

He popped his soda tab. "There is. They're driven in ways that I'm not. Being on the A-list is important to them. It isn't to me. But why are you the black sheep? You are in the family business."

"I water plants. I cut off dried leaves. I pack dirt. I can't do PR like my dad, or balance the books like my brother, and Robin is a front person like my mom." She felt a return of the weight on her heart. "Was. Robin was. And see, I'm the black sheep in this, too. My mother wants the machines on, my brother wants them off, my father wants what my mother wants. Me, I just want what Robin wants." But how to know that? It was the same dead end. Needing to lighten up, she said, "Want to see my favorite spot?" She led him to the stairs at one end of the living room.

"This would be my favorite, too," he said when they reached the loft. "What kind of plant is that?"

"Aphelandra squarrosa, fondly known as a zebra plant. It's native to Brazil. It was dying in my dad's office, so I brought it here. It doesn't love direct sun and needs shade when it's done blooming. After dormancy, though, it'll re-bloom if it gets a couple of months of strong light. In the meantime, we get to enjoy this beautiful striped foliage."

David bent to study the pot underneath. "Beautiful earthenware, too."

"That's from Rio," she said, pleased that he'd noticed. "Robin bought it for me when she marathoned there. She always brought me gifts. This one's from Valencia," she said, pointing to the pot holding a schefflera, then at one containing a palm, "and Helsinki." She grew nostalgic. "I can say Robin was self-absorbed, but she never came back without a gift. I have a hair clip from Luxor and sweaters from New Zealand and Cornwall. She always knew what I wanted. So why don't I know what she wants now?"

He straightened. "Because knowing the gifts a person appreciates is easier than knowing how a person wants to die."

Simply spoken, but true. She didn't even wince at the word "die." She could say it. She had come that far. Robin was dying.

That said, she wasn't a rock. She didn't want to be packing Robin's room. That had *end* written all over it.

With only four nights left, though, it had to be done. And with David here to buffer her emotions, Robin's room was the place to start.

She led him down the stairs to the first bedroom. There, centered on Robin's bed, was the cat. She was sitting up, eyes unblinking, ears alert.

"She's very small," David observed.

"And not a baby, but she's been abused. Poor thing. I haven't been much help." She crept forward. When the cat didn't run, she dared a little more. She held out a hand and bent over. "Come here, little sweetie," she cooed. "I know you've been eating." When she tried to bridge the final gap, the cat bolted off the bed and out the door.

David swiveled to watch. "Her color is striking. Will those cuts leave scars?"

"Her fur will cover them up. The scars inside? Time will tell. Right now, she's between two lives. She doesn't really know who she is." Like her grandmother, Molly realized, and she felt a need to visit again. Despite what Kathryn said, Marjorie handled what she could and let the rest go. Alzheimer's disease notwithstanding, it was an enviable trait.

Sinking onto the bed, Molly ran a hand over the quilt. "People really did love Robin. This was made for her by the mother of a running friend. The woman lives on an island off the coast of Maine. Her work is exquisite."

David admired the quilt, then looked around, seeming curious but appropriately so. He wasn't rushing to touch Robin's things. He wasn't going gaga over the laurel wreath she had won in Boston. He wasn't fixated on the bed.

Molly tried to view it all through his eyes. Had he not known Robin before, he would now. This room had a single focus.

That heightened the qualm Molly already felt. "If my sister is anywhere, it's here. Taking this room apart feels like I'm rushing her to the grave."

"Can you postpone the move?"

With a frustrated tug, she removed the band from her hair and regathered it. "I've called my landlord twice. He's a nice guy, but he isn't giving an inch." She had a sudden thought. Running back to the kitchen, she thumbed through the local phone book. She put through the call as she returned to Robin's room.

The line rang once on the other end before the realtor picked up. "This is Dorie."

"It's Molly Snow."

There was a low gasp. "Oh my gosh, Molly. I'm so glad you called. No one seems to be able to get through to your mother. I understand things are bad."

"They are," Molly admitted, "and in the middle of it, I'm supposed to be packing. I've begged Terrance Field to give me an extra few days, but he insists I have to move out Monday so that his contractor can start Tuesday. I know you're his realtor, and I was thinking . . . I mean, maybe you could explain . . ."

"Hold on, sweetie. I'll call him on the other line."

Molly quickly heard a click. "My landlord's realtor," she explained to David. Clamping the phone to her ear, she reached for the quilt, thinking to fold it along with the rest of the bedding and use the mattress as a staging area for the closet junk. Then she noticed patches of amber fur on more than one spot. "Looks like my kitty really does like this." She neatened the quilt. Then she paused. David had now seen Robin's room. If that was why he had come, he might conveniently remember something he had forgotten having to do.

That was what Nick had done. On the few occasions he had come to the house, he had wandered from room to room, remarking how much he loved it. Typically then, his phone had rung. He was the paper's best reporter and was in demand.

With the brilliance of hindsight, Molly realized the truth. He had seen what he needed to see—namely, no Robin—and was ready to leave.

Accepting this now, she didn't feel angry or hurt. She was actually relieved to be of one mind with her mother and sister.

Lighter of heart, she led David to the cartons in the front hall. That was when a voice came from the phone at her ear.

"Molly. The man is impossible. I told him that a few days wouldn't make a difference. I offered to call Mike De-Lay—that's his contractor—but Terrance says no. He argues that you should have been packed two weeks ago. Should I give Mike a call anyway?"

But Molly was resigned. "No. Thanks, Dorie. The truth is, this won't be any easier in a month."

And here was David, with his sleeves rolled to the elbows, assembling cartons without her having to ask. If Nana was to be believed, the reason for *that* was that Molly was meant to move.

They returned to Robin's room and worked their way around the periphery, packing books from the night table, notes from the corkboard, race hats from hooks. They packed two bookshelves' worth of mementos before Molly opened the closet door, at which point David sucked in a breath.

"I heard that," she said quietly.

"Where do you *start?*"

She had asked herself the same thing more than once, but she was suddenly motivated. "Get more cartons. This is Robin's war chest. I'll just pack it all up. My mother can go through it once it's home."

There was no "just" about packing it all up. Memories were crammed in right along with the things. While David untangled headsets, MP3 players, and iPods, Molly folded clothes; but each tee shirt recalled a story, so she discussed those, and told more stories about the plaques and trophies that were unearthed once the clothing was gone. When Molly warned David about mice, he searched the back of the closet for droppings but found none. More comfortable then, Molly dug armfuls of CDs from the far corners. They talked about Robin's musical taste, even played a U2 CD of hers while they worked. When David said he was hungry, Molly realized she was starved.

She thanked him over bowls of Ok Dol Bibim Bop at a nearby Korean restaurant. "I needed this break. You're very soothing." He was also very good-looking, with his gray eyes and chestnut hair. On the tail of that thought, her smile faded. "What kind of person has a good time while her sister is dying?"

"One who is still alive," he said gently. "Hey, it's not like you're partying. You've been working. You have to eat. Besides, it's hard to sustain grief 24/7. And is it necessary? You've been there for Robin. Even what we just did was for her."

That was the bottom line right now, Molly realized. "Tell me what you learned."

"About Robin? Or you?"

"Robin." Even though the final decision on what to do lay with Kathryn, it would help if Molly found clues. All the while they were packing, she had been looking for them. She wondered if she was too close to the forest to see the trees, hence her question to David.

He was thoughtful. Tentatively, he said, "I learned that she wins a lot. I hadn't realized how much until I saw all those trophies."

No clues there. Molly waited.

"I learned how much she inspired others," he went on. "The notes on the board were good, but there were all those others stuffed into trophies. Their sheer number is impressive. And she kept most of the trophies in the closet. What does that say?"

"That she already had too many on display."

"Maybe it says she was embarrassed by the glut?"

Molly felt a pang of amusement. "Robin embarrassed? Not a chance. She loved winning. She loved knowing those trophies were there. She called that closet her war chest for a reason. It held what she needed to conquer the world."

"Well, that's the last thing I learned. Running is her life. There isn't much else."

"Does that disappoint you?"

He shot her a puzzled smile. "Should it?"

Molly hesitated for only a minute. "When I first met you, you said you recognized her name. You called her every runner's idol. Someone who idolized her would have offered to help pack just to be near her things."

"Not me. I offered to help *you*; but I'm helping myself, too. I'll always wish I could have done more Monday night. You ask what I learned? Not much more than I already knew. I've known a lot of people like Robin, and their accomplishments are amazing. But sometimes there's a price to be paid. I'm sad that she didn't have other things."

Looking at it that way, Molly realized it was true. She had always envied her sister. But viewing Robin's life through another's eyes provided a new perspective.

"Maybe the problem was time," Molly mused. "Running consumed her. Maybe as she got older, she would have done other things, too."

"Which makes the tragedy all the greater," he said, pulling a phone from his pocket. He studied the panel.

She gestured that he should take it. She had kept him long enough. He did have a life, had tomorrow's class to prepare for, maybe even a call to make regarding the girl who was sick.

He frowned. "This guy keeps trying me, but I don't know a Dukette."

Coughing on a last sip of tea, Molly held out a hand, took the phone, looked for herself. Furious, she opened it. "Why are you calling this number?" The ensuing silence was long enough for her to say, "Don't you dare hang up, Nick. Why are you calling this man?"

"Molly?"

"Good ear," she taunted. "Where did you get this number?"

"The school directory."

"Why?"

"David Harris and I have something in common."

"You do not. He's an honest person. You are not."

"Molly—"

"I'm going to hang up now, Nick; and when I do, I'm going to tell this man exactly *why* I hung up." She snapped the phone shut. David was looking startled. "I know Nick Dukette," she explained. "He's a major writer for the local paper, and he's looking for a story, *always* looking for a story—except when he's scheming for ways to be with my sister. They dated for a while, and after she broke up with him, he used his friendship with me to stay near her. I thought he valued me as a friend. Robin saw him for what he was. So if you learn one thing today, it's that my sister is smarter than I am."

She held out the phone.

He set it on the table. "Why is he calling me?"

Molly didn't know, but the possibilities made her squirm. "He must want information on Robin. He saw me talking with you the other night and wanted to know who you were. I gave him your first name but not your last, and I said you were visiting someone else. If he knows you're the Good Samaritan, he got it from the cops."

"They don't know. You're the only one who does."

"Then he doesn't know. He told me you looked familiar, and he's really, *really* good with faces. Are you sure you've never met him?"

David seemed wary. "Is he a dedicated journalist?"

"Dedicated?"

"Ambitious."

"Definitely," Molly confirmed, trying to be professional now. "New Hampshire is a stepping-stone. He says it's about connections. He'll be leaving here as soon as he has the clout."

"Would he go to Washington?" David asked, sounding subdued.

"In a heartbeat. He knows everything about the papers there."

"Then he knows about my family. My dad is the publisher to meet. Look at a picture of him, and you see me in thirty years. Our features are identical."

Molly sat back. "He saw that then. I'm sorry. If he hadn't seen me talking with you, you'd be safe."

"Hey, I don't regret it. Besides, chances are he won't call again."

"You don't know Nick. Be careful. He's a user."

David snorted. "I was weaned on those." He handed the signed tab to their server. "Are we packing more?"

BUT MOLLY WAS STARTING TO WORRY ABOUT HER MOTHER. Returning to the hospital, she found Kathryn alone with Robin. With artwork and two comfortable chairs, the new room was more like a real bedroom. Though the ventilator made the same soughing sound, there was less sense of urgency. That frightened Molly.

"Where's Dad?"

"Home."

"Did Chris come by?"

Kathryn nodded.

"Can I get you anything, Mom?"

She shook her head.

"If you want to go home to sleep, I'll stay here." When Kathryn didn't respond, Molly said, "Nick and I are no longer friends."

That won her a small glance.

"You were right. He was using me."

"Are you okay with it?"

"Yeah. Actually relieved. I'm tired of fighting you."

Kathryn simply turned back to Robin.

"I've done a lot of packing." Molly told her about the war chest. She didn't mention David—didn't want to upset her mother, though Kathryn seemed half-comatose herself. Given the shadow hanging over everything she herself did, Molly could only begin to imagine the depth of Kathryn's grief.

Something had to help. Determined to search for whatever it was, Molly returned home and attacked the next layer of Robin's closet. With yet another armload of CDs off the floor and no sign of mice, she was starting to wonder about Robin's warning, when she hit pay dirt.

chapter 13

A CD. IN HINDSIGHT, IT WAS OBVIOUS. AFTER SO many years of keeping a journal, Robin wouldn't have suddenly stopped. She simply shifted format. Instead of using a book, she would use a computer—but not just any old folder, since she had Molly checking her e-mail all the time. If she wanted to record private thoughts, she would type them on a CD and lock it away.

This one wasn't exactly locked away, but was where Robin knew Molly wouldn't go snooping around if there was the possibility of mice. That said, the CD did look insignificant, sandwiched between Norah Jones and Alicia Keys, with hand-doodled cover art. Except that Molly knew Robin's doodles, and while another person might have missed the letters hidden in the art, she did not. *My Book,* she read, and her heart skipped a beat.

Hurrying to the den, she put the CD in her computer. Where to *begin*? Each folder had a title and focused on an event in Robin's life. The majority related to marathons she had run, like *Boston 2005, Austin 2007, Tallahassee 2008,* and a quick look inside each showed details on training, pre-race events, and the race itself—offered in the same dry format as in her earlier journals. There were separate folders for speeches, also listed by location and date. Molly opened a few, but she had heard them. She had even written a couple herself.

But here was something new, a folder named *Speeches I Will Never Give,* and the files in it were not to be believed—titles like *Why I Hate My Mother, Competition Sucks,* and *Why My Sister Is Wrong.* Molly wasn't sure she wanted to read that one. She knew she was wrong; she was wrong all the time. She wasn't sure she wanted to read *Why I Hate My Mother* either. Kathryn was suffering such agony now that the idea of Robin hating anything about her was awful.

Who Am I? Molly wanted to read that one, along with, *Do I Need A Shrink?*

First, though, she went back to the folders, because there was one under *Speeches I Will Never Give* that registered. *Men.* Perhaps it was habit; Molly's initiation into the dating world had come through sneak peeks at Robin's journals. Perhaps it was pure curiosity, or wanting something light before she hit the heavy stuff, but she quickly opened the folder.

Inside were three files: *Nick Dukette, Adam Herman,* and *Peter Santorum.* Robin had dated Adam before Nick, but Peter Santorum was a new name. She clicked on this one.

What do you do on the day your life changes forever? she began reading and was instantly hooked.

A phone call. One phone call. I can't even believe I was home when it came. I'm NEVER home. I train. I travel. I hang out at Snow Hill. I run to the Café for a latte and stay for hours because someone always wants to talk. So how did he know I'd be home on THAT day at THAT hour?

It's a month before Boston, and I'm going for an eight-mile run. I'm worried about my hamstrings, so I shake myself loose outside. I jog down the driveway to the street and back. And there's another thing. If the phone had rung while I was at the street, I would never have heard it. A highway truck was out there trying to repair the road—pretty ridiculous, since mud season is barely over—but they're chugging and scraping along, making enough noise to drown out five phones.

Nana believes in sprites. She says they know your destiny in life and sit on your shoulder steering you where you're supposed to go.

So I'm there on the house end when the phone rings, and I consider ignoring it. I don't want to talk now. But I'm supposed to meet Mom for lunch, and I have to know where. Her current favorite is 121 Garrett, but they have LOUSY salads, so if she's going to suggest going there, I want to suggest somewhere ELSE.

I stick my head in the door and grab the phone. If it isn't Mom, I'm not going to answer. Then I see this name: Peter

Santorum. Never heard it before, and I don't give out my num-
ber to anyone who isn't a friend. But Sarah had asked if she
could give it to a guy. I broke up with Adam a month ago, and
I'm starting to feel lonely. Peter is a nice name.

"Hello?"

I hear nothing at first, then a voice that is definitely too old
to be Sarah's friend. "Is this Robin Snow?"

"It is," *I say, because my next thought is that this may be a*
guy from USATF wanting to talk about the selection process for
the Olympic Marathon team. My sprite would know that was
coming.

"My name is Peter Santorum," *he says. I don't tell him I've*
already seen that. He sounds close in age to my dad, who is
always shocked when I pick up and right off say "hi." CID
isn't intuitive to him. "Does the name ring a bell?" *this man*
asks.

Quickly, I try to remember every name on the USATF com-
mittee, but the list keeps changing as new people come on. "I
don't think so," I say politely.

"Did your mother never mention it?"

Not from USATF, then. I start to fear it's another of those
third cousins who call to ask me to speak in their town.

"Your mother is Kathryn, right?"

"That's right. But she never mentioned your name." *I shake*
out my legs. "Are you a relative of hers?"

"Of hers? No."

"Do you KNOW her?" *I ask, growing impatient. I want*
him to speed it up. I'm ready to run.

"I did. It was a long time ago. So, she never mentioned me to you?"

"No. Who are you?"

"Your father."

I stop kicking and think, Oh God, a crackpot with this number.

I'm about to hang up when he says, "Don't hang up. Your mother's name was Kathryn Webber, and she worked at a flower shop in Boston. I was there playin' tennis." A pause, then a self-conscious sound. "I was kind of hoping you'd recognize the name, but it's a generational thing, I guess. I played the big tournaments in the seventies and eighties. Google me and you'll see. I really am a person. I played Longwood for nine years. That's in Chestnut Hill, just outside Boston."

"I know where Longwood is," I say. I had run Boston enough to know the area.

"Google it. You'll see my name there. I was staying at the Ritz—it's called something else now—but your mother used to do flower arrangements for the lobby there, which was where I got her name. I wanted to send flowers to someone special, so I went to your mother's shop. We hit it off and spent some time together. I left town and thought it was over. She called me a few weeks later sayin' she was pregnant."

"And I'm the result of that?" I don't know why I'm continuing the conversation. His claim is ridiculous. My mother doesn't believe in quick affairs. She doesn't believe in premarital sex, PERIOD, though we've stopped discussing that.

I should just hang up. Only this man doesn't sound deranged.

And I did have that sprite on my shoulder, so there has to be a purpose to this.

"I have a father," I say. "My parents got married nine months to the day before I was born."

"Look," he says, "theirs wouldn't be the first marriage certificate to be altered. Or the first baby born a couple weeks early. Hey, I've agonized over this. Believe me. I've not been part of your life. Your mother never once called me to ask for a thing. I have three children of my own. They're a little younger 'n you. One of them is affected by what I'm going to say, which is why I'm calling you."

Uh-oh. One of them is affected. Here comes the pitch, I think, and ask, "How did you get this number? It's unlisted."

"I know the right people," he answers so dismissively that I know he's telling the truth. He hurries on. "A couple of months ago I found out I had a heart problem. It was an artery thing, but while the doctors were treatin' it, they diagnosed a hypertrophic heart. An enlarged heart. It's common in athletes, especially ones at the top of their game. I may not compete anymore, but I still play hard. So there was reason enough for me to develop the condition. But when they said it can be inherited, I realized it wasn't just me involved. I was five when my father died. He was forty-one. He had a heart attack."

"Caused by an enlarged heart?" I ask. I'm still skeptical, but I'm being sucked in. *If this is a solicitation, it's a novel approach.*

"We don't know. But if I got the condition from him, there was a chance one of my children got it from me. Turns out my

youngest daughter did. She's twenty and plays Division I vol-
leyball. It's rigorous. She's on the court six hours a day. She
doesn't have to change that since she's asymptomatic, but she
knows what symptoms to look for."

Still I wait. I keep thinking that he has a special request,
something to help his daughter.

Instead, he says, "Once I realized she had it, I knew I had to
get in touch with you. I didn't even know your name, but a lit-
tle research brought it up. Some surprise THAT was. You're an
accomplished runner. But it means you're at risk."

I am not, I'm thinking, because his claim is absurd. "Well,
thank you for the warning," I say sweetly and am about to dis-
connect when his voice continues with force.

"If I were you, I wouldn't believe me, either. Here's some
guy callin' out of the blue saying he's your biological dad. But
hey, here's my number. Write it down?"

"Sure." I start limbering up again as he reels it off. He actu-
ally says it twice.

"Got it?"

"Yup."

He sighs. "Okay. You probably didn't write it down, but it'll
be listed on your phone. Check out a reverse directory, and it'll
connect with my name. Santorum, Peter. Or go to the cops.
Have them check me out. If you still don't believe me, see your
doctor. And if he gives you a clean bill of health, forget this call.
But watch yourself. If you feel dizzy or short of breath, get help.
Please?"

"I will," I say, and this time I do end the call. I wait for him

to call back. A lunatic would do that. I'll have to change my number anyway.

He doesn't call back. I wait ten minutes, which is all I care to spend on a nut. Then I run my eight miles, but all the while I'm wondering whether he actually thinks I'd believe him. Charlie Snow is one of the most upstanding men I've ever met. If I'm not his daughter, something is seriously wrong with the world.

Running clears my head. By the time I return home, check my phone, and find that he hasn't called again, though I'm starting to imagine that, wherever he is, he's shrugging and saying, "Well, I warned her. That's all I can do."

I feel let down.

He's right. His number is there on my phone. I'm tempted to try calling him back—but if this is a hoax, I'd be playing into his hands.

I Google Peter Santorum. Unbelievable. If the guy who called me is an imposter, he picked a visible guy to imitate. Peter Santorum lives in California, which is consistent with his area code—and, yes, I put his number in my BlackBerry. I figure I need a record in case I decide to call the police. For all I know, Peter Santorum is a crazy man.

I look at his picture and see no resemblance. But I don't look like Dad, either. Mom always says I look like her Aunt Rose. Just to be sure, I dig out my picture box. There she is, Aunt Rose. We have the same widow's peak, same broad brow, same tapered chin. The resemblance is marked.

There's no way he's right, I'm thinking. I have these pictures as proof. Family portraits, vacations, milestones—there's a whole life in this box. My mother wouldn't let me believe in it *if it wasn't true. I'm THIRTY, for God's sake. That's old enough to be told.*

But he didn't sound delusional. So I check out his daughter on the Web. She is twenty. She plays volleyball for Penn State, which is a Division I school. So this part of it is true. And there's something he didn't say, printed there in his daughter's bio. Her aunt—his sister—is Debra Howe. I know that name before I even check it out. Debra Howe was one of the first women to run Boston.

Something about Peter Santorum seems legitimate. He didn't gloat when he called. He did sound a little nervous, but wouldn't that be appropriate if he was talking to his biological daughter for the very first time? He didn't even sound eager to be calling—just concerned about doing the right thing. He didn't ask for anything. He just warned me.

I'm having trouble absorbing this. If you aren't who you thought you were, who ARE you?

There's an easy way to find out. I can ask Dad. I can ask Mom. But would they tell me the truth after all this time? Does Dad even KNOW?

Then I realize there's an easier way to find out. I call my doctor. She sees me the next day and does a chest X-ray, but the results are inconclusive. She refers me to a cardiologist, who does an echocardiogram. And guess what?

I'm shocked, but only partly, at discovering something that might kill me. I'm shocked at discovering that someone I don't know might have been the one to give me life in the first place. I think about Nana's sprite and wonder if it could be a coincidence that this man and I both have this condition.

Mine isn't severe. They don't recommend medication, but they tell me every last possible symptom. Sweet. They warn me against pushing too hard, but they don't say I can't marathon. And that's good. It's my body, my life, and I want to run.

I haven't told Mom about the heart. I can't yet.

And I can't ask her about Peter. I'm afraid she'll lie. And then I won't be able to believe ANYTHING she says.

It's been a week now, and he hasn't called back.

There are times when I wonder what his life is like and whether we would hit it off if we met. There are times when I consider calling him. Or I could just show up at his door. He owns a group of elite tennis schools. I know where to find him.

Then I feel disloyal to Dad—to Charlie—for even considering it.

But what if I didn't tell anyone I was going? What if this was my own secret? I mean, if the guy is my biological father, I want to meet him. What if I could create a whole other life, like a parallel universe?

Right now, it's a dream. Too risky. And maybe I'm just being spiteful. I'm trying to adjust to the idea of a bad heart and a different father, and I start to BURN. I don't think I will tell Mom about my heart. If she can hide my father's name, I can hide stuff, too. It's my body, my heart, my life.

MOLLY WASN'T ANGRY WHEN SHE FIRST FINISHED READING the journal. She was just unable to believe it was true. The idea that Robin had a different father was ridiculous. She was a Snow. She had always *been* a Snow. Besides, the chances of Kathryn keeping such a monumental secret for so long was improbable.

The trouble was, Robin seemed to believe it.

Needing proof it wasn't so, Molly went into Robin's room and dug her picture box from the junk that remained in the back of the closet. Sitting on the bed, she opened it and began sorting through the photos. Robin was right. Here was the documentation of a life—and yes, the snaps of Aunt Rose with her heart-shaped face, looking so very much like Robin. That would have been convenient for Kathryn.

And still, Molly wasn't angry. What she felt was threatened. Someone was saying that everything she had been raised to believe was based on false assumption. Robin was right. *If you aren't who you thought you were, who are you?* Molly had asked herself that question more than once in the past few days.

The life she had known was coming apart.

Clinging to the familiar, she slept with the box—actually kept it on her bed with her hand touching its nubby leather. Her first thought when she awoke was that she had to share these pictures with her grandmother, but it was too early to go to the nursing home. There was no going back to sleep, though.

She showered and this time put on a tunic over capri leggings. Brushing her hair, she pulled it back in the clip Robin had brought her from Egypt, then headed for Snow Hill.

Chris's car was parked in the lot. Concerned, she went to

his office. He was slouched in his tall leather chair, his head back against the headrest, his eyes tired.

"Have you been here all night?" she asked.

He raised a shoulder. Yes.

"I'd ask what's wrong, only what a stupid question is that? Chris, does the name Peter Santorum mean anything to you?"

He looked blank. "Should it?"

"No. No. Just wondering." She left before he could ask why. Four days ago, she might have blurted everything out, but it seemed more prudent now to wait.

The greenhouse helped with that. There was no sense of loss here, but rather the sense of renewal that came each day at dawn.

The nursing home was something else. As lovely as it was, there was a sadness to it. The same visitors parked in the lot. When a car stopped coming, it meant someone had died.

Her grandmother was finishing breakfast in the small dining room on the third floor. Leaning over Nana's shoulder, Molly gave her a hug.

Marjorie looked up in surprise. "Hello."

"It's me, Nana. Molly. You look like you're done eating. Can we take a walk?" She helped her grandmother up and, threading an elbow under Nana's frail arm, guided her out. Thomas was staring from the next table, but Marjorie seemed unaware. The day was young; she hadn't met him yet.

Molly talked softly as they went down the hall. "You look pretty today, Nana. Is that the sweater Mom gave you for your birthday?" It was pale blue, finely knit. When Marjorie didn't reply, she asked, "Did you sleep well?" Then, when they reached the solarium, she remarked, "What a *beautiful* day." Awning windows were open. The air smelled of fall.

Molly settled Marjorie in a brightly cushioned wicker chair and pulled another close. Then she leaned forward and took her grandmother's hands. "Okay, Nana," she began, "this is really, really important. I'm going to say a name. I want you to tell me if it sounds familiar." She watched Marjorie's eyes. "Peter Santorum." There was no flicker of recognition. "Peter. Santorum. Does that name ring a bell?"

Marjorie turned in alarm. "A bell? I . . . I didn't hear."

"No, Nana. There's no bell." She tried again. "Have you ever heard of a man named Peter Santorum?"

Marjorie tipped her head, but her eyes were blank. Seconds later they fell to Molly's tunic. "Pretty color."

"It's lilac, your favorite. But this is important, Nana. Your daughter is Kathryn. Did she date Peter Santorum? He played tennis."

Her grandmother frowned. "I was running." Her eyes brightened. "Did I win?"

Molly wasn't alarmed by Marjorie's confusion. She had seen it in her grandmother many times. Marjorie was pulling a memory from the messy closet of her mind and, in the process, was thinking it applied to herself. Those memories, like the nerve cells in her brain, were all tangled up.

Peter's name wasn't registering.

Molly tried a different angle. "You have a granddaughter named Robin. Who is Robin's father?" A light went on, but only in her own head. "Last time I was here, you said robins come early. Was your Robin born early?"

Marjorie seemed worried. "I don't know if I finished. I . . . I can't remember."

Easing back, Molly removed the box from her tote and pulled out a picture of Robin. There were others around Marjorie's room, but this was a fresh one. "Here she is. Do you remember her, Nana?"

Marjorie studied the photo. "Did she finish?"

"She did," Molly said encouragingly, though she felt a catch inside. She was referring to an imagined race—*any* race—certainly not life itself, and that was the crucial one right now. Pulling out a second photo, she said, "This is Kathryn. She's your daughter." Marjorie stared at the picture. Molly put the two photos side by side. "Kathryn and her daughter Robin. Is Robin's father Peter Santorum, Nana? Think back. Do you remember?"

Marjorie went from one picture to the other.

"It's really important, Nana," Molly said, applying more pressure. "I need to know if this man is for real, and you would know. You're Kathryn's mother. She would have told you if she was pregnant before she got married.

Think, Nana. If I've ever asked you anything important, this is it."

Marjorie studied Molly with worry-filled eyes.

Coming out of her chair, Molly took her grandmother's face. Her hands were gentle, but she was desperate. "I need to know this, Nana. *Think.*"

The older woman's eyes filled with tears. "I . . . I was supposed to run my race." She started to cry.

Molly's heart broke. She wrapped Marjorie in her arms. She was sorry she had pushed, sorry she had expected more than her grandmother had in her, sorry because if something this shocking hadn't jarred the woman's memory, nothing would.

What hit Molly then went beyond an intellectual understanding of her grandmother's illness. She knew what Alzheimer's meant—had used the word often enough—but for the first time, its meaning was visceral. Marjorie's mind had deteriorated beyond repair, taking much of Molly's past along with it. The loss was staggering.

She wondered if this was what her mother felt and why she couldn't visit. Thomas was an excuse. The real reason was the pain of loss.

Molly didn't want to feel it either, but she couldn't close her eyes and turn away. That would be abandoning someone she loved. Her grandmother had comforted her more times than she could count. Now the tables were turned, and Molly had to be the one to give comfort.

The key, she realized as she held her grandmother, was

letting go. The past was gone. She couldn't get it back. Here was a new reality.

Sad as it was to accept that, it brought calm.

MOLLY WANTED TO SHARE THE INSIGHT WITH HER mother. Letting go wasn't a betrayal, but rather a pure form of love. But letting go entailed acceptance of reality—and in the case of Robin's life, did reality include Peter Santorum? That question had to be faced.

chapter 14

KATHRYN LAID HER HEAD BY ROBIN'S HAND. SHE had no energy—couldn't think, couldn't go down for lunch, couldn't talk on the phone. She could barely remember how busy her life had been four days ago. When it came to Snow Hill, she just didn't care.

Charlie touched her head. She struggled to open her eyes.

"Hey," he whispered.

She tried to acknowledge him with a smile, but failed.

"Want anything?" he asked.

She moved her head no.

"I can't convince you to go home for a while?"

She repeated the motion and closed her eyes.

"This isn't good, Kath," he said softly. "You shouldn't be

here all day. It isn't healthy—not emotionally, not physically. You've barely slept in four days."

"I can't sleep."

"Then it's time to talk with someone. Therapist? Minister? Your choice."

"Maybe tomorrow," she whispered wearily.

"Which one?"

"I'll let you know."

"Is Mom okay?" Molly's voice came from the door.

Charlie answered, "She's upset. This will pass. Come on in, sweetheart. Maybe if you talk with her it'll help. She's feeling sorry for herself."

Kathryn wasn't being goaded. "With good cause," she murmured and turned the other way. "Try again."

For a minute, there was silence. Then, from close beside her, Molly said, "Peter Santorum."

The name startled Kathryn. She opened her eyes. Lifting her head, she looked at her youngest child. "What did you say?"

"Who is he?" Molly asked.

Kathryn shot Charlie a quick look, but he seemed as startled as she was. And Molly was waiting with a determined look on her face.

"Where did you hear that name?" Kathryn asked.

"I read it on Robin's computer."

"Where did she hear it?"

"He called her. He learned he had a medical condition that was hereditary—an enlarged heart. He wanted to warn her."

Kathryn's thoughts began to scramble. She struggled to sort them out. "When was this?"

"A year ago last spring."

A year and a half ago. And Robin hadn't said a thing? Feeling a stab of defeat, Kathryn closed her eyes. Suddenly the years evaporated, and she was back when it began.

She wasn't thinking of having a child when she met Peter Santorum. She was twenty-two, newly graduated and working at a flower shop in downtown Boston. Her job entailed creating floral arrangements for some of the best hotels and restaurants in the city.

Peter was a tennis player, in town for the U.S. Pro Championships at Longwood. The Ritz bar was his off-hours hangout. Impressed by Kathryn's lobby arrangement, he came to the shop looking for a bouquet for his latest squeeze. He and Kathryn struck up a conversation and went out for drinks. One thing led to another, until Kathryn *became* his latest squeeze.

It lasted one night. When she discovered she was pregnant, she dug his contact information from the flower shop files and tried to call him. Getting through his handlers wasn't easy; she was a nobody. She didn't even know why she was calling. They had little in common. He loved crowds; she loved flowers. He loved the road; she loved home. A tiny part of her, perhaps, dreamed that he hadn't been able to forget her, and that he was footloose simply because he had never found the right girl.

To his credit, he didn't try to deny his role in Robin's conception. Nor, though, was he excited. "If you're calling for money," he said quietly, "I'll pay. We'll make some kind of legal arrangement, but I can't be tied down. I'm going other places right now."

He didn't go far on the professional circuit, though he subsequently established a lucrative tennis school, with branches in several cities. Not for a minute, though, did Kathryn regret having turned down his offer of money. She had pride, and she had a career. She also had supportive parents.

Then she met Charlie. Like Peter, he just walked into the flower shop one day, but there the similarities ended. Charlie wasn't buying flowers for a girlfriend, but for his secretary as a thank-you for making his life less miserable. It was a powerful opening line, delivered with such a rueful smile that they got to talking, but there was no tumbling into bed this time. For the next three days, Charlie stopped by the shop on one pretense or another. Then he gave up pretending and simply stopped by to see Kathryn. Director of marketing for a local bank group, he called the shop his oasis from the pressures of work. They talked about his work and about flowers. Already a plant person, he asked lots of questions.

It was a week before he got up the nerve—his word, confessed much later—to ask her out, at which point she told him she was pregnant. He felt a moment's qualm—another belated confession—wondering whether she was looking for a soul mate or a father for her child, before deciding that Kathryn was worth it either way. When he simply came back and asked what kind of food sat best in her stomach, she knew she had a keeper.

From that moment on, their lives were a tandem endeavor. They eloped the following week and, after researching locales as only a flower person and a marketer could do, moved to Vermont and opened Snow Hill. When Robin arrived seven weeks early, not a single brow was raised.

Kathryn had thought of Peter Santorum so infrequently over the years that he might well have not existed. She had assumed that would always be the case. She had everything she wanted without him. *Robin* had everything she wanted without him—everything except, perhaps, a healthy heart.

"It's true then," Molly said because the flow of emotions on her mother's face, not the least of it guilt, left little doubt.

Kathryn shot Charlie another look before nodding, but that brief look told Molly something else. "You knew?" she asked her father in disbelief.

"Yes."

"She *cheated* on you?"

"No. Your mother was pregnant when I met her."

Which meant Charlie had been in on the secret all these years. Suddenly little things made sense, like his mystified shrug when Molly first mentioned the enlarged heart, his perplexed frown when she told him what Robin had told her doctor. He had never outwardly lied. Nor, though, had he told the whole truth.

Molly felt completely disoriented. "Are you *my* father?"

she asked, because anything seemed possible now. Charlie shot her a chiding look. "I need to hear the words."

"I'm your father. And Chris's. Your mother was with Peter Santorum once. Robin was the result."

"Which makes her only my half sister."

"There's nothing 'only' about it," Charlie said. "Her biological origin can't change thirty-two years."

But Molly was shaken. "Does Chris know?"

"Not unless you've told him."

"But you wouldn't have told him yourself, if this hadn't happened? And if Peter hadn't called Robin, she would never have known?" She turned on her mother, prepared to argue about honesty and trust—about *fairness*—but Kathryn was looking at Robin.

"She must have hated me," she said, sounding devastated.

At least she was talking, Molly realized. If raising the issue of Peter had shocked her back to life, it couldn't be all bad. "We'd have accepted what happened easily if you'd told us when we were kids."

Kathryn spoke in a beseeching tone. "I couldn't, Molly. Times were different when Robin was born—or maybe it was just me and the values I was raised with. There was a stigma. Then the years passed, and with each year it would have been harder to say. Call me a coward, but I'm only human. Robin knew for eighteen months, and she didn't tell you either. What does that say?"

Molly hadn't thought it through yet. "Maybe she was embarrassed. Maybe she was afraid that if I knew she was only a half sister, I wouldn't do her wash. I don't know, Mom. What she said was she was afraid that if she told you, you wouldn't tell her the truth."

"Wouldn't tell her the truth?" Kathryn echoed. "She made up her mind? Can I see the CD?"

"I have it at home." It was a small lie in the larger scheme of things. The CD was in her computer, which was in her car. This was her connection to her sister now, and there were still other entries to read.

"Will you go home and get it?"

But Molly had questions of her own. "Peter Santorum implied he was a big-time tennis player. I've never heard of him."

Kathryn gave her a tired smile. "If you were into tennis, you would have. He was top tier for a short time, not long before you were born."

"Was he the reason you pushed Robin into sports?"

"Your mother didn't push her," Charlie said. "Robin pushed herself."

But Molly had seen too much, sitting on the sidelines all those years, watching the investment of mother in daughter.

Kathryn looked stricken. "I wanted her to shine."

"Because she was illegitimate?"

"She wasn't illegitimate. I was married to your father when she was born."

A technicality, Molly thought, but she was suddenly re-membering dozens of sex talks that stressed abstinence over indulgence. And now to learn that her arrow-straight mother had been unmarried and pregnant? "Did you *not* use birth control?"

"I didn't think," Kathryn said awkwardly, but Molly didn't stop. She was picturing her grandmother, whom Kathryn criticized for holding hands with a man. *Holding hands.*

"Do as I say, don't do as I do? That's horrible, Mom. Did you love him?"

"It was only once."

"But you knew who he was before that. Did you have a crush on him?"

"No. It happened out of the blue. He was charismatic. And I was young."

"He told Robin you called him when you learned you were pregnant. Did he want you to get an abortion?"

"No, but I wouldn't have even if he'd asked. Single motherhood wasn't common then, and I didn't have much money. But I wanted the baby. I figured I'd do what I had to."

"So you married Dad," Molly concluded, angry on her father's behalf, but also angry *at* him. He was standing silently by—perhaps then, certainly now. Surely he had thoughts on the subject.

"I married your dad because I loved him," Kathryn replied. "And he loved Robin from the start. He never once favored you or Chris."

"You favored Robin. You poured all of your energy into her."

Kathryn hung her head and for a split second Molly regretted the charge. Robin was being kept alive by machines. In a matter of hours—days—weeks she would be dead. This wasn't the time for accusations, particularly ones rooted in jealousy. But she was too raw for self-restraint.

Raising her head, Kathryn sighed. "Maybe I felt she was starting at a disadvantage. That I had to give her a little extra to make up for it. Maybe I felt like you and Chris were inherently stronger."

"Stronger?" Molly was amazed. "Are you kidding? Robin was always the strongest, always the best. She was the one who gave you the most pleasure. She was the one who made you proud."

"You make me proud."

"*Mom,*" Molly protested, "Robin *wins.* If she'd gone to the Olympics, she'd have won *gold.*"

The words hung in the air, a hope that would never be. Robin wouldn't go to the Olympics. Not next year. Not ever. The tragedy of that tore into Molly, and in the next breath she felt the walls closing in. Needing air, she went out to the hall. She was bending over, hands on her knees, when her father joined her. He massaged the back of her neck until she regained composure and straightened.

Bewildered, she asked, "How did things get bad so fast? Have our lives been built on a deck of cards?"

"No, sweetheart. We're just lucky. Most families face crises earlier and more often."

And through it all he stayed calm. She studied him. Oh, he was pale. But definitely calm.

"Are you comfortable with this?" she asked.

"With knowing Robin isn't my biological daughter? It never made a whit of difference."

"Because you knew from the start." He nodded. "Did you ever wish you could talk about it with Robin?"

"It wasn't my place to wish. I took my lead from your mother."

"But were there ever times when you disagreed with her about it? What if Robin had gone to the Olympics? Would you have thought Peter might want to watch?" He shrugged a maybe. "Would you have called to tell him?"

"Your mother would have had to do that."

"She wouldn't have. What if Robin wanted it?"

"Robin could have done the calling."

"What if she really wanted him here but was afraid of upsetting Mom?" Molly asked. "And what about now? Do you think someone should tell him what's happened?"

"Your mom will call if she thinks it's right."

"What do you think?"

"I think your mom should decide."

"But what about what Robin wants?" Molly asked, frustrated. When Charlie simply shook his head, she said, "I just came from seeing Nana. I thought I had it figured out—accepting and letting go. Nana's not going to remember the past. I accept that. I'm at peace with it. No more what-ifs. Let it all go. With Robin, it's harder. I want to accept. I want to let go. But the ground keeps shifting under my feet. When will it settle?"

KATHRYN LOOKED UP WHEN CHARLIE RETURNED TO THE room. She gestured at Robin. "She knew. All these months. How could I have missed it? Wouldn't there have been anger? Tension? Maybe an odd question? I've been sitting here trying to remember; but I swear, I didn't notice anything. Was I that obsessed with everything else not to see it?"

Charlie put an arm around her. "If you didn't see it, she didn't show it."

"Something like this—how could she *not*? She must have been furious with me. I never imagined she'd learn about it that way." She waved a hand, trying to explain. "It was just so irrelevant to our daily lives. I would have told her at some point, maybe if she was getting married or having a child. Charlie, how could *he* not have called me first?"

"She was thirty, Kathryn. A grown woman."

"But I'm her mother."

"*A grown woman.*"

Kathryn heard him this time. Leaning forward, she touched Robin's face. "I'm sorry, baby," she whispered through a sudden rush of tears that blurred Robin's pale features. "You should never have had to deal with this alone. I was wrong." Taking the tissue Charlie passed her, she wiped her eyes. With the next breath, exhaustion returned; but it wasn't the debilitating lethargy from before. This was one that cried out for sleep.

But first, she asked, "Is Molly okay?"

"She will be. She has a solid head on her shoulders. Right now, she's Robin's surrogate."

"And Chris? Do we tell him?"

"I will," he offered.

Kathryn was grateful. She didn't think she had the strength. "Won't that put you in an awkward position?"

"As the father who wasn't?" he chided softly. "Come on, Kath. You know better. I've always been fine with it."

Yes. He had been. Always. "It's been me," she said with resignation. "Mothering is precarious. You try to do the right thing—you think you have—then wham." Her eyes returned to Robin. "I don't know what to do here, Charlie."

"You will in time."

She sighed. "How long?"

WHY *I HATE MY MOTHER*. MOLLY WAS INTRIGUED. LOOKING at Kathryn and Robin together was seeing two people in to-tal sync. Molly was the one who went from love to hate and back, not Robin. *Why I Hate My Mother?*

With her laptop resting on a small table on the hospital patio, Molly opened the file. It was written several months after Robin had learned about Peter Santorum.

This is new. If you'd have asked me two months ago, I'd have said I LOVED my mother—why not? She's been behind me in absolutely everything. I always thought she was my best friend.

But best friends don't lie to each other about the most basic thing in life. Well, maybe she didn't lie. I never asked her if my father was really my father—why would I DO that? But it's an interesting thing to consider. What if I had? Would she have told me the truth? No. The truth would have been a distraction, but she wants me focused.

"That's how you get things done," she always says. "Focus. Make yourself good at that one special thing. Don't let distracting thoughts pull you away."

So I didn't ask—and she didn't exactly lie. But she didn't offer the truth, and, PLEASE, the thing about distraction doesn't cut it. A person has a right to know who her father is. Did Mom think I couldn't handle it? Did she think I was so fragile I would break apart? Did she think I wouldn't love Dad as much? Did she think I wouldn't want to be with Chris and Molly? Like I really have somewhere else to go? Like this father of mine is calling and sending gifts and wanting me to be part of his life?

Yeah. I think Mom was afraid of all that. Because she doesn't TRUST me. Why else would she keep her finger on everything I do? And I let her. I tell myself it's nice letting someone else run the show. I just go along for the ride. I mean, I was never as smart as Chris or as reliable as Molly. Maybe I wouldn't be good at running my life.

But maybe I would. I'LL never KNOW.

I do know a couple of things. Learning about Peter Santorum changes the way I see things. Like sports. One of the reasons people think I'm so incredible is that I come from a family that isn't athletic—like I popped out of the womb with this incredibly fluky talent.

HAH. Turns out my biological father is an athlete. Same with a half sister. And my aunt is a runner. Makes me less of a wunderkind.

Molly paused. She remembered a conversation now: Robin wondering whether Charlie could have been a good golfer—a *great* golfer, she had actually said—if he played more regularly. *Do you think it's strange,* she asked, *that I'm the only athlete in the family?* To Molly it had seemed like a purely philosophical discussion, prompted by Charlie and Kathryn's trip to watch the Pebble Beach National Pro-Am the January before. Should Molly have read more into it?

I have athletic ability thanks to Peter. Turns out I got a bad heart from him, too—and there's another thing. I'm THIRTY, for God's sake. Don't I have a right to know what I've inherited? Mom kept her secrets, but did it ever occur to her that maybe I'd want to know if I have a family history of breast cancer or diabetes or HYPERTROPHIC CARDIOMYOPATHY?

Learning who I am changes the way I see things. Mom always says I'm the one driving my career—what does that mean, driving my career? What drives my career is expectations and pressure. MOM is the force behind both.

Why do I run? Why do I push myself? Why do I want to win? I do it because it means so much to her. And why is that? Maybe she wants to show HIM just how good SHE made me.

I hate her for doing that without telling me. I feel like a TOOL—like the one thing she withholds from me is the one thing that underlies everything she does. She imagines him seeing the pieces in Sports Illustrated *and in* People. *Both of those magazines had pictures of us together, and her looks haven't changed much. She assumes he'll see my age and connect the dots. She wants him to know she raised me better than he ever could.*

Well, what about ME? Aren't I a person? Don't I have a say in this? Who is living this life anyway—Mom or me?

"Molly?"

Startled, she looked up. Nick was there, standing on the opposite side of the small table, staring over the top of her laptop. He wore his usual open-neck shirt and slacks, but his face was pale, his blue eyes hollow. His trademark arrogance was gone, which should have satisfied her. But he was an intrusion.

Closing the laptop, she folded her hands.

"You hate me," he concluded after a minute.

She made a show of considering it. "Close."

"I'm sorry."

She waited. "Is that it? You want to be friends again? Please, Nick. Fool me once, shame on you, fool me twice, shame on *me*." It was one of her grandmother's favorite lines. Thinking of Marjorie made her calm.

"I'm sorry for using you. I was wrong."

Again, she waited. Nick was nothing if not glib. She had to hand it to him; he did look unhappy. But he had toyed with her before.

"I love Robin. I should have told you that." He looked off. His hand was on the phone at his hip, fingers shifting nervously. "When you want something really badly, you forget there's a right and a wrong. I wanted Robin to see me. I wanted her to realize I wasn't giving up. I wanted her to know I would be loyal to her forever."

"So you pretended to be my friend to get information on her?" Molly cried. "Didn't you think Robin would *get* it?"

He looked back. "Like I said, you forget what's right and wrong."

Molly remembered what she had just read . . . *like the one thing she withholds from me is the one thing that underlies everything she does.* There were parallels here. Nick looked more than unhappy. He looked like he was in pain. Molly actually felt bad for him . . . but not bad enough to cave in. She wanted full disclosure. She owed that to Robin.

"What do you want?" she asked quietly.

His fingers shifted again. "To see her."

"Not possible."

"I want to tell her what I feel."

"She won't hear."

"I will."

But Molly was protective of Robin. And of Kathryn. "Write it out. I'll read it to her."

"It wouldn't be the same."

"No one but the immediate family is seeing her, Nick. You're a writer. Someone else wouldn't be able to do this, but you can."

He opened his mouth, then closed it and looked away. After a minute, he turned and walked off, just as he had done in the parking lot Tuesday night. Molly had assumed he wanted to make a phone call, but if she believed what he said now, he had simply been stunned by grief.

Alone again, she felt sorry for him—then foolish for feeling sorry. She wondered what Robin would have said. Reopening her laptop, she clicked this time on *Why My Sister Is Wrong.*

Molly is one of those people you want to shake. She can't see what's right in front of her nose.

Hell, I couldn't either until all this happened. I bought into the hype. I believed that Mom had spotted a skill in me and was directing me to greatness.

WRONG. She knew what the skill was when she saw it. She had cause to push me. Running was all I could do. I inherited athletic skill. I wasn't good at anything else.

That's where Molly comes in. She looks up to me—always has. She's like my little servant, an extension of Mom, helping me out. Okay, so she can be stubborn. And impulsive. And she can't run a mile—absolutely CANNOT do it—though she's been through it enough with me to OWN the motivational tools.

She calls me a star. But stars flare and fade fast, while Molly, she's the good earth. She's grounded. She renews herself.

Mom takes her for granted, but what would I do without Molly? She found the house. She keeps it up. She pays the bills because we both know I'd never do it on time. She also keeps things going at Snow Hill. If people there have a problem, they don't come to me. They go to her. I have a fancy title—Director of Community Events—but my assistant does all the work. She's MUCH better at it than I am. That's why Mom hired her.

Molly likes saying she's only a greenhouse person—HAH. Mom relies on her. Mom respects her. Mom doesn't look over HER shoulder at everything she does. Mom isn't constantly calling her to remind her of things, because she KNOWS they'll be done.

How can Molly not SEE that? She wants to think she's a flake who can't do much more than repot a plant. Maybe that's a good approach. When expectations are low, it's easy to exceed them.

I envy Molly for that. She's driving her own life. I'm not. I'm in a great big fat rut. Maybe it's because of the heart thing. What'll I do if it acts up? They tell me to watch for shortness of breath, but during a marathon the only people who aren't short of breath are the ones at the BACK OF THE PACK. And if I can't run? Oh sure, I can coach, but the only reason people want me is because I'm a great runner.

Smoke and mirrors. Dad uses that expression when he talks about the work he did before he met Mom. Marketing is about creating an illusion, he says, and that's the way I feel. My sister is real. I'm an illusion. Mom may not use smoke and mirrors, but she created the illusion that I could do anything. So there's another kind of expectation, and when I can't live up to it, people will see the truth—which IS that I do one thing well. I run to the finish line, and I do it faster than everyone else in the race. As for the rest of life, I run away. I don't apply myself at Snow Hill because I know I'll mess up. I don't date men who are keepers, because they want women who are, too. I don't cook because I'm lousy at it. I don't do well with babies, because they don't care about running ONE mile, let alone twenty-six.

I run. Period. And when the running is done? Who will I be?

I wonder if Peter misses the high of competing. Or if he felt like a failure when he quit the circuit. I wonder if he started the tennis school because he didn't know what else to do or if he finds it rewarding. I wonder what he expects of his daughter.

I could take Molly out there with me, like we're doing a sister trip. She can keep a secret. Maybe I should tell her.

MOLLY WAS HEARTSICK, WHICH SEEMED TO BE COMMON-place lately. She had no idea Robin was tormented. She had bought the image of a woman making it big and loving what she did. Smoke and mirrors. Omigod, *yes.*

Nearly as tragic as the idea that Robin had suffered in silence was the realization that Molly hadn't known her sister well enough to see it.

But there were answers. A phone call would get them, but not from here. From home.

chapter 15

MOLLY BLASTED THE RADIO ON THE WAY HOME, singing aloud, taking interest in absolutely everything she passed as a diversion from what she was about to do. Kathryn wouldn't be happy, but Molly's focus was Robin. When it came to Peter, her wishes were clear.

Parking under the oak, she let herself in the door and went straight to the kitchen. Robin's BlackBerry was on the counter by the phone, right where she had left it when she had gone out for Monday's run. It was dead. Typically. But the charger was nearby. In a matter of minutes, Molly had fired it up to get Peter's number.

It was mid-morning on the West Coast. She tried to picture what he would be doing. The phone rang twice before she heard a winded, "Santorum here."

Hang up, Molly. Once it's done, there's no taking it back. Mom will not be happy.

But Robin would be. Molly believed that. So, quelling a final qualm, she said, "This is Molly Snow. I'm Robin's sister."

There was a brief pause on his end, then a curious, "Robin's sister? How are you?"

"Not good." Unsure of her welcome, she rushed the words out. "I wouldn't be calling if this weren't an emergency. There's been an accident. Robin is in bad shape."

Several beats passed. "What kind of accident?"

"A massive heart attack. It was the problem you told her about. She was running Monday night and collapsed. Another runner got her heart beating again, but we don't know how long she was out. She never regained consciousness."

"What does bad shape mean?"

"They've declared her brain dead."

He groaned, clearly upset. His voice was raspy. "Oh God. I was afraid—just felt it. Did she see a doctor after I called?"

"Yes. They told her she had the condition but that it was mild. No one said she couldn't run."

"Brain dead," he repeated in a defeated tone. "Hold on a second. I'm on a treadmill. Lemme get off. I can't think here." He said "think" with a hint of a twang.

She heard voices, the squeak of a background machine, then silence. "Better," he said. "Is there absolutely no hope?"

"They've run the definitive tests. The machines are all that's keeping her alive—so it's not like there's anything you could do if you came here—but I'm trying to figure out what she would want us to do long term. The only thing I've learned is that she wanted to meet you." That put the ball in his court.

"She's on life support?"

"Yes."

"For how long? What will your family do?"

"I don't know. It's only been a day and a half since the last test was run. We're kind of torn."

"Torn enough to end up in court?" he asked, forceful for the first time. "If you're involving me to tip the balance one way or th'other, I opt out. I haven't been part of Robin's life. I won't have a say in her death."

Molly heard only the first of what he said. It hadn't *occurred* to her that he might weigh in on the decision. For all she knew, he might take them to court himself. That would be a *nightmare,* not to mention the fact that Kathryn would never forgive her.

She was wondering if she had made a major mistake calling, when he said, "I won't take a stand. I talked with Robin once. She never called me back. That told me something."

Molly did hear him this time, but she remained wary. She didn't know this man, had no idea if he meant what he said or would call a lawyer the minute he got off the phone. She wanted to make it clear he would have a fight on his hands if he did that.

In her best Kathryn voice, she said, "No one wants you to take a stand. We'll decide what to do. My family is very close. We always reach agreement, and we always do what's best for Robin." Returning to what he had said last, she added more gently, "And Robin did want to call you back. But she was afraid."

"Afraid of *me*? I didn't ask for a thing. I was careful about that."

"She was afraid of hurting Mom. I am, too, and it's possible this call will upset her."

"That raises an interesting question. Why isn't she calling me herself?"

"Because she hasn't seen Robin's diary. I have. Robin didn't know what to believe after you called. She wanted to think you were making it all up, but she checked out the information you gave her, and the heart thing clinched it. Mom had no idea Robin knew about you. Robin didn't tell her about the heart either."

There was a pause. "That's a surprise. I got the impression they were close."

"They were. But this was different." Molly tried to articulate it without being critical of Kathryn. "I think that when Robin learned about you, she decided she hadn't been in full control of her life. She wanted to change that."

That was why Molly was calling—why, acting in

Robin's stead, she had a ready answer when he asked quietly, "What would you like me to do?"

"Come see her. She wanted to meet you."

"Does your mother want that?"

"I don't know. But Robin does. That's what matters."

UNCERTAINTY SET IN THE INSTANT MOLLY HUNG UP THE phone. Of all the impulsive things she had done in her life, this held the greatest potential for disaster. Oh, she had no doubt that she was doing what Robin wanted. But Kathryn might never forgive her.

Peter was taking the red-eye and would be arriving the next morning at dawn. His seat was booked.

Seeking reassurance that she had done the right thing, she went to Robin's bedroom. It was starting to look bare, but the bed was intact, and there was the cat on the quilt, raising its head when she sat down. After staring at her for a minute, it put its head down again. It had decided to trust her. She took that as a sign.

"Sprite," Molly murmured. Definitely a sign.

Calling Peter had been the right thing. But what to do now? She could tell Kathryn or not. She could tell Charlie or not. She could make up a wild story about Peter having a premonition and calling. Or she could say nothing at all.

She needed an objective opinion, but the only person she could think to call was David. So she dug out his card and pressed in his number. His "hello" was low.

"Omigod," she realized, "you're in the middle of a class."

His voice remained soft, cautious now. "Everything okay?"

"It's the same. I'll call you back."

"No, I'll call you. Give me two minutes," he said and that was literally all it took. His tone was normal now, pleasantly soothing. "Class was just ending," he explained. "I had to go over the assignment. I don't usually keep my phone on, but there's an issue with Alexis."

"How is she?"

"I'll let you know soon. She was asking for me, so I'm heading to the hospital now. Where are you?"

"Home, but I'd like to run something past you. Can we meet there?"

They arranged a time and place. Satisfied, she ended the call and went into the den. Within minutes, she had saved Robin's files on her own computer and burned a new CD.

This was for Kathryn. And no, it wasn't the original. Molly wanted that one for herself. She believed that her sister meant these files for her, and while she couldn't keep their content from Kathryn, a copy would have to suffice.

SHE MET DAVID IN THE HOSPITAL PARKING LOT. HE LOOKED like a really cool school teacher—in shirt, tie, and jeans, with a leather backpack that he lowered to the ground. His warm smile said she had been right to call. She trusted him with private information. She didn't know why—maybe because he wasn't a Snow Hill person and didn't know the Snows' friends, or maybe because her mother had blasted him and he hadn't withered. But he felt safe to Molly.

There in the parking lot, leaning against the Snow Hill logo on the door of her Jeep, she told him about Peter.

"Amazing," he remarked when she was done. "You had no clue."

"None. I mean, I've been remembering little things she said—like when one of her friends adopted a baby and she wondered how an adoptive parent would feel if the child ever wanted to know its birth parents, or when she told me I should try tennis, maybe sign up for a week at one of the really good tennis schools—but was I supposed to ask *why* she was saying those things? If Robin had sprung this on me last week, I'd have said she had sunstroke. I'm also amazed that I called him—who am I to do that?"

"You're Robin's sister, and her wishes were clear."

"But what do I do now? He's practically on his way. If I asked him to hold off, I'm not sure he would. He wants to come. He called me back in five minutes with his flight plans. I've stuck my neck way out."

David thought a minute. "I'd have done the same."

Which was probably why Molly had sought him out. He was an ally at a time when she needed one. "Will my family be happy? My mother?"

"Maybe not short term. Long term, yes. It's what Robin wants."

"Robin is only here in spirit. My mother is here in the flesh. Should I tell her?"

"You said that mentioning his name snapped her out of a stupor. That's a good thing, isn't it?"

"Mentioning his name is different from his walking in the door."

"Did you sense she was hostile toward him?"

Molly thought back. "No. But she's been private about Robin's situation. Only immediate family in the room. That's her order. She won't even let her friends come to the hospital. She may feel he has no right to be there."

"You have Robin's CD. That's strong stuff."

Yes, but Molly was still apprehensive. "Mom will be furious with me for calling him without asking her first."

David smiled sadly. "That's the dilemma with family. When it comes to our parents, we're always children. At what point do we grow up? They raise us to function as individuals, but when do they allow us to act independently?"

"Never," Molly said. "We have to do it on our own. But how do we know if we're right?"

"When the facts say so. Robin's journal speaks volumes."

"And you'd really have done the same thing?" she said, needing his reiteration.

"Yes. Not that I'm an authority. My family didn't appreciate what I did. The Ackermans may be the same, but I still think I did the right thing."

Molly didn't hear stubbornness. She didn't hear pride. What she heard was conviction, which was what she felt on the matter of Peter. "Mom could still refuse to let him in."

"Would she do that once he's there?"

"Probably not. But she could refuse to be there herself."

"Would that be so bad? This is really about Peter and Robin."

Put that way, it made sense. "So you think I should tell her?"

He studied the ground before finally raising his eyes. "I would. She's been through so much. It's only fair to prepare her for this."

Molly was touched. "Amazing you can say that after how she treated you."

"She was upset." He made a diffident sound. "Not that I'd ask for a repeat."

Molly straightened as nearby movement caught her eye. "Oh no." Her mother was heading their way. She looked exhausted; her step lacked its characteristic resolve. But her eyes didn't waver.

As she neared, Molly became her parent's child again, timid and unsure. "Mom, you remember David. He's a teacher. One of his students is here."

Kathryn nodded but said nothing.

"Mrs. Snow," David acknowledged nervously, then said to Molly, "I'd better head in."

As soon as he was out of earshot, Kathryn said, "Our Good Samaritan."

Her voice, like her step, lacked something. In the void, Molly gained strength. The time for half-truths had passed.

Taking her mother's arm, she headed for Kathryn's car. "He's concerned. He keeps checking back."

"He's the one who might have gotten there sooner."

"No," Molly reasoned, choosing not to remind Kathryn of her earlier tirade, "he's the one who got her heart going and called for help, so any hope there was wouldn't be wasted. If it hadn't been for him, she might have been lying there for hours. She might have been hit by a car in the dark. Trust me. He agonizes over not having been able to do more."

Kathryn stopped walking. "Have you and he talked much?"

"Some." Molly got her walking again. "He's a good person. Like I say, he's a teacher."

Kathryn seemed suddenly distant. When they reached her car, she asked, "Did I really favor Robin?"

"Yes."

"I didn't mean to. Her running just took so much time. But you're the one I count on. You do make me proud."

Molly wasn't ready to believe that, especially with what she had to say. "I called Peter."

Kathryn gave a start. "You what?"

"He's coming here. I read more of Robin's diary," she

said and pulled the CD from her bag. "She really wanted to meet him."

Kathryn had blanched. She stared at the CD in horror.

"Read it, Mom," Molly urged. "Not all of it is fun, but if we're looking for direction from Robin . . ."

Kathryn's eyes rose. "You *asked* Peter to come?" When Molly didn't deny it, she cried, "How *could* you? I have gone out of my *way* to give Robin a full and complete life without him. He has *no right* to see her like this."

"She wanted to meet him, Mom."

"She did not."

"Read what's on the CD."

Kathryn closed her eyes and hung her head. When she raised it again, she put a hand on the back of her neck. "When is he coming?"

"Early tomorrow."

"Can you call him back? Tell him this isn't the time for a visit?"

"If not now, when? This is his last chance. It's something Robin wanted."

"She didn't envision this," Kathryn chided. "Oh, Molly. Do you have any idea what I'll feel if he comes here? Did you stop to think of that? Or what your *father* will feel? He's the only father Robin has ever known. Inviting Peter here is a slap in the face to him. And what about *Chris*?"

"Chris will handle it. If not, he needs to grow up. There's so little we can do for Robin. Would you deny her this?"

"She didn't want to see Peter. She would have *told* me if she had."

"Like she told you about her heart?" Molly asked and, seeing Kathryn's stricken look, softened. "Read her journal, Mom," she begged. "Robin had thoughts and feelings we never knew about, and it's not your fault or mine. We tried to be there for her. But she was more than just a Snow. She was her own person."

Molly was actually thinking that there was something redeeming in that, when Kathryn said, "I don't want to see him."

"You don't have to. He can come when you're not here."

"I don't want Robin alone with him."

"I'll be with her the whole time."

"What if he decides to stay? What if he claims parental right and wants a say in what we do?"

"He doesn't. He told me that, and he was really firm. He knows he hasn't been part of Robin's life. And he didn't ask to come here. I did the asking, because it was what Robin would want. You're right that she may not know the difference, but we will. When it's over, I want to know that I did what I could in the time she had left."

Her mother fumbled in her purse and brought out the keys.

"Don't you?" Molly asked.

Kathryn got in the car, but when she tried to close the door, Molly held it. "Talk to me, Mom."

"What can I say? It's been a harrowing week, and the worst is still ahead."

She sent Molly a look so startling that Molly released the door. As she stepped back, it struck Molly that her mother, who controlled so much of her life but couldn't control this, was terrified.

chapter 16

ALEXIS ACKERMAN WAS IN A PRIVATE ROOM ON THE
hospital's elite floor. David approached with some trepida-
tion. As it happened, she was alone—sad for Alexis, not bad
at all for him. She had the television on, but turned it off as
soon as she saw him.

Smiling, he left the door open and came in. "You look
better," he said in an upbeat tone, though it was more wish-
ful thinking than reality. With her dark hair pulled tightly
back, she was as pale and waif-like as ever. But, of course,
he couldn't say that. Instead, trying to make light of the situation, he glanced at the IV. "Filet mignon with broccoli
and a baked potato?"

She didn't smile. "I don't eat beef." She looked past him,

seeming relieved to find him alone. "I want to ask you something, Mr. Harris. What are the other kids saying about me?"

He wasn't sure they were saying much at all. She was something of a nonentity at school. Unable to say that either, he fudged it. "I think they're worried."

"They must have been talking after I was carried out."

"Most of them were at lunch." He smiled again. "You picked a good time to collapse."

No smile this time either. "They think I'm weird anyway, but I don't want them saying things that are wrong. I'm not anorexic. I'm just thin. Dancers have to be thin. Can you tell them that?"

David wasn't saying any such thing. Alexis wasn't thin; she was *emaciated*. There wasn't an ounce of fat on her face, and still her head seemed too large for her body. Not even the big, fluffy robe she wore could hide the protrusion of her collarbone.

"Maybe you'll be able to tell them yourself," he tried. "Any idea when you'll be back at school?"

She made a face. "They won't *tell* me. They're *evaluating* me. I don't know how long it'll take. My parents want me to go somewhere and rest awhile, but then I'll miss too much."

"Rest might be good," he said and, pulling at the strap on his shoulder, dug into his briefcase. "I talked with your other teachers. I have their assignments for the week."

Her eyes widened. "What did you tell them?"

"Nothing, Alexis. All they know—all anyone knows—is that you're in the hospital."

"I am *not* anorexic. I'm just tired. Will you tell them that? I don't want rumors starting, Mr. Harris. I don't want people staring at me when I get back."

"No one will stare at you."

"They *will*. They'll be thinking I have an eating disorder—which is *such* a joke. Do you know how many of them make themselves *throw up* in the lav? I have *never* done that. I'm just thin. But they'll be comparing me to my brothers, who are huge; they play *football*. It's different for a girl. Especially with dancing." She lowered her voice. "I wanted you here so you could see that I'm fine. Can you tell everyone that?"

"Mr. Harris?" came an authoritative voice from behind him.

He turned. Alexis's mother had arrived.

"He brought my assignments," Alexis explained quickly. "He's just leaving."

Donna Ackerman nodded.

"I'll check back on you another time," David told the girl.

"Oh, I'll be home soon and back at school. I'm feeling much better."

He smiled. "That's a relief. I'll let people know." He left the room and was halfway down the hall when Donna called his name.

She jogged up. "I appreciate your coming. She was asking for you."

"She's worried about what people are saying."

"So am I. If she'd told me she wasn't feeling well, she

could have stayed home yesterday and we'd have avoided all this."

"Do the doctors have a reason for keeping her here?"

Donna gave a long-suffering sigh. "You know the medical profession. Doctors can find *anything* if they look hard enough. Alexis is anemic. She just needs a little boost. We'll get her home and take it from there."

David wasn't sure where they would "take it" if they denied the problem, but that was for the doctors to say. Whether Alexis's parents would listen was something else. For now, he was simply glad the girl was here.

"Let me know if there's anything I can do," he offered.

"I will," the woman said and turned back to her daughter's room.

He watched her for a minute, thinking of his own parents and his brother's drug problem, even of Kathryn Snow with Robin. Self-delusion was a tricky thing. A product of pride? If so, he was just fine being modest. It might be a whole lot easier on his own kids some day.

Wondering how Molly was doing, he took the elevator down and was crossing through the lobby when he saw a trio of familiar faces—mother, father, and son—from his student-teaching year. Breaking into a smile, he approached.

"This can't be the same Dylan Monroe I taught when he was in first grade," he teased. "That guy was little. This one's gettin' pretty big."

Deborah Monroe smiled back and extended her hand.

"David. *You* have not changed. Dylan, you remember Mr. Harris, don't you? He taught you to read."

"Oh no," David cautioned. "Denise Amelio taught him to read. I just nudged him along when he started thinking about songs and not books."

The boy's eyes were large behind glasses that seemed even thicker than David remembered. "You loved Springsteen."

"Still do," David said. "And you?"

"Dylan," he said with a grin.

"Good choice. Still playing the piano?" When the boy nodded, David turned to the parents. "What brings you folks all the way up here?"

The dad answered. David couldn't remember his name. Both parents worked—Deborah as a doctor—but she was always the one who made it to school.

"Marvin Larocque," he said. "Dylan has a corneal problem."

"Two," the boy put in. "Both eyes." He seemed proud to acknowledge the problem. David found that refreshing.

"Marvin is the best transplant person in town," the father explained.

"We're still a year or two away," cautioned the mother, "but it doesn't hurt to do the legwork now. Dylan's father lives near here. That makes it easy."

"And my dog—*my* dog—has a mom and brother living with Dad and Rebecca. That *really* makes it easy."

"*You* have a dog?" David asked.

Grinning, Dylan nodded.

Deborah put a hand on his head and turned the boy toward the elevator. "This could be the start of a long conversation, but we have an appointment upstairs. Good seeing you, David. Didn't I hear you were teaching in this area?"

"Sure am. Twenty minutes from here. But hey, you go on. Good luck with Dr. Larocque. I taught his son the year before last. The kid loves acoustic guitar." He winked at Dylan. "A little inside tip." He held up a hand and watched the threesome leave, then turned to find a new face.

David had never formally met Nick Dukette, yet that was the name that came to mind. Something about intense eyes made David think of the people he had known growing up. This man was close to his age.

His guess was correct. "David Harris? I'm Nick Dukette, here to rebut what Molly told you. I am not evil," he said, but what little humor might have been in his voice ended there. His face was tired and tight.

"She didn't use that word."

"No, but I'm sure that was the gist."

David wasn't about to relate what Molly had said, and Nick didn't appear to expect it. He went right on. "I've met your dad."

"Really."

"Several times, actually. He's one of my idols."

"If I tell him that, will he recognize your name?" David asked, well-trained to detect phonies.

"I doubt it," Nick said without balking. "I had nothing to offer then. Now I do."

"What's that?"

"A bio of Robin Snow. I've been writing about her for a while. Molly's actually encouraged me to do it. It's exactly the kind of thing your dad serializes in his papers. I'd offer an exclusive."

David wasn't surprised by the offer, only the speed with which it came. Nick was all business. "Why not just approach a publisher in New York?"

"I don't know one personally. On the other hand, New York might see what your dad publishes and take notice."

True, David thought. *And blunt.* "Give him a call, then."

"Like I say, he wouldn't recognize the name. I was hoping you'd give him the heads-up beforehand. You can vouch for me. You live here. If you read the local paper, you read me."

"Actually," David said in a moment's perversity, "I get my news on TV. Journalists today don't write the way they used to. They overlook basic questions. They stress irrelevant details for the sake of drama."

Nick smiled smugly. "My bio of Robin is different."

"Did Robin know you were putting together a bio while you were dating her?"

"Ah. Molly told you that Robin and I dated. Actually, yes. She knew. She loved it."

"The attention or the bio?"

His smugness wavered. "She hasn't had a chance to read the bio." He swallowed. "That's what makes it so timely. I mean, here she is, hanging by a thread between life and death. It's the kind of hot story that your father loves."

It was, but David wasn't his father. "What about the Snow family?"

"Like I say, Molly gave me the go-ahead. Besides, authorized or unauthorized, I have more information than anyone else. If your dad doesn't want it, I'll go elsewhere; but I thought that since there was this connection, you being here and even knowing Molly, it would make for a good fit. What do you think?"

"I think, maybe, no," David replied easily. "I'm not involved in my father's work."

"You don't have to be involved. All you have to do is call him. What about your brothers?"

"I tried it in journalism, but my instincts suck. They know that. Trust me, if I were to push your name with them, it could do more harm than good."

"All I want is an intro. Tell them you have a friend who wants to call. Once I get through on the phone, I can take it from there."

"Tell you what," David suggested, thinking that Molly would be interested in seeing what Nick was hawking, "show me what you have. If I'm comfortable with it, I'll see what I can do."

Nick grinned. "Deal." He raised his eyes, and his expression flipped from pleased to worried. "Chris!" he called and said to David, "Do you know Molly's brother?"

David recognized Chris from the ICU floor, but even if he hadn't, the resemblance between brother and sister was marked. Nick made the introductions. Chris looked distracted.

"How's Robin?" Nick asked.

Chris shrugged.

"You heading upstairs? Want company?"

"No. I have to talk with my dad." Darting David a parting glance, he walked off.

DRIVING TO THE HOSPITAL, CHRIS HAD BEEN FIXATED ON his own agenda. When he reached Robin's room, though, Charlie was the first to speak, and what he said pushed Chris's agenda aside.

Not that Chris was entirely surprised to learn about Peter. It explained his mother's emotional investment in Robin. He hadn't taken that personally, but he knew Molly had. He wondered how she felt learning the truth.

The one he had immediate questions for, though, was his father. They were in Robin's room, leaning side by side against the wall, their voices low, eyes on Robin, the machines, the flowers—anything but each other. It was easier that way.

"You knew all along?" Chris asked.

"Not details," Charlie said. "I didn't need to know those."

"But you knew his name."

"Sure did. Even back then, I read the Sports section first. Longwood was a big deal in Boston."

"What'd you think about Mom being with a star?"

"It was only one night, Chris."

"But he was famous."

"Your mother barely knew that. I followed his career more than she did."

"Before you knew about Mom and him?"

"After, too."

"For Robin's sake?"

"Mine. I like tennis."

Chris's situation was different. There had been overlap between his time with Liz and his time with Erin. But Erin didn't know about Liz. He wondered how he would feel if he learned she had been with someone else, too.

"Did it bother you coming after him?" he asked quietly.

"If you're talking about sex, let's not. If you're talking about love, there's no contest. Your mother wasn't pining for him. She loved me."

"You saved her. You offered her marriage. You supported her."

"Hold on," Charlie warned and did look at Chris then. "If you're saying she used me, you're wrong. Before we ever went on a date, she told me about Robin. I had a choice—go for it or walk away. I chose to go for it. Your mother and I hit if off from the start, and it was mutual. She gave back as good as she got."

"But she was having another guy's baby."

"So? Look around. Blended families are common. We were just ahead of our time."

"Okay. Then her fixation on Robin. Did it bother you?"

"No. I understood it. And I agreed with her. Robin needed more help."

Chris made a face. "In what?"

"School, for one thing. It didn't come easy for Robin."

That was news to him. "She won every prize."

"Actually," Charlie said with quiet authority, "if you go back and look, the prizes weren't for academics. They were for things like improvement and congeniality."

What Chris remembered most was the big deal they made of any prize Robin got. Conceding his father's point, he said, "She's always been hyper-social. Is that because her father was?"

"I'm her father, Chris."

"But the rest of us are reserved."

"Not your mother. Robin may have inherited physical traits from Peter, but she learned behavioral ones from Mom."

Christopher wasn't sure that was correct. You could inherit behavioral traits. Hadn't Chloe been born with the ability to pacify herself? She was sucking her thumb, then rubbing the edge of her blanket, then kicking her mobile to make it jingle. She inherited resourcefulness from Erin, yet she certainly hadn't seen Erin sucking her thumb.

But he didn't want to argue with Charlie. So he said, "Does it bother you knowing Robin's been in touch with him?"

"No. I wish I'd known. I'd have talked with her about it. But her behavior toward me never changed, Chris. She knew I loved her."

Christopher envied his father's unflagging faith. He wished he could be as sure about everything he did. "I have a problem, Dad."

"With this?"

"No. Liz Tocci. She's threatening to make trouble. When I first met her? We were together."

Charlie was slow to register what Chris had said. Then he was startled. "Together like . . . ?"

"Yuh." Chris put his hands in his pockets. "Not exactly one night like Mom and this guy, more like a couple of weeks and around the same time I first met Erin."

"Liz Tocci?" Charlie asked in disbelief.

Chris felt the same disbelief. "I was a senior. I didn't go looking for it, but there Liz was. Kind of like a last fling."

"Did you bring her here for that?" Charlie asked disapprovingly.

Chris looked at his father. "No. It was over before I graduated. She knew I was seeing Erin. She even knew we got married, but she kept in touch. When she was looking to leave the city, I set up her interview with Mom. She was an old friend. She never suggested anything more than that until now, when she needs a weapon. The fact that Molly fired her is driving her nuts. She wants to be reinstated."

A nurse came in. Charlie took Christopher's elbow. "We'll

be right outside," he told the woman and waited only until the door was closed before murmuring, "She's all hot air."

Chris kept telling himself that, but there was a catch. "She says she has pictures."

"Compromising ones?"

"They can't be. I wasn't with her but that one stretch, and there were no pictures." He paused, then said, "My relationship with Erin was just getting off the ground. I didn't want her finding out."

"Did she?"

He shook his head. "Liz knows that. It's her ace in the hole."

"What do you want to do?"

"Tell her to take a hike."

"There's a risk. If you told Erin, you'd eliminate it."

Chris let out a breath. "Easier said than done. She'll be upset."

"Explain why you did what you did."

"Last fling?" He made a disparaging sound.

"You have to tell her something."

"We've, uh, had some differences lately. She says I don't talk enough."

"Maybe you don't."

"*You* never did."

Charlie slid him a puzzled look. "I talked enough."

"I never heard it."

"Were you in the bedroom with Mom and me?" Of course not. "Parents don't talk about everything in front of their kids," Charlie went on. "Your mother and I talk at night when we're alone. She always knows what I'm thinking."

"I thought that with Erin, but she says no. You and Mom work together, so you don't have to come home at night and give a play-by-play of your day."

"Erin can work at Snow Hill."

"That's not the point."

"Maybe it should be. She's been a help this week. I'd rather have her with us than somewhere else. She could even bring the baby."

"Snow Hill's no place for a baby."

"It worked for you kids. But if you don't want it, find a better solution. Come on, Chris. Be positive."

"This week?" He snorted. "Fat chance."

His father was quiet. "Life goes on, Chris. You raised the issue of Liz. It'll be here with or without Robin. Same with you and Erin."

"Erin's being unreasonable. So what if I'm quiet. You're quiet. That works for Mom. Erin just doesn't get it."

"No, Chris, *you're* the one who doesn't get it if you don't acknowledge her needs. Sharing feelings is hard. If someone disagrees, you feel offended—especially if that someone is the person you love. But the solution isn't to clam up. Mom would be upset with me if I didn't express my thoughts. I just do it in a way I'm comfortable with. You have to find what you're comfortable with. To refuse to do it at all is cowardly. You could start by telling Erin about Liz."

Chris didn't like that idea. But it might be the only way to neutralize Liz. "You wouldn't vote to reinstate her?"

"And undercut Molly? No."

"What about severance?"

Charlie considered that. "Four weeks' pay, maybe. That'd be a compromise."

Chris wasn't sure she would go for it, but that took him to the next step. "She'll fight me. Will you make the call?"

"Oh-ho no, my boy," Charlie said, pushing off from the wall as the nurse left Robin's room. "This one's all yours."

AT HOME, KATHRYN SAT ON HER BED WITH HER LAPTOP. SHE was wearing her robe, its pockets filled with tissues she had used, crying as she read Robin's files. She was glad she was alone. She couldn't be strong, just couldn't. To be able to cry, to sob, to shriek without anyone hearing was a luxury.

Molly was right. If these files were to be believed, Robin wanted to meet Peter; but there were other wants that Kathryn hadn't imagined, either. Reading about these made her look twice at the mother she had been, and what she saw didn't please her. Her heart might have been in the right place, but she had missed the core of who Robin was. She had chosen to see a Robin who was made in her own mold, rather than one shaped by Peter, Charlie, even Molly. This other Robin was a revelation.

That was why, at last, she was drawn to *Who Am I?* Craving the answer, she opened the file.

I'm a fraud, Robin began but caught herself. *Maybe that's an overstatement. Let's say I'm an actor. I play the part of the star, and I do a convincing job. Do I love giving speeches? No. And cutting ribbons is boring as hell.*

The part about running is real. I couldn't fake that. But I have my mother to thank. She gave me the motivation when I had none myself.

So I'm a RUNNER. Who else am I?

I'd say I'm a DAUGHTER, only I don't do much for my parents. They're the ones doing things for me. Same with being a SISTER. Molly does more for me in a day than I do for her in a month. And the bitch of it is, I now know that I'm not even completely a SNOW.

So who am I?

In order to BE someone, you have to be passionate. Molly is passionate. She LOVES her greenhouse and LOVES her cats. She LOVES the house, even when I criticize it for every little fault that I see. She LOVES being the traveller, which may not be obvious to her, because she also LOVES being home. But when she's with me on the road, we actually SEE the city we're in. When I'm alone, I'm in and out. Could be Dallas, could be Tampa, could be Salt Lake City. I barely notice.

I have lots of friends. So I'm a FRIEND. But they're not here in the middle of the night, and besides, they're more like an entourage than a group of friends. If I stopped running, we wouldn't have much in common.

Who do I WANT to be? I want to be all of the above, only I don't have the time. OK, I don't MAKE the time. Because I'm too busy being an actor playing the part of a runner who is so busy racking up wins that she doesn't HAVE a clue about who she wants to be.

Nana used to slow me down when I was little. She'd catch me there in her arms and hold me without saying much at all. When I squirmed to escape, she said, "Just be, little Robin. Just be."

I think that if I could do that, I would be able to decide who I am.

I'd like to JUST BE, for a little while at least. Nana doesn't say those words anymore, but they're coming to me now. Must be her sprite.

Kathryn was sobbing again, loudly and unrestrained— this time for Marjorie. She missed her mother. Marjorie would have had something down-to-earth and sensible to say about what had happened to Robin. Or she might have simply called it the work of sprites. But hadn't Charlie, too, said that things happened for a reason?

Struggling to make sense of it all, Kathryn set aside the laptop and went downstairs. The kitchen looked like a party waiting to happen, with covered casseroles on the counter, dropped off only that morning. Others filled the freezer. Moreover, there were flowers in every room, not a one brought back from the hospital.

Preparation for a wake? No. Kathryn was past the point of cynicism. These gifts were to sustain her through this horrendous time.

She had friends, though she hadn't done much to earn their loyalty. She had a successful business, though its success was truly the work of a larger team. She had a mother she had deserted and a family she didn't hear. And *Robin* called herself a fraud?

With their lives in such flux, Kathryn had no idea who she was herself. Nor could she see the future.

At this moment of sheer exhaustion, the idea of just . . . *being* . . . sounded nice. Except that her firstborn was on life support pending a devastating choice, Charlie was deferring, Molly was arguing, Chris was silent, Marjorie was absent, and Peter was coming.

Focus, she told herself. But on *what*?

chapter 17

MOLLY WORE A SUNDRESS ON SATURDAY MORNING. As Robin's emissary, she wanted to look good. In order to recognize Peter when he arrived, she pulled up pictures of him before she left home.

The airport was small and the plane a private one. He emerged from the terminal alone, with a single bag on his shoulder, and looked exactly like his photographs— same lean build, same polo shirt and chinos, same tanned face.

Recognizing him was the easy part. The hard part was knowing what to say. She did fine with the greetings— *How was your flight? Do you have any other bags? Have you been to this area before?* Once they were in the car, though, she found herself unsure of what he expected, of what she expected, of what *Robin* expected.

"Excuse the ride," she said when he shifted his legs in what looked like an attempt to get comfortable. "We don't have a limo."

"This is fine. The company Jeep?" he asked in a nice-enough way.

"My Jeep. The logo is good advertising."

"Is advertising your field?"

"No. I do plants."

"Do?" he asked with either mockery or simple curiosity.

Giving him the benefit of the doubt, she said, "I run the greenhouse. Plants are reliable. Once you know them, you know them. No surprises."

He was quick; he got it in one. "Surprises like me?"

"And Robin and my mother. They both knew and never told."

He was quiet for a minute. Then he said, "I didn't know Robin Snow was my daughter until I went lookin'. I haven't been in touch with your mother. I never even knew if the baby was a boy or a girl."

Molly resented that on Robin's behalf. "Weren't you curious?"

"I didn't want to know. Didn't want to feel anything."

"But didn't you feel anyway?" she asked.

"Maybe. Once in a while."

She shot him a look. He seemed serious. "How many kids do you have in all?"

"Back home? Three. One loves me; two hate me. That's

not a great track record. Robin was better off with your dad."

Stopped at a traffic light, Molly studied him. "I don't see any of Robin in you."

"She's fortunate then."

"Actually, she's not," Molly said with mild annoyance. "I'd rather she inherited your looks than your heart." The light changed. She drove on.

"You were the one who asked me to come," he reminded her gently.

Duly chastised, she softened. "I'm sorry. This is weird."

"Does your mother know I'm here?"

"She does. Does your wife?"

He made a derisive sound. "Which one? Wife number one, two, or three?"

"There are three?"

"Four, actually—only the last took off with our financial adviser, so she has no idea where I am. For what it's worth, neither do the other three."

"Why not?"

"I respect Robin's privacy. Did she tell *you* about me?"

"No."

"Enough said."

Molly smiled wryly. "That's something my brother would say. He's an accountant."

"Then he's no friend of mine," Peter said, but with humor. "Does he know about me?"

"My father told him last night."

"So your father does know."

"Oh, he has all along. For the record," she said, needing to stress this because she was feeling like something of a Judas, betraying the family by bringing Peter here, "he's been the best father Robin could want. He adores her. Please do not go in there talking about wishing you'd been a father to her. She's had a wonderful father."

"Hey," he reminded her again, this time chidingly, "*you* were the one who invited me here."

She forced herself to take a breath. "You're right. I'm just worried. It's been an awful week. I don't want to make things worse, but I want Robin to know that you've come."

He might have remarked that Robin wouldn't know it. When he didn't, her regard for him rose a notch. She said, "Your sister is a runner. Does she know about Robin?"

"She doesn't know Robin is my daughter. None of my kids know either. Again, for Robin's sake."

"Robin's or yours?"

He winced. "How old did you say you were?"

"Twenty-seven. And this is just my personality. If Robin were sitting behind me, she'd be kicking the back of my seat." She paused. "If she were here, though, she'd be asking these questions herself."

"She's lucky to have a sister like you."

"I'm the lucky one. She's been an awesome role model. Talk about determination and self-discipline. I could never do what she does."

"Did she ever try to convert you?"

"Of course. Runners are missionaries. She just never succeeded."

"What else did she do besides run?"

"Ate yogurt and drank herb tea," Molly said fondly. "And gave speeches. She inspired girls who wanted to run competitively. She helped raise millions of dollars for charity. You have my mom to thank for that. She taught Robin good values."

He seemed pensive. Then he looked at her. "Tell me about your mom."

"She is deeply in love with my dad," Molly said, just so he'd know.

"She's been happy, then?"

"Very. Until now. This has thrown her."

"Will I see her?"

Molly shot him a look and, for an instant, they were conspirators. "That's anyone's guess. We'll know soon. Almost there."

KATHRYN HAD NO DESIRE TO SEE PETER. IF THERE WAS physical fault to be found in what had happened to Robin, he bore it. But Robin had collapsed on her watch. That was a mark against her, and it went beyond pride. Facing Peter meant facing her guilt for missing signs that had to have been there.

The alternative, though, was letting him visit Robin

alone. Oh, one of the others could sit in, but it wasn't the same. Kathryn had shepherded Robin through everything else in her life. She couldn't quit now.

That thought made for another night of sporadic sleep. She awoke groggy, and even a long shower and three cups of coffee barely helped.

Arriving early at the hospital, she put Robin's arms and legs through range-of-motion exercises—not caring that the doctors had stopped suggesting it—but her eyes kept returning to her daughter's face. Robin had always had beautiful skin, and that hadn't changed in four days. Kathryn wondered if it would after a week. She wondered if it would after a year. Other things would definitely change, such as muscle tone. She couldn't remember a time when Robin hadn't been lean and strong. Watching her run was like watching a thoroughbred.

Her heart ached at the paradox—the same sport that had made Robin the picture of health had been her undoing.

The door opened, and despite twelve hours of dread, she thought at first that Peter was just another hospital employee. Robin might have seen recent pictures, but Kathryn had not. Thirty-two years later, he looked different.

She must have been staring blankly, because he gave her a wry smile. "Were you expecting someone else?" he asked. His voice, with its seductive West Texas drawl, compressed the years.

She rose. "No. It's just that the hospital sends so many people in here."

He closed the door. "Have I changed that much?"

His body hadn't. He was as tall and lean-muscled as he had been when they first met, and exuded the same athleticism. He'd had few wrinkles on his face then but there were plenty now. Conversely, he'd had plenty of hair then but little now.

"I pictured you the way you were," she said.

"You haven't seen me since?" He pressed a hand to his heart. "You wound me. I'm still in the news sometimes, and my face is all over my Web site."

But Kathryn was at a loss. The last time she had seen Peter Santorum, he had been stark naked. They had just had sex, and she was dressing to leave. She tried to think of what else they had said or done during their twenty-four hours together. But sex was all she could recall.

Focus, she thought, and turned to Robin. "You wanted to see him, so he's come," she said softly, then to Peter, "Isn't she beautiful?" So beautiful. So still. The tragedy of it made her emotions raw.

He hadn't moved from the door. "I could see it from her pictures. She takes after her mom. You look good, Kathryn."

"I can't. It's been a week from hell. I've barely slept."

"Still you look good. The years have been kind to you."

Angry, because this wasn't a party and flattery was *absurd,* she said, "I'd give up every one of those kind years if I could turn back the clock. I'd sell my soul to the *devil* if it would spark Robin's brain back to life."

His eyes did shift to Robin then, but they seemed tentative, as if they might skitter away at the slightest provocation. It struck her that he was frightened. Oddly, that made him less of a threat.

"You can come closer," she dared.

Cautiously, he came to Robin's side. "This is not how I imagined meeting my daughter."

"No. I wish you'd seen her in action."

"I did," he said to Kathryn's surprise. "A couple months after I called, she ran San Francisco. I watched from the Embarcadero just past Pier 39." He smiled. "My luck, she was in the first wave of runners. I had to get up at dawn for a four-second glimpse. I'd call that devotion."

Kathryn would call it curiosity—*cowardly* curiosity. Robin had run a personal best that day, placing second among women runners.

Devotion? Not quite. "Did you *never* think of her all those years before?" she asked in dismay.

He didn't flinch. "What would have been the point?"

"She was *your child*. How could you *not*?"

He held up a hand. "I'm not you, Kathryn. I didn't carry her for nine months. I gave up my parental rights before she was even viable. Besides, would you have wanted me involved?"

"No."

"Enough said."

Kathryn made a guttural sound. "You sound like my son."

"Molly told me that."

"She tends to run at the mouth. What else did she tell you?"

"That you have a great marriage, that your husband has been a wonderful father to Robin, that you've been happy."

"I have. I've been lucky."

He waved his hand. "We make our luck. It's about making smart decisions."

But Kathryn had learned too much about herself in the last few days to agree. "I don't know if the decisions I made were always smart. When something like this happens, you start second-guessing your life."

"What's to second-guess? You raised a wonder with this one. Her sister's pretty sharp, too, and I haven't even met your boy."

You haven't even met Charlie, Kathryn thought, because at that moment, he seemed a far more stable parent than she. "Molly's heart's in the right place," she said quietly. "She's hell-bent on doing what Robin wants, hence her call to you."

Leaving her side, Peter walked around the bed. He put his elbows on the far rail and studied Robin. "Part of me wishes she hadn't. This isn't fun."

Kathryn shot him a withering look.

He got the message. "Y'know," he said, sounding defensive, "some of us aren't good at the hard stuff. I play tennis. I teach kids. I run schools. I am not good at family. Any one of my wives—excuse me, my *ex*-wives—can attest to that.

So I stick to the light stuff, and maybe that's a character flaw. But my father died when I was a kid. So I knew I could die young, too—even before I learned about my heart. We'll never know for sure whether my father had it, too, but he was a rancher. His work was as physical as any athlete's. But that isn't the point. I can't stress over stuff I'd fail at. I am who I am. I play tennis. That's what I do."

Kathryn was pressing her heart. Substitute the word *run* for *play tennis,* and he could have been quoting Robin's journal. She had felt a sadness reading that, and now felt the same sadness hearing it from Peter.

"So I accept the reality of the thing," he went on. "People have limitations."

"But isn't it important to try to expand on them?"

"Yes. That's why I'm here."

She had no retort.

"But it doesn't change who I am," he insisted. "If I'd married you back then, sure, I'd have known Robin, but we'd have all been miserable. Instead, look at you. Married to the same guy all these years? Know how special that is?"

She did. Taking Robin's hand, she held it to her throat.

"I'm glad Molly called me," he said, straightening. "Being here is right for me. If I'd learned about it afterward, I'd have felt worse." He paused, looking from one machine to the next. "Mighty intimidating."

"You get used to them. You get used to the whole situation. You go from numbness to tears and back."

"What are you gonna do?" he asked with just enough gravity to explain what he meant.

She shook her head—*can't go there*—and clung to Robin's hand, her own lifeline. Then she cleared her throat. "So you still love playing tennis?"

"Yeah. I do it well."

"Do you miss the high of competing?" she asked, because Robin had wondered that.

"I miss winning. I don't miss losing. When you start losing more than you win, you know it's time."

"Did you feel like a failure when you quit?"

"If I let myself think about it, I would have; but I was already starting my school. Surround yourself with kids who think you hung the moon, and you don't feel like a failure."

"Did you ever want to do anything else?" He made a *who-me?* face.

"Did anyone ever suggest you do something else?" Kathryn asked, wondering if she should have suggested it to Robin.

"My wives did. Lotsa different ideas to make money."

"What about your mother? Is she still alive?"

His face softened. "Sure is. She wants me happy."

"I wanted Robin happy," Kathryn mused. Robin's journal haunted her.

"Wasn't she?"

"When she was running. But it bothered her that running was the only thing she was good at—at least, that's what she wrote in her journal. She kept looking at the rest of us and thinking she should do more."

"Did you pressure her?"

"No. But I always equated her with running. I never pushed her to do other things. Maybe that was the problem. She began thinking she couldn't *do* those other things and worrying about what would happen when she couldn't compete. If I'd known she worried about that, I'd have said I didn't care what she did, as long as she was happy."

"That's a mother thing—happiness is."

"I didn't get a chance to say it. She didn't share those thoughts."

"I had a dozen years of therapy before I could share them."

She should have talked with you, Kathryn thought and, feeling responsible for the lack of contact, quietly said, "Maybe you could tell her some of what you learned from your therapist? She'll hear. It's really important." Gently, she set down Robin's hand. "I'm going to leave you alone with her, Peter. Please tell her what you just said?"

MOLLY WAS WAITING OUTSIDE THE ROOM. CHARLIE AND Chris were there, but neither of them wanted to barge into Robin's room, either. Charlie looked worried when Kathryn came out, but Molly felt worse. She was the one who had brought Peter here.

Kathryn motioned briefly to let Charlie know she was

all right, but Molly was the one she turned to. "I lost sleep over this," she said with an edge.

Molly's heart fell. "I'm sorry. It's just that Robin was so insistent."

Kathryn took a deep breath. Settling against the wall beside Molly, she folded her arms and asked, "So what do you think of him?"

The edge had softened. Relieved by that—and flattered to be asked—Molly said, "He seems nice. How was he with Robin?"

"He was okay. Do you think she'd like him?"

"Not like she loves Dad," Molly said on a note of loyalty.

Charlie must have sensed their need for space because he quietly moved Chris down the hall. Molly was grateful. It was hard enough talking about Peter with Kathryn, but even harder with Charlie listening.

"Would she understand?" Kathryn asked.

Molly was a minute following. "Understand your having been with Peter? Omigod, yes. You may be hung up about having been with someone other than Dad, but my generation is not. He's really good-looking even now, and he does have charm. I don't fault you for being with him, Mom. It was a shock—the *secret* of it—especially because you've always been hard on us on the subject of men."

"Do you understand why?" Kathryn asked beseechingly.

"Yes. Now. If we'd known about Peter, we might have understood sooner."

"How could I tell you—and still try to keep you from

doing what I did—without suggesting Robin was a mistake? She wasn't, Molly. I was raised on Nana's sprites, too. Robin's conception had a purpose. It gave me focus. It made me ready to love your father."

Robin had certainly believed in those sprites. "So you read the CD?" Molly asked.

Kathryn nodded. "Not fun to read. But enlightening. I just never knew."

"None of us did. You can't beat yourself about that."

"Some of what she felt, he felt, too."

"Like competition sucks?"

Smiling, Kathryn reached for her hand. "Mmm. That, and the business about doing only one thing well. They were both insecure about that."

Molly loved her mother's grip. It suggested forgiveness, even approval. Her selfish heart felt full in what should have been an impossibly grim situation. "How does he deal?"

"He lets go. He gives himself permission to be good at one thing and lousy at other things." Linking their fingers, she frowned. "He accepts who he is."

"You accept who Robin is."

"Do I? I didn't allow her to think about much else." Her eyes found Molly's. "Maybe I didn't love her enough."

"Omigod, Mom. You did."

"She said I didn't trust her. Maybe I didn't."

"You wanted her to do what she did best."

"Maybe I just couldn't let go."

"Would she have done anything differently if you had?"

"Maybe not, but she should have had that chance. I gushed over her running, but I should have gushed over *her*. I should have let go and loved her for *everything* she did."

"Well, that's how I feel about Nana," Molly burst out. Kathryn looked at her in alarm, but the comparison was too strong to ignore. "She is who she is, which is a different person from who she was. When I let go of who I want her to be and love her for who she is, I feel calm."

"Nana is a whole other can of worms."

Molly *hated* that expression. "She is the sweetest person in the world, and she's stuck somewhere between this life and the next. You sit with Robin for hours, even though the tests show she's not here. But what about Nana? She *is* here. She's still your mother. Why do you visit Robin and not her?"

Releasing Molly's hand, Kathryn folded her arms. "I can't talk about this now."

Back off, one part of Molly cried, but the other didn't listen. A window was open. "Then when? Nana has lucid moments. Do we wait until they're gone, too? Her brain isn't totally dead yet, Mom."

Kathryn seemed ready to argue when Peter emerged. Straightening, she turned. Molly couldn't see her face, but she saw Peter's. He looked upset.

"Did you tell her?" Kathryn asked.

He nodded. "I don't know what she heard."

"It doesn't matter. At least you told her."

He nodded. He looked at Kathryn for a minute, then at Molly.

Kathryn kept her arms folded. "You know my daughter."

She hitched her chin toward Charlie and Chris, who were approaching. "My husband. My son."

The men shook hands.

Then they stood there, all of them, in awkward silence. What to do next? Feeling responsible, Molly said to Peter, "Would you like a tour of my sister's life?"

He seemed relieved. "Yeah. I would."

MOLLY WAS PLEASED WITH HERSELF. ROBIN *WOULD* WANT to show Peter around.

Leaving her parents at the hospital, she began at their house. From there, she showed him the schools Robin attended, the club where she worked out, the track where she trained. She drove him around the perimeter of Snow Hill but didn't take him inside. "Too many questions about Robin," she explained quietly. He seemed to understand.

Then she drove to the cottage. When they turned off the road, she waited for a *wow, this is nice*; but if he noticed the roses, the hydrangea, or the oak, he made no mention. He was pensive. An emotional time for him, perhaps?

Inside, she showed him around. She saved Robin's room for last, but by the time they reached it, he was sneezing. Turned out, he was allergic to cats.

Not so perfect after all, Molly thought, though she apologized profusely. Still he seemed determined to look around the room, and she felt guilty that so many of Robin's things

were boxed up. Guessing that he might want to take something of her with him, she pointed him to a box of tissues
and went into the kitchen. On the counter beside Robin's
BlackBerry was the fanny pack that Robin had been wearing Monday night, home after its time on the floor in the
ICU. Her wallet was inside.

Its contents were mainly plastic—a VISA, two store
charges, a health insurance card. There were also her US-
ATF membership card and her driver's license. Both had
photos. The one on the license was barely a year old and
flattering, as most pictures of Robin were. This one cap-
tured her looking carefree, definitely an expression Peter
might like.

Molly was about to follow the sound of his sneezes when
she spotted the small heart that designated Robin as an organ donor.

An organ donor. By self-request.

Pulse racing, Molly slid the license into her pocket. Taking the USATF membership card, she gave it to Peter
instead. He studied it, seeming genuinely touched, and
thanked her. Moments later, they were out at the Jeep
again.

"That's really it," Molly said. "Did you . . . want to see
Robin again?"

Kathryn might not like that, but Molly didn't know
what else to say. She had invited him here. For what? A
one-hour visit?

He sneezed a final time and blew his nose. "No. I'm

okay. But I thought I'd hang around town for a couple days. Since I'm here anyway." Stuffing the handkerchief in his pocket, he seemed cautious. "How long. . . . Has your mother said what she'll do?"

"She won't discuss it." But Kathryn hadn't seen Robin's license. She had been adamant against organ donation when the doctors mentioned it Thursday morning. Once she knew Robin's feeling, that might change.

"I've booked a room at the Hanover Inn," he said in a voice that was still vaguely nasal. "Think you could drop me there?"

Molly gestured him toward the car and drove the short distance. Once there, though acutely aware of the license in her pocket, she was reluctant to let him go. Guessing that the reluctance was what Robin would have felt, she suggested lunch.

Peter ordered a thick, home-cooked burger. Robin might have challenged him on it and spent a while arguing. Molly? She couldn't think of a thing to say, but she wasn't sure Peter noticed. He seemed lost in thought. It was a quiet meal.

When they finished, he took out a card and jotted a number on its back. "Here's my cell. Will you call if anything happens?"

She took the card and studied the number. Her mother might be upset. She might feel Peter had no right to any continued contact. But Robin would have taken the card.

Slipping it into her purse, Molly headed for the hospital.

Kathryn was alone there. She looked like she had been cry-ing again.

Molly hesitated, wondering whether the license would help or hurt. But she couldn't ignore it. Taking the small plastic card from her pocket, she handed it to Kathryn.

chapter 18

KATHRYN WAS A MINUTE FOCUSING. SHE HAD seen Robin's license before. Puzzled, she glanced at Molly, who pointed to the small designation. As she grasped its meaning, Kathryn's heart began to pound.

Oddly frightened, she asked, "Did you know about this?"

"Not until today. I took it out because I thought Peter might want a small something of Robin's. Then I saw the notation."

Kathryn studied the license again. "One more thing I didn't know," she murmured and raised her eyes. "Wouldn't she have wanted to mention this to her family before she signed on?"

"It's not a big thing, Mom. Very PC right now. Her friends have probably done the same."

"Have you?" Kathryn asked.

"No, but I'm not into yogurt and herb tea," Molly said quietly. "But it's a good practice, like boycotting fur or refusing to eat veal. I'm green when it comes to plants, but I don't do those other things. Don't ask me why."

The answer was obvious to Kathryn. "You don't do them because Robin does." She looked at the license again. "I wish she'd told me."

"She figured she'd outlive you."

"So did I," Kathryn mused and again was hit with the unfairness of it. Angry at that, she said, "Were you really going to give this to Peter?"

"Robin won't need it, Mom."

"But to give her things away so soon?"

"He's here now. He came all this way. And he's not staying long."

"Did he say that?"

"No. But he knows he's not welcome."

"It isn't that he isn't welcome," Kathryn said, trying to figure out exactly what she felt. "I am glad that he came. You were right to call him. Robin did want it. Besides, it brings things full circle. I just don't want pressure." Her eyes fell to the license again. She studied it, then looked at Robin. Still breathing. Still alive. Still here—her daughter, her child. How to end that? "I don't know what to do."

"Maybe it would help if we knew more about it. Should I look into it?"

Kathryn's head came up fast. "Into what?"

"Organ donation. Find out what it entails."

"It's too *soon*."

"Not to actually do it, Mom. Just to find out."

"No one will be able to use her heart."

"There are other organs. Shouldn't we explore the options?"

But any option involved ending life support. Kathryn took a shuddering breath. "Thinking about this exhausts me."

Molly was clearly upset. "I'm sorry. I thought it might help."

"Because it tells us what Robin wants?"

"Because it would be doing something good."

But Kathryn was so afraid of making a mistake. "What if Robin had something entirely different in mind when she signed on to be an organ donor? What if she was thinking of a sudden accident—like a car crash—where you're gone in an instant? Or, God forbid, a murder?" She let out a tired breath. "Listen to me—'God forbid, a murder?' A car accident is bad enough. Every mother fears that, especially when her child first starts driving. But murder is every mother's greatest nightmare. Or so she thinks." She looked at Molly. "This is worse. This decision. How does a mother *make* it?" She didn't expect Molly to know the answer, but was still surprised by her silence. "No argument?" she asked with a sad smile. "Where's that brashness?"

"It's hard to be brash in here."

"Or is it the dress? You look very mature."

"I feel very mature. Something like this happens, and it makes *everyone* feel old. I don't disagree with you, Mom. This *is* worse. I'm just trying to help."

Kathryn studied her youngest—hazel eyes troubled, sandy hair escaped from its clip, wide mouth somber. She was every bit as attractive as Robin, if in a softer way. Her tongue, which could be tart, more than made up the difference. But Kathryn wasn't complaining. Taking Molly's hand, she said, "You *do* help. You and Robin are two sides of a coin. She tells me what I want to hear, you tell me what I don't. Both need to be said. Maybe it's just been easier to listen to her."

"I have to learn to be quiet. I say things without thinking."

"But they aren't stupid things. Like about your grandmother." Rapping Molly's hand against her thigh, Kathryn dropped her head back. Painful as it was, it had to be addressed. "You have a point. I just can't deal with it yet."

"I was thinking that if you could reconnect with Nana, it would help make up for this loss."

"In my mind, your grandmother stands for loss, too."

"She still gives me comfort."

"Does she? Or is it the memories?"

"Comfort is comfort."

"Here with Robin, too," Kathryn pointed out. Closing her eyes, she put her cheek on Robin's hand. It didn't smell like her child's anymore—no remnants of muscle cream or sweaty gloves, and Robin had long since stopped eating fluffernutters. She had loved them once, though. Welcoming the escape, Kathryn took refuge in memories of seesaws and swings.

CHRIS WAS AT THE PLAYGROUND WITH ERIN AND CHLOE. They often walked here on weekends, so that the baby could see other children, and there were plenty this Saturday afternoon. Chloe was intrigued. As he pushed her in the baby swing, her head swung back and forth following a little girl in the not-so-baby swing beside her.

Erin came close and said in a low voice, "Tell me more about him."

Chris didn't want to discuss Peter. He didn't want to think about Robin at all. He had hoped the playground would be an hour's respite.

But Erin had asked. And he was being accused of not wanting to talk. So he said, "He was nice enough."

She took a turn pushing the swing. "Was it weird seeing him with your mother?"

"Only when I thought about it."

"Did she behave any differently with him?"

"Like slip him a little love note?"

When Erin was quiet, he glanced her way. She seemed reproachful. "That's not what I mean," she said under her breath. "I'm wondering what she felt seeing him for the first time after all those years."

"She didn't say. At least not to me. Maybe she told Molly. Dad and I were down the hall."

"I can't imagine keeping something like that a secret. I can't imagine living with the fear that it would come out."

"My father knew."

"But Robin didn't. What do you think she felt getting that phone call?"

"Surprised?"

"*You* were surprised. She must have felt more—like shocked, afraid, even angry. I can't imagine keeping something like that from Chloe."

"Well. You're not my mother. You haven't walked in her shoes. Circumstances sometimes make us do things we'd rather not have to do." How true was *that*?

"Boy, did it backfire," Erin said and gave the swing another push. "Think about your *father* seeing him there. I mean, it's one thing meeting someone your wife used to know, but someone she'd had an affair with? That has to be *humiliating*."

Chris shot her an uneasy look. To hear her talk, she knew about Liz and was goading him to cough it up.

"What?" she asked innocently.

He shook his head and stopped the swing. "Sandbox time," he told Chloe as he lifted her out.

Erin persisted. "What was that look for?"

Carrying Chloe to the sandbox, he set her down and, scrounging up a pail, put her little hand around the shovel and helped her scoop in the sand.

"Talk to me, Chris," Erin said.

"This is a playground. No heavy talk here."

"I'm not being critical of your mother. I'm just trying to understand. You have to be feeling plenty."

"You don't know the half," he muttered.

"So tell me," she begged.

Tamping down the sand, he leveled it off, then said, "Watch me, Chloe. Watch what Daddy does." He flipped the pail quickly, and more slowly lifted it, but the sand was too dry to hold. "Uh-oh. We need water." He glanced at the water bubbler.

"What half don't I know?" Erin asked, but he took the pail and went to the bubbler. Seconds later, he returned and dribbled water on the collapsed pile of sand.

Next thing he knew, Erin had picked herself up and was walking off. He didn't think anything of it until she passed the stroller, went out the playground gate, and started down the street.

Dismayed, he dropped the pail and scooped up Chloe, who instantly started to cry. He tried to soothe her as he strapped her in the stroller. When soft cooing didn't work, he pulled a bottle from the back. Then he pushed the stroller as fast as he could. Erin was well down the street and around the corner before he caught up.

"What's *with* you?" he said when he finally closed the gap.

She turned and glared.

He held up a hand against her anger, but dropped it quickly. She wasn't the one in the wrong. "I have a problem," he said.

"Tell me something I don't know."

"I knew Liz Tocci when I was in college."

Erin recoiled. "What does *that* mean?"

"I knew her."

She went pale. "As in . . . had a *relationship* with her?"

"It only lasted a couple of weeks and ended right after I started seeing you, but there was a little overlap."

"You were sleeping with *both* of us?"

"No. I broke up with her before you and I ever slept together."

Erin swallowed. "You never told me this."

"What was there to tell? It was over and done."

"*Liz Tocci?* She's old enough to be your *mother.*"

"She's only ten years older than I am."

"And you thought it was *great*?"

He reached for her hand, but she snatched it away. Feeling no small amount of self-disgust, he said, "It was fun. I was flattered. I was a senior, and I was feeling my oats. I'm not proud of it, Erin. That's why I never told you."

"But you brought her to Snow Hill."

"No. I didn't. She wanted to get out of the city. She heard through one of our suppliers that we were looking for a design person. She called me. I arranged for her to meet my mother. That's the sum total of my involvement."

"But you put in a good word for her."

"I did not. She got the job on her own. Her credentials were good."

"How could you *have* her here?" Erin cried, sounding dismayed.

Chris had been totally naïve—either that, or disengaged. Either one was pathetic, not something he wanted to discuss with someone he cared so much about; but hadn't his father said sharing feelings was hard? *If someone disagrees, you feel offended, especially if that someone is the person you love. But the solution isn't to clam up.*

So he pushed the words out. "Honestly, I thought, 'This is someone I used to know, an old friend, and if she can do the job, that's fine.' There was *never* anything between us after we broke up. I just didn't think about her that way."

"Then what's the problem now?"

Chris leaned forward. Chloe had fallen asleep, the half-finished bottle fallen to her lap. Straightening, he looked at his wife. "The problem is that Molly fired her, and she's out for revenge. She says if she doesn't get her job back, she'll make something of our relationship."

"What can she make?"

"Trouble between you and me. She'll show you a picture from back then and one from this year's design conference, and she'll hint that we've been together."

"Pictures from *this* year's conference?"

"Snow Hill had a booth there, and I'm a Snow. There are pictures of me with Tami, Deirdre, and Gary, too. Hell, they're all posted on the board near Mom's office, and the one with Liz is just like the others. I haven't been with her, Erin. You're my wife. I chose you because I love you. I love Chloe. I love my life. Liz Tocci is an angry person. Apparently her life hasn't gone the way she wanted."

Erin studied him for the longest time. Finally, she moved behind the stroller and began to push. Her pace was measured.

"Well?" he asked, falling into step.

"Well, what?"

"Are you okay?"

"Of course, I'm okay," she said angrily. "Did you think I'd go berserk, whine, cry, ask for a divorce because you were with someone before me? I'm annoyed because it took you so long to tell me, that's all. Was it *so hard*?"

"Yes. I feel like a heel."

"You should. You were wrong. But I'm not an unreasonable person, Chris. If you'd told me about her when we were first dating, it would be a nonissue."

She pushed the stroller faster. He kept pace. She looked angry. That made him nervous.

After a bit, she returned to a saner speed.

He kept glancing at her. "Liz means nothing to me." When Erin nodded, he said, "Do you believe me?"

"Given the problem you have talking and what you just managed to say, yes, I believe you." She shot him a sharp look, but slipped her arm through his.

That was reward enough for him to say more. "You were right. Things changed after we got married. But so did the issues." They walked on. Her silence became a prod. "I'm good at my work, and I thought I communicated like Dad did at home. Looks like I didn't know what he did." Her arm draped his more comfortably, but still she didn't speak.

So he said, "Turns out he does his talking when he and Mom are alone. How was I supposed to know? An accounting degree doesn't include courses on how to talk to your wife. It isn't that I don't want you to know things, Erin. I just don't like to talk."

"But don't you feel better when you do?"

He did. Stopping the stroller, he pulled her to him and held her tightly.

"Say it," she said.

But feeling better about Liz only made room for other emotions. "My sister's dying. I don't know what to do."

Erin rubbed his back.

"She was a good sister," he went on. "I didn't always like what she did, but she loved us. Remember the toast she gave at our wedding? Remember how she cut short a trip when Chloe was born? Chloe won't ever know her." His throat tightened. He didn't say anything for a while, but Erin seemed to understand. She continued to hold him, there in the middle of the sidewalk. It didn't occur to him to move.

"I think they should turn off the machines. But maybe I'm wrong. If Chloe was lying there like that, I'd want to keep her as long as I could."

"If she wasn't suffering."

"Robin isn't. She's comfortable. Sounds awful, but we're getting something out of this. If it had ended last Monday, we wouldn't have known about Peter. Molly wouldn't have been so stressed that she fired Liz, Liz wouldn't have threatened me, you and I wouldn't be talking." Drawing back, he said, "I don't know what to do."

"You're there. You're at Snow Hill. That's enough."

He raised his head. "You're at Snow Hill, too. Dad wants to hire you."

"Do you?"

"If it's what you want."

"Do you want me there?"

"Do you want to be there?"

"*Chris.*"

"*Yes,* I want you there. It's a family business, and you're family. And you're good."

"At what?"

"Anything that involves diplomacy. You're tactful."

Erin made a sputtering sound. "Not always. I was cheering Molly on when she fired Liz. What'll you do about her, Chris?"

"Call her. I discussed it with Dad. We don't want her reinstated. I'll offer her generous severance."

"Maybe you shouldn't be the one to call?"

Chris sure didn't want to. But he agreed with his father. "I made the mess; I have to clean it up. This is my decision. She needs to know it."

HE WAITED ONLY UNTIL THEY GOT HOME, BEFORE LOcating her number in the company directory and making the call.

"It took you long enough," Liz said when she heard his voice. "I'm assuming you'll make the wait worth my while. Do you know your sister actually had the lock to my office changed? I was over early this morning and couldn't get in! I'd like that new key."

Even if Chris hadn't discussed the situation with Molly, Charlie, and now Erin, the arrogance in Liz's voice would have clinched it.

"No key, Liz. No reinstatement."

"Excuse me?" she asked in the same haughty tone.

"We'll give you four weeks' pay and two months' health coverage."

"You'll *give* me that?" She laughed. "Apparently you didn't get my point. I can ruin you, Chris."

"I believe you've been neutralized," Chris took pleasure in saying. "My whole family knows that you and I were together once. So does my wife. And I honestly don't think anyone else cares. Four weeks' pay, two months' health coverage."

There was a pause. "Are you ready to see pictures in the paper?"

He angled the receiver away from his mouth. "Pictures in the paper?" he asked Erin loudly. "From the Concord design conference?" He was starting to enjoy himself. "That's good publicity for Snow Hill, don't you think?" He spoke back into the phone. "Great idea, Liz. My wife's covering for Dad—did you know she has a background in PR? We'll get the story to the paper Monday morning, along with a couple of other shots. They may not run them. But it's a good idea. Thanks for suggesting this."

DAVID'S PHONE RANG. HE WAS DRESSED TO RUN BUT WAS procrastinating. He hadn't exercised since Monday night.

"Hello?"

"Wayne Ackerman, here. Are you around?"

"Uh, sure, Dr. Ackerman. Is Alexis okay?"

"That's what I want to talk about. Be there in ten minutes." He hung up before David could tell him where he lived—but, of course, his home address was in the staff file.

His apartment was small and messy. Knowing he couldn't do much about either in ten minutes, he went down the stairs and outside. He was in the parking lot when the BMW purred down the street.

Ackerman parked and climbed out. He wore khaki pants and a black shirt. "Thanks. I know it's Saturday."

David dismissed that with a hand. "How's Alexis?"

"She was depleted, hence the collapse. She's already feeling stronger. There are some issues that we'll be dealing with, but I'm hoping you'll help us out."

"Anything. Alexis is a terrific girl."

"We want to minimize stress, and right now she's stressing about what people are saying. The official diagnosis is exhaustion. She's been burning the candle at both ends. She'll be out of school for a week or two to rest and recoup. Think you can keep collecting her assignments and get them to my office at the end of each day? Better still, can you drop them at the house once she's home? It'll be good for her to have contact with someone from school."

What he meant, David knew, was that it would be good for the school to know that one of their own was there. It freed anyone else from stopping by and perhaps guessing the truth. With David as the only conduit, what little news hit the outside world could be sanitized.

David wasn't pleased to be used this way. It put him in a terrible position. But what choice did he have?

"I can do that," he granted politely.

"You'll be our spokesperson. People will know to ask you how she is."

"Uh-huh."

"If there are any questions, just give me a call. The goal is to think ahead and make Alexis's return to school as smooth as possible."

"A good goal," David said. Stepping back, he watched the superintendent drive off. And he did go running then. He ran hard and fast, pounding the pavement in self-punishment at having been a coward; but by the time he reentered the parking lot, he was enumerating the facts. Alienating Dr. Ackerman would hurt Alexis. *She* knew David knew the truth. When the time was right, she might open up. For now, he would play by the rules.

Frustrated that he had to rationalize this, he wasn't in the most receptive of moods when the honk of a horn stopped him, just as he was back home, about to go inside. It was Nick Dukette, who didn't have school files to give him David's home address, but who had learned it anyway.

Sweaty and disgruntled, David stood with his hands on his hips and let Dukette come to him. He was holding a large manila envelope. "The papers I promised," he said, giving the envelope to David.

"That was fast."

"I've been working on this for a year. It's only a partial. But what's here gives you a taste of what I'm doing." His voice lowered. "Any news on Robin?"

David shook his head.

"She's still on life support?"

"As far as I know. Look, I don't know if I can do anything with these. I'm not in my family's inner circle."

"Is anyone else visiting Robin—friends, other runners?"

"I don't know."

"Have you visited?"

"No. Why do you ask?" David had no intention of making things easy.

Nick studied the gravel, then the trees. "Hard to eat, sleep, carry on . . ." He looked at David. "Have you ever loved someone?"

"Not yet."

"Well, it sucks," he exclaimed with a rawness that gave authenticity to the words. "How do you explain thinking about someone all the time? I sure as hell can't. The bitch of it is that we were probably all wrong for each other. We are both headliners. Paired up, that can be lethal. But I figured she could only run so long, and then it'd be okay. But now she's on life support. How do I live with that?"

He looked like he might cry. David did not want to see that. He didn't want to believe that anything about the man was honest.

But Nick Dukette, standing there trying to get a grip on his emotions, did seem sincere.

Giving a little, David said, "Listen, I'll read what you've written. Can I get back to you?"

Nick didn't even seem relieved. He remained grief-stricken. "Sure. My number's inside." He looked at the trees, then back. "You have no cause to like me. No cause to *trust* me. You know what newspaper people do. But this is not for the paper. I haven't been in the city room for two days. Don't even know when I'll go back. Don't *care*. But I'm begging you, if you hear anything about Robin—if anything changes—will you let me know?"

David agreed to do that.

chapter 19

$\mathcal{M}$OLLY KEPT UP ON THE LATEST IN HORTICULTURAL thinking. There were always new blights, new treatments. She believed that if she was familiar with them, she would be ready to act should her plants get sick.

She felt the same now about organ donation. Familiarizing herself with the process would make things easier when the time came. Kathryn couldn't think about it yet; but when she was ready, Molly wanted to be able to help.

Had it not been Saturday, she would have called the social worker who had been at Thursday's meeting. Her second choice was her favorite of the nurses caring for Robin. The woman was pleasantly plump, as physically soft as her nature was warm. When Molly asked if they could talk, the nurse guided her to an empty room.

"Organ donation," Molly said, but quickly cautioned, "Please don't mention this to my mother. She's not there yet. It's only been two days since it became an option." Hesitant, she eyed the nurse. "How long does it usually take?"

"That depends on the person. Your mother and sister were unusually close."

Molly made a sound of agreement. "Unusually close" was putting it mildly.

"Your mother hasn't wanted to see a minister," the nurse observed.

"Her qualms aren't religious. They're personal. She isn't ready to let Robin go—not that I am," Molly added quickly, "but Robin did register as an organ donor. Can you tell me how that works?"

"Of course. It's really very easy. When the time is right, you let us know. We contact the New England Organ Bank, which sends representatives here to meet with you. They explain the procedure and obtain consent. They're experienced in this, Molly. They counsel families on the emotions involved."

"What are those?"

"Ohhh," the woman breathed, "they run the gamut. Some family members are angry; they don't want to be doing this. Some are resentful that another person gets to live while their family member does not. Most are simply heartsick at losing a loved one. Organ donation can sometimes even be a comfort. Some people want to know everything about the recipients, some want to know nothing."

Molly was curious. "Would we actually get names?"

"No. Privacy laws prevent that."

"But I've seen clips on TV of recipients meeting donor families."

"When a recipient wants to thank the donor family, the organ bank may put the two in touch, but only if the donor family agrees. More often, anonymity holds. The representatives from the organ bank may say, 'We have seven patients in Boston waiting for hearts, six waiting for kidneys,' and so on, but they don't give specifics."

"Then the recipients would be in New England?"

"Not necessarily. The local bank works with a national network to get organs to the right recipients. If the right patient is in the Pacific Northwest, the organ goes there."

"Can we specify a recipient?" Molly asked, thinking that if Kathryn could hear stories, even physically *see* the people who were waiting for transplants, it might move her in that direction.

But the nurse gave a small smile. "Other than a family member donating, say, a kidney to a relative, that isn't done. Can you imagine the mess if it were—charges of favoritism, lawsuits claiming discrimination? Once in a while, you hear about a famous person being popped to the top of the list, but that's usually rumor, not fact. Organ banks are dedicated to fairness."

That was actually okay, Molly decided. Robin would

want her organs doing the most possible good. "How soon is it done after a person dies?" she asked, for the first time actually moving beyond the decision itself. Though it had to be asked, the question chilled her.

She must have shown her qualm, because the nurse put an arm around her shoulder. "As soon as possible. In the case of someone like your sister, once a decision is made to turn off the machines, the wheels start turning. Recipients are located, often hospitalized even before the withdrawal of life support is complete. Once the death is confirmed, a doctor performs the procedure. Representatives of the organ bank whisk the organ to the recipient."

It was all very clean and efficient—less so, though, when Molly thought of Robin. "Once the machines are turned off, how long would it take for her—"

"For her heart to stop?" the nurse finished in an understanding voice. "Without cerebral activity? Not long."

"Would she suffer?"

"No. She feels nothing."

Molly swallowed. The end seemed so near. "So, once it happened—once her heart stopped—she would be wheeled out of the room."

"Taken to an operating room."

"And afterward? I mean, like, at a wake, would we see anything?"

"You mean, disfigurement?" the nurse asked insightfully. She was either used to the question or simply attuned to Molly's thoughts. "No disfigurement. Great care is taken, so that even with an open casket, the loved one looks like herself."

Molly nodded. Her eyes met the nurse's. "If I'm having trouble with this, I can imagine how much more my mother will have."

"She's a strong woman. She simply needs to come to it in her own way."

KATHRYN KNEW TIME WAS SHORT. NOTHING, ABSOLUTELY nothing about Robin's condition had changed, yet her daughter was slipping away. Finger-combing Robin's dark hair, Kathryn restored a bit of the look of a physically active runner; but Robin's forehead was too cool, her eyelids smooth. With each day, she became less the Robin Kathryn had raised.

Or perhaps it was Kathryn's own mind making the adjustment. Accepting.

Part of her was frightened by that.

Elbows on the edge of the bed, she took Robin's hand in hers and, kissing it, studied her daughter's face. "I love you," she whispered. She wanted to say more, but her throat closed up; and when she would have thought she was all cried out, her eyes filled again.

Charlie touched her arm. "Let's take a walk," he suggested softly.

And still Kathryn looked at Robin. She didn't speak. Robin no longer heard. Her mother accepted that—though the thought brought more tears. Blotting them, she rose. Charlie's arm was a solid support as they went down the hall.

Leading her to the lounge, he pointed outside. Far to the left was the river, but closer, on a patch of grass well shy of the bluffs, was a sign: *We're praying for you, Robin*. Nearby, seated in a loose circle, were a group of Robin's friends.

"Other friends have brought signs," he said, "but this is the first group that guessed the right spot. I've been fielding calls from the press. So far, they're holding off."

We're praying for you, Robin. Kathryn started crying again. She pressed her face against Charlie's arm until she regained control. "This is *so* not like me," she finally whispered.

"Crying?" he asked, drawing her close.

"Falling apart."

"You're acting as any mother would. And you're utterly exhausted."

"I'm torn—pulled here, pulled there. Final has never been so *final* before. What should I do, Charlie?"

"Oh, sweetheart. I can't make that decision for you."

That struck her as being unfair. "Beginning of life, end of life—why is it always the mother's choice? When I was first pregnant, I had to decide whether to have a baby alone or to abort. Peter didn't offer an opinion. It was me. My choice."

"At least there were choices."

"They were both daunting. Choosing to abort is *painful,* even when it's done for all the right reasons. I would have suffered for years afterward and never have known Robin. This choice is even worse."

"It's the cost of having a life worth living. Choices are easy when you have nothing to lose. Would you rather have led that other kind of life?" She was feeling perverse enough to say *yes,* when he added, "You couldn't do that, Kathryn. It's not in your nature. I've always loved your determination—the wholehearted way you go at things."

"But now I'm giving up," she said in self-reproach. This was the frightening part of accepting what was happening. Giving up was a betrayal.

Charlie answered with startling force. "No, Kathryn. If anyone has fought these last few days, it's you. No, it's not about giving up." His voice gentled. "It's about letting go, and I say that in the most positive sense. At some point, you'll decide there's nothing else you can do and that hanging on only brings more tears."

"Have you reached that point?" Kathryn asked.

He was silent, his eyes troubled. "I want to start remembering Robin the way she was. That'll only happen when this is done."

"Is that enough reason to turn off the machines?"

"Not alone. No."

"What would be reason enough?" She was looking for something. One concrete thing. A reason to rest on in the years to come.

"Your having made peace with the situation."

That wasn't concrete, she thought. It was *nebulous.* Spoken by Charlie, though, it was a challenge. "But she's not in pain," she reasoned frantically. "She isn't suffering. There has to be a reason why that's so—why we can keep her heart beating indefinitely even while her brain is dead."

"Some people do it to buy time until a miracle cure is found."

"You believe in miracles," she reminded him, wondering if even a tiny part of him would be willing to wait. That would be something to grasp.

"Miracles within reason," he qualified. "When the odds are against something and it does happen, we call it a miracle. But in this case, the odds are too long. I've searched the Web, Kath. I've pulled strings with friends who know doctors. Not one of those physicians felt that with test results like hers there is any chance of recovery. Yes, we're buying time, but it's for *our* sake, not Robin's."

"My sake," Kathryn murmured. "Robin's been a major player in my life. I can't picture my life without her. Once this . . . this *vigil* is over, once I'm not coming here every day, there'll be a huge hole in my life."

"It'll close. You'll fill it with other things."

She couldn't think of what. Her mind was numb.

The sun had begun to slant low over the river, but Robin's friends remained on the grass. "Someone should thank them."

"Molly's down there."

Kathryn tried to see, but her eyes were too tired. "She's pushing for organ donation."

"Not pushing," Charlie cautioned softly, "just saying that Robin was interested."

Which was precisely what Kathryn couldn't dismiss. If there was one thing she had learned in the last few days about her relationship with her daughter, it was that honesty had been lacking. Here was honesty. She couldn't deny what was on that license, any more than she could deny the content of Robin's journals.

"What you said before," she asked, "about picturing her the way she was? Would you be able to do that if her organs were gone?"

"Of course I would," he said spiritedly. "Remember my mother—how much she suffered before she died, how thin and gray she seemed after so much surgery? I don't picture her that way anymore. I picture her as she was before she got sick. That'll happen with Robin, too. As for her organs, the truth is, if she keeps them, they'll return to dust sooner. Letting other people use them will prolong their lives."

It was a comforting thought. "Then you do favor organ donation?"

"Probably. But it can be done next week or next month. It doesn't have to be today."

Looking north, past the grass to a stand of birches that were already starting to turn yellow, she whispered, "I keep hoping—this is such a horrible thing to say—hoping that one of the machines will malfunction and the alarm won't ring and no one will rush in, so the decision will be taken out of my hands. Am I a horrible mother?"

"No, sweetheart. You're human. This is hard."

She wanted to ask when it would get easier, but he had already answered that. It would get easier when she made peace with the situation. She was getting there. But the closer she got, the more frightened she was.

She remembered a distinct moment, early in her labor with Robin, when she realized that she was actually going to have to push a full-size baby out of her body through an impossibly small opening. What she had felt then, just hours before welcoming Robin to the world, was panic.

With death closing in now, she felt the same thing.

MOLLY HADN'T PLANNED ON SITTING WITH ROBIN'S friends. She had wandered out along the bluff to pass time until David arrived, and there they were, waving her toward them, hugging her, making her sit. When she braced for the inevitable questions, none came. These friends knew the situation. They focused on memories instead, and the memories were good. Molly even laughed with them over a few.

When she saw David on the patio, though, she hurried back. She had a mission.

"That should make you feel good," he said with a glance at the sign.

"It does. Were you able to reach your friend?"

With the hitch of his chin toward the building and a light hand at her arm, he guided her back to the hospital. One flight up and down the corridor to the central station, he introduced her to John Hardigan. A staff doctor, John was in his forties. David had taught his son two years before. They had hit it off then and occasionally ran together now.

John led them to the small lounge. When the door was closed, he cautioned, "Organ donation is a very personal thing. How much do you want to know?"

"Whatever you can tell me," Molly said.

The doctor shot David a look.

"Whatever," Molly insisted. "Please."

That seemed to be all the man needed to realize she meant business. "Organ donation is the stuff of which dreams are made," he began. "Literally. In a given year, there may be 4,000 people waiting for 2,000 donated hearts, and 4,000 people waiting for 1,000 donated lungs. Livers? Probably 18,000 people will wait, 6,000 will get, and another 2,000 will die waiting. And the numbers are even higher when we talk about kidneys—60,000 people waiting, 15,000 getting, 4,000 dying while they wait. By the way, the survival rate for these transplants is impressive, often up in the 85 percent range."

Molly didn't say anything. She couldn't argue with figures like those.

"Right now, here at Dickenson-May?" he went on. "We have a woman with pulmonary fibrosis, probably the aftereffect of an infection. She's thirty-five, which is young for the disease, and she has two children. Pulmonary fibrosis causes scar tissue to form in the air sacs, making breathing difficult. That limits her to a sedentary life, which will lead to other problems down the road. A single lung will give her a new lease on life.

"Also in-patient right now, we have a guy in his twenties who contracted hepatitis from a blood transfusion when he was a kid. He gets chronic liver infections that require hospitalization several times a year, and he still managed to graduate from Dartmouth last June. He wants to go into medical research. All he needs is half a liver. Another patient can use the other half, and they'll both survive."

"Half?" Molly asked.

"Just half," the doctor confirmed. "The liver regenerates itself. And then upstairs are the kids. One is a seven-year-old girl who has cystic kidney disease. It goes without saying what a kidney would mean to her." He went on, speaking generally about cases he'd seen where a donated heart, a pancreas, even an intestine had saved a life. He spoke of donors and donor families, and of new techniques being tested.

By the time he was done, Molly had heard enough to understand why Robin had registered as a donor. Then David told her about Dylan Monroe.

"This is the nicest little guy," he said. They were on the back patio of the hospital now, finishing dinner. With visiting hours nearly over, there were few other diners. "He's a musical whiz—hears a song, plays it by ear. Academics are a problem. He's slow to catch on, but once he gets it, he's fine. Same with sports. He's a little plugger. What trips him up is his eyesight, which is why music is so great. His ears matter more than his eyes. He has thick glasses, but his corneal condition makes the world a hazy mess. When he's old enough, he'll have a corneal transplant. Until then, he has to work twice as hard. This isn't a matter of life and death. It isn't even technically organ donation, since the cornea is only tissue. But if you saw this little boy trying to keep up with his friends, it'd break your heart."

"My mother would feel for him," Molly said.

"Can you tell her?"

"No. But I'll have to. No one else will." Pushing the last of her chicken around, she set down her fork. "Funny, Robin was self-absorbed in some ways and totally selfless in others. She loved doing clinics, loved working with kids who needed extra help. And organ donation? You're right. The boy needing a corneal transplant may not be a matter of life and death, but she would care about him, too."

David sat back, smiling at her.

"What?" she asked.

"Remember Thursday when I helped you pack and you asked what I'd learned about Robin? I really learned more about you. What you just said confirms it. You loved your sister. You're realistic about her shortcomings, but you admired her. You've been loyal in everything you've done this week."

"*After* I blew her off," Molly reminded him. "I'll never forgive myself for that."

"You will," he said and, grabbing her tray, carried both to the trash.

"How do you know?" she asked when he returned.

"Because you're practical."

"Practical?" They headed back into the hospital. "Me? I'm emotional. I fly off the handle. I act without thinking."

"But once you calm down and think about what you've done, you're practical. You're doing things that no one else in your family can do, because someone has to do them. You'll tell your mother what you learned about transplants because it'll help her with the decision she has to make. You'll forgive yourself for not taking Robin on that run, because she'd have had that heart attack whether you were there or not—just as she would have had it whether I'd gone running earlier or been running faster." He opened the door.

Molly went through. "You've forgiven yourself, then?"

"Intellectually. I'm still getting there emotionally. It doesn't mean I'm not sorry I didn't get there sooner. But I didn't." His eyes met hers. "Are you going back up?"

Molly nodded. "I have to talk with my mom." She entered the elevator. "Are you heading home?"

He checked his watch and joined her. "There's five minutes left before visiting ends. I want to run by my student's room. If her parents are there, I'll just keep on running. I'm no masochist." He pressed floor buttons for her, then himself. The door closed.

"Thank you," Molly said quietly.

"Elevators are easy."

"No. Thank you for having your friend talk with me. Thank you for listening to my whining and helping me pack and boosting my ego. You've been a bright spot in a dark week." Which was putting it mildly.

"The feeling's mutual," he said and opened his arms.

Hugging David was as natural to Molly as waking up to the sun, watering plants, stroking cats. She no longer thought of him as the Good Samaritan who had found Robin. They saw eye to eye on so much. In an incredibly short and stressful time, he had become a close friend. That made her feel really, really good.

The elevator stopped. The door slid open. "My floor," he said.

Grinning, she held his gaze until the door cut him off. By the time it opened again, on Robin's floor, her grin was gone.

DAVID MEANT WHAT HE SAID TO MOLLY. HE WALKED CA-sually down the corridor, prepared to saunter right past Alexis's room if her parents were inside. Only when he saw her alone did he stop. She looked up and actually smiled.

"Hi, Mr. Harris. Come on in." She pushed herself higher. "Last chance. I'm going home in the morning."

"You are?" he asked as he neared the bed. "That's great news. How're you feeling?"

"Fat," she said, patting her middle. "They have been making me eat *huge* amounts of food. But that'll be over once I get home. I mean, like, just one more day of rest was all I needed. They want me to rest more at home, and they don't want me dancing right away. At least, that's what the doctors say. My parents know better."

That was what David feared. But even aside from the fact of who this particular student was, he had taught long enough to know never to directly contradict a parent to a child. "I'm really pleased for you, Alexis. I'll make sure you get your homework, and if there's anything else I can do—"

"Tell everyone how well I look. Don't I look well?"

He studied her face. The shadows under her eyes were marginally lighter. "I think you look more rested," he said.

"Oh, I look *much* healthier. Please let the kids know. The doctors here say I'm perfectly healthy. This was a totally false alarm—and I don't blame you, Mr. Harris. The nurse was the one who sent me here. She overreacted."

David might have pointed out that the doctors had admitted her for two days. But again, he wasn't the parent.

"Well, it's always good to check things out," he said. "So you'll let me know if you need anything?"

She smiled and nodded. "Thanks, Mr. Harris. I really appreciate your help."

As good as David had felt moments earlier with Molly, he felt bad leaving Alexis's room.

Then he spotted Donna Ackerman. She was leaning against the wall not far from her daughter's door, lips pursed, hands in her pockets. From the way she straightened expectantly, she had been waiting for him.

When he was close enough, she asked, "Did she tell you she's going home tomorrow?"

"She did. That's good news, Mrs. Ackerman."

But the woman was shaking her head. "She's going to a center that specializes in this."

David was relieved, but surprised. "She said the doctors gave her a good report."

"They didn't. She hears what she wants to hear. You know she has a problem."

He hesitated. But Donna appeared to want the truth. So he said a quiet, "Yes."

"Well, I appreciate that. You've been tactful. I doubt it's been easy." It was the closest she would come to criticizing her husband. "There isn't a quick fix to this problem. Alexis will likely spend a couple of weeks there, with ongoing therapy after that. But she likes you, David. You're her link to school. She'll need your support."

"Anything," David said.

"Anything? Okay. How do I break it to her?" the woman asked bluntly. "I've raised four boys. Never had this kind of problem. You know how to deal with teenagers. She doesn't have a clue what's coming."

"She may," David cautioned. "What she told me may have been pure bravado. Kids this age are conflicted. I've heard Alexis use the word anorexia once too often. I'd be direct. She's too bright for anything else."

Donna was quiet. Then she sighed. "I was afraid you'd say that," she said and, pursing her lips again, headed in to see her daughter.

THE INSTANT MOLLY ENTERED ROBIN'S ROOM, SHE KNEW she wouldn't be discussing organ donation. Kathryn was clearly upset. She was watching Robin from the window, hands braced on the sill behind. Her eyes flew to Molly. She moved one hand but quickly put it back, seeming to need the support. Her eyes returned to the bed.

Frightened, Molly looked there, too. "Did something happen?"

"No," Kathryn croaked and cleared her throat. "No. She's the same."

"Are you sick, Mom?"

Kathryn brought her arms forward and folded them tightly over her middle. "Just emotional."

She had been crying. Molly could see. Between her reddened eyes and marked lines of fatigue, her mother looked fragile.

"I shouldn't have brought Peter," Molly said. "That caused more strain."

"It's not him, it's this," Kathryn said without shifting her gaze. "I'm okay one minute and panicky the next. I feel like time's running out."

"They'll keep the machines on—"

"Time's running out," Kathryn repeated.

Molly was worried. "Where's Dad?"

"I sent him home. He was exhausted."

"So are you. Go home, Mom, please? Nothing's changing. Robin will be here like this tomorrow morning."

"Every night is precious."

Molly tried a different approach. "Did Robin live at home? No, she didn't want to be sleeping under your nose. Maybe she wants to sleep alone now."

Kathryn's eyes filled. "*Enough* of what Robin would want," she cried and pressed a finger over her lips. After a minute, she refolded her arms. "This is what *I* want, Molly. Besides," she added, "I don't think I could drive right now."

"I'll drive you," Molly offered, feeling worse at that moment for Kathryn than for Robin. "Dad can drive you back tomorrow."

For a minute, Molly saw a small softening and thought her mother was relenting. But Kathryn only shook her head. "No. I need to do this."

MINUTES AFTER MOLLY LEFT THE ROOM, THOUGH, Kathryn changed her mind. *No, I don't need to do this,* she thought. *This isn't what I want. I want my mother.*

The thought startled her, but she couldn't shake it. She wanted Marjorie—wanted to pour out her heart and cry in the arms of the one person whose job it was to listen. It didn't matter how old or how independent Kathryn was. She needed her mother.

Taking her purse from the chair, she fumbled inside for her keys. Her comb fell out. In the process of picking it up, she stumbled against the IV pole. Grabbing it, she steadied herself, and, mercifully, the IV continued to drip.

Keys finally in hand, she kissed Robin's cheek. "I'll be back. I'm going to see Nana." It was okay to leave to do that.

She stopped at the nurse's station, theorizing that if they knew Robin was alone, they would check her more often.

As the elevator descended, though, Kathryn wished she had a video cam in the room. For all she knew, they *never* came in. They could monitor the machines from their station.

The elevator opened. She was about to press the button and go back up, when she thought of Marjorie again. She needed her mother. It was irrational, of course. Marjorie wouldn't say anything that would help. She wouldn't know *what* Kathryn was talking about. She wouldn't know *Kathryn*, period.

Still she continued on to the parking lot. Night had fallen, but large overhead lights pinpointed the cars. There weren't many left. Still it was a minute before she found hers, parked where she had left it that morning. Fumbling, she dropped her keys and had to pick them up from the pavement before she finally got the door open, and once inside the car she could barely breathe. The air was stifling.

She was upset. She was tired. She was frightened.

Rolling down the window, she took a deep breath and started the engine. She backed out of the space and left the parking lot. The main road was dark. Only when a passing car honked and passed, plunging her into darkness again, did she realize she hadn't turned on her headlights.

The omission shook her. Her mother had Alzheimer's disease. She wondered if this was an early sign of it in herself. But it *couldn't* be, not with everything else that had happened this week. No God could be so cruel.

Bereft, she began to cry. When her vision blurred, she drove more slowly, hands tight on the wheel, but even then she came within inches of hitting a large flower-shaped mailbox. *Pull over,* said a little voice, but she swung too quickly and sharply. The car careened off the road into a meadow. Foot still on the gas, she tried to correct the error. Instead, she lost her bearings completely and ran into a tree.

chapter 20

KATHRYN WAS SHORT OF BREATH. IT WAS A MINUTE before she raised her head, another before she moved her limbs. Nothing hurt.

The car wasn't as lucky, to judge from the noise it was making. Wanting to silence it, she turned off the engine, but when she tried to restart it, it refused to turn over.

One headlight still burned. Climbing out under low branches, she used its light to see what she'd done. The front of the car was pleated in a dozen odd angles against the tree. There was no smoke, just an odd, sweet smell of antifreeze and grass.

Belatedly, her knees began to wobble. Stumbling back to the car, she sat for a minute regaining control. The damage might have been worse—to her, to a passenger, even to the car—but she had trouble feeling grateful. This was one thing too many on top of the rest.

And the grand purpose of an accident now, Charlie? she wondered. *Your sprite, Mom?*

At least, she wasn't crying. That was something.

She was pulling out her phone when she saw a car zip by without stopping—but of course, she was easily twenty feet from the road, with her one headlight aimed away. A passerby wouldn't see her. Nor, from where she sat, could she see any houses. But there was that flower mailbox.

She would need a tow. But who should she call? No one was hurt, no other car involved. But if the police came, there would be questions, and she wasn't in the mood. She started to call Charlie—but she wasn't up to telling him, either. The one she wanted, she realized, was Molly.

The girl picked up after a single ring. "Mom?"

"Where are you?"

"Just got home. What's wrong?"

Kathryn might have laughed hysterically. Where to start? "Think you can come pick me up?"

"Of *course.*"

"Not at the hospital. I had a little accident. You'll have to kind of look for me."

"Accident?" Molly cried in alarm.

"I'm fine. I hit a tree."

"Mom."

"I'm fine, Molly. Really. I'm walking around. Nothing hurts."

In the short silence, she pictured Molly composing her-self. "Tell me where to look." Her voice was bobbing, like she was already heading outside.

"I'm on South Street, maybe four minutes from the hos-pital. Know that flower mailbox?"

"Yes."

"I passed it just before I went off the road. One of my headlights is still on. Park on the side of the road, and you'll see me."

"I'm getting in my car right now. Are you sure you're okay? Have you called the police?"

"And start the whole world talking?"

"Okay," Molly said. Her engine started. "Did you call Dad?"

"No. He'll be sleeping. He thinks I'm still at the hospi-tal." In the time it would have taken Charlie to get out of the house, Molly would be here. Besides, Molly was the one Kathryn needed.

She didn't tell Molly what she wanted, though—until Molly finished exclaiming over the car, turned off the lone headlight, and guided Kathryn to the Jeep—at which point Kathryn said directly, "Drive me to the nursing home to see Nana?"

The darkness couldn't hide Molly's surprise. *"Now?"*

"You've been wanting me to go."

"Yes, but during the day. It's nearly eleven at night."

"Are you worried she'll be in bed with that man?" Kathryn asked.

"I'm worried she'll be asleep," Molly said with simple

logic. "We'll go first thing in the morning. She really does sleep alone, Mom. Thomas has his own room at the other end of the floor."

Kathryn was soothed by her voice. Feeling surprising calm, she said, "I just find it so hard to understand."

"I know, Mom. Don't you think his family has trouble with it, too? But they're just like children meeting for the first time each day. They don't remember what's come before, and there is no after. They live in the here and now."

"She gets so excited seeing him," Kathryn remarked. Something about the dark made discussing this easier. Or maybe it was hitting a tree and freeing a gaggle of tied-up thoughts.

"That's how she shows pleasure. Whether it's him, me, you, a tea sandwich—it doesn't matter. She doesn't know the cause, only that something makes her smile."

Simple logic again. Kathryn was considering it when Molly said, "Why don't I drive you home?"

"No. Not home." She had left the hospital needing her mother, but if that was on hold, she wanted to *do* something. Being constructive was part of who she was. She had felt too helpless all week.

"Then my place," Molly suggested. "Robin's place."

Robin's place sounded right. Nodding her assent, Kathryn leaned back against the headrest. After a minute, she began to relax. It was nice to be driven, nice to yield responsibility for a short time.

Tired as she was, though, she didn't sleep. She raised her

head when they turned off the main road. The path to the cottage was dark, but she could smell trees, flowers, rich earth. They were the sedative she needed.

MOLLY STILL THOUGHT OF THE COTTAGE AS IT HAD BEEN before packing—furnished simply, cozy and comfortable. Seeing it now as she opened the front door, she was apologetic. "I'm sorry everything's a mess."

Kathryn barely seemed to notice. She wandered around the room, touching a windowsill, a bookshelf, the sofa. Watching her, Molly was frightened. She had felt her mother shaking when she helped her into the car. She looked steadier now, but that didn't mean she was okay. She could have a concussion. There could be internal damage. She could keel over in an instant and be gone.

After Robin, anything seemed possible.

But Kathryn didn't look injured. In a natural show of surprise, she jumped when Molly's cat scampered out from between cartons and ran down the hall. "Is that what I think it is?"

"Yes." Quickly, Molly explained. "It was abused. I've rescued it."

"But you're moving home Monday," Kathryn argued, sounding like herself.

"Not my fault, Mom. The vet begged me to take her. She needs a quiet, no-other-pets place, and this was the only one I could think of."

Kathryn studied her. "Why do I sense that the vet didn't have to do much convincing?" she finally asked, less in disapproval than resignation. "Your sister didn't tell me you had a cat."

"She didn't know. I just got this one on Monday. That's why I was late getting home. The poor thing has led a traumatic life. She's skittish."

"Not a good sign. She may never socialize."

"She will. I can tell. She doesn't hide as much as she did at first. She loves Robin's bed."

Kathryn cleared her throat loudly. "And after next Monday?"

"She won't be a problem, Mom. I've thought this out. Cats don't need much space. She'll stay in my room until I find another place."

"That could take a while."

For the first time, though, Molly realized that she would be looking alone. "No," she said sadly. "It's just me. A smaller place will be easy to find." But it wouldn't have the character of this one. "I keep hoping Mr. Field will relent." Kathryn wasn't listening. "Are you sure nothing hurts, Mom?"

"I'm sure."

"Want a hot bath?"

"No. It was a nothing accident. I wasn't watching where I drove."

Molly guessed it was more than that. Kathryn's emotions had to be frayed. Wanting to see Marjorie was telling in and of itself.

"I'd better call Dad and let him know you're here before someone finds the car and reports you missing."

When Kathryn didn't argue, she made the call. Charlie was groggy until the words *crashed the car*, at which point he grew alarmed. "Put your mother on," he said.

Kathryn waved her hand no, but Molly insisted, knowing her father wouldn't rest until he heard Kathryn's voice.

"There," Molly teased when her parents were done. "That wasn't so bad." At Kathryn's look, she offered to make tea.

Kathryn seemed ready to protest, but stopped. "That'd be nice."

Molly pointed her toward a chair, but when she headed for the kitchen, Kathryn followed. At least there were no cartons here, which would mean a late night packing on Monday. For now, though, Robin's tea was still haphazardly piled in the cabinet.

Kathryn smiled sadly. "Your sister loved tea."

"I keep trying different ones, thinking that somehow I'll reach her." After studying the choices, Molly removed a box. "I'm making you jasmine chamomile. It's a stress reliever."

"I don't feel stressed."

"You're stressed."

"Not right now. Will you have some?"

Molly put water in the kettle. "No. I've tried, Mom, but tea isn't my thing. I'm not Robin."

"You don't need to be Robin."

"But you love her."

"I love you, too."

"Not like you love Robin."

"That's true," Kathryn admitted, but her eyes were steady. "No mother loves her children the same. Each one is different."

"Robin has so many good points."

"Had," Kathryn corrected quietly.

It was a sobering moment for Molly, a sign of how far her mother had come. Kathryn's use of the past tense was a nod to reality. A tiny part of Molly would have fought it, if Kathryn hadn't gone on.

"You have your own good points."

"Y'think?" One minute Molly believed it, the next she did not.

"Robin saw your strengths. She envied you. Remember what she wrote?"

How could Molly not? She had read *Why My Sister Is Wrong* many times now. It wasn't what she had thought to find in any journal of Robin's—and made her all the sadder that Robin wasn't there to argue.

She dropped the tea in a mug, but by the time she covered it with simmering water, Kathryn had wandered off. Listening, Molly heard a small, upsetting sound. She followed it to Robin's room, where Kathryn was weeping, one arm wrapped around her middle and the other hand pressed to her mouth. Molly hugged her from behind.

"Who would have imagined . . . ," Kathryn gulped between sobs.

Molly waited until she quieted, which was when she noticed the cat, sitting alert in the middle of the bed, eyeing Kathryn warily.

Kathryn eyed it back. "Did this cat come with a name?"

"No. I'm calling her Sprite."

"You know that once you name her, she's yours."

Molly did. But this cat was hers anyway. She had come to her on the evening Robin left—maybe even at the exact same *minute*, though Molly would never know for sure. She did know she wouldn't be giving the creature away.

Kathryn wasn't wild about cats; but with the rest of the room dismantled, the bed would have to be shared. Plumping up pillows, Molly settled her against the headboard. The cat didn't budge.

Wanting to give Kathryn a little time alone with memories of Robin, Molly went back to the kitchen. After a while, she returned and sat cross-legged on the quilt.

"How do you feel?" she asked, watching Kathryn drink her tea.

"Better. It's strange. I don't feel Robin here. This is her bed in her room, but the cottage is you."

"It always was."

"I'm sorry you have to move. Want me to call Mr. Field for you?"

Among all the possibilities for stalling the move, Molly had considered that one but had ruled it out. "It won't do any good," she said. As desperate as she felt, she was trying to be realistic. "He has compelling reasons for needing to sell. I have to move anyway. Robin and I were splitting the rent. I can't handle it myself."

"I'll help."

"No. He needs to sell and I need to get over it. It won't be any easier in six months or a year."

Kathryn folded her legs sideways, then looked around again. "This place suits you. Like Snow Hill." Growing pensive, she sipped her tea. "Snow Hill never made Robin happy."

Molly knew it, but was surprised by her mother's admission. "What would have?"

"A week ago, I'd have said she would race for another few years, then coach."

"Like Peter? Were you thinking of him?"

"Not consciously."

"He's a nice person, Mom. Lonely."

"His fault."

"But still lonely. I think he was deeply affected by seeing Robin."

Kathryn was quiet. "Yes," she finally said. "I think so. Meeting Robin was probably something he needed to do at some point in his life. This gave him an excuse. Your call dragged him here. Men are funny that way."

"What way?"

"They're not proactive when it comes to emotional things. If they can avoid something tough, they do."

"Dad doesn't."

"Dad's an exception."

"David Harris doesn't. He could have run right past Robin and just phoned for help. Do you still wish he had?"

Kathryn was a minute answering. "No. He wanted to help. If Robin's problem had been less severe, he might have saved her life. He had no way of knowing how bad it was."

"He's a nice guy. Very honest. And reasonable."

"Unlike Nick."

"Oh, Nick is so in love with Robin he can't *see* straight."

"Are you defending him?" Kathryn asked.

"Dismissing him, more like," Molly remarked. "But maybe I am. Defending him, I mean. I let him use me."

Kathryn sank deeper into the pillows, setting the mug on her middle. "You were too busy living in Robin's shadow. Too busy thinking that everything she had was the best."

"Did you know he was still in love with her?"

"The cynical part of me guessed it."

"But you do know it was one-sided. She didn't want him."

"Yes," Kathryn said. "I know that now." Finishing her tea, she put it on the nightstand, slid lower, and reached for Molly.

Molly wanted to think about that particular concession and about other things her mother was saying. But stretching out in her mother's warmth, she was lulled. She was Kathryn's daughter, would always be that. The fit seemed better.

She didn't hear another thing until morning. Kathryn slept on. Gratified to be able to give her mother this additional brief respite, Molly crept out of the room.

KATHRYN HADN'T BEEN TO THE NURSING HOME IN SIX weeks. As Molly drove her there now, she kept telling herself that Marjorie wouldn't know the difference; but when the rambling Victorian came into view, she felt unbearable guilt. And fear. She wanted her mother to be the mother she knew. She wanted—*needed*—that woman.

The nurse at the front desk lit up, worsening her guilt. "It's good to *see* you, Mrs. Snow. It's been a while. Sunday brunch is always special. Will you be joining us today?"

"Oh, I don't think so," Kathryn said. She wasn't sure how she would feel seeing her mother, and then there was Robin. Charlie would be with her by now, but Kathryn had to get to the hospital herself. This was the longest she had been away from Robin's bedside.

Of course, Robin wouldn't know. Kathryn just wanted to be with her daughter during the little time they had left.

"Go on up then," the nurse said. "She's in the lounge."

Trying to keep pace with Molly on the stairs, Kathryn felt stiff. A week of sitting would do that, and driving into a tree hadn't helped. Determinedly, she lifted one foot after the next.

Halfway up, she stopped. Last time she was here, the pain had been intense. Now it all rushed back—the sadness, the hurt, the profound sense of loss.

"Mom?" Molly asked softly from the step above.

"I can't do this," Kathryn whispered, gripping the bannister tightly.

Molly was suddenly beside her. "You can. She's your mother. You love her."

"She isn't the same as she was."

"Neither are you. Neither am I. Neither is Robin. We all change, Mom."

Kathryn eyed her beseechingly. "But will she know it's me?"

"Does it matter?"

Simple logic. How to argue? Love was love. Kathryn loved Robin, though her mind had ceased to function. In its finality, that was oddly easier than this. Marjorie might know her. Or she might not. But yes, she was still her mother.

Taking strength from Molly, Kathryn started up again. The instant they came within sight of the lounge, she spotted Marjorie, looking so pretty—so *peaceful*—that Kathryn might have thought she didn't belong there. Eyes half-closed, Marjorie sat alone on a love seat, listening to soft church music. Her gray hair shone, one side tucked behind an ear to show off a pretty pearl earring. She wore a baby blue sweater and white slacks. A small smile played in the corners of her mouth.

Heart melting, Kathryn crossed the room and, kneeling, took her hand. "Mom?"

Marjorie opened her eyes. They grew bright with a small burst of pleasure. "Well, hello."

Kathryn wanted to believe the pleasure was from recognition, but she remembered what Molly had said. Anyone new would generate this little spark. It was an ingrained social response.

"It's me, Mom. Kathryn."

Marjorie gave her a puzzled smile. Babies were like that, Kathryn realized. They wanted to please even before they knew what they were doing. Robin had been that way. And Kathryn had loved her for trying.

And so, in that moment, she loved her mother. "You look beautiful, Mom," she said. "Were you enjoying the Sunday music?"

Marjorie's face was blank. "Sunday?"

"Church. We used to go—you, me, and Dad. Do you remember the music from church?"

Marjorie considered that for a time before saying, "I sing."

"You *do*," Kathryn replied with enthusiasm, as though she were talking to a child. Retrieval of even a tiny thread of memory was encouraging. "You were in the choir for a while. You *loved* singing."

"I didn't know Nana sang in the choir," Molly remarked.

"Oh yes. She did for the longest time. My father and I loved watching her."

"Why'd she stop?"

Kathryn hesitated. She hadn't discussed this with her

mother in years, but it might elicit a response. Watching Marjorie closely, she said, "I got pregnant."

"But you were with Dad by then. So who knew?"

"Mom did. It bothered her."

"But she *loved* Robin."

"She came around," Kathryn said, her own memory jogged. "There was a watershed moment right before my wedding. Remember that, Mom? I was running around trying to pack, because Charlie and I were moving. I had bad morning sickness, and I was scared of marriage, scared of having a baby, scared of leaving home." Marjorie appeared to be listening—finding her daughter's voice familiar, Kathryn hoped. "So many changes in such a short period of time. I accused you of wanting me gone. You said I was wrong—that you wanted me *there*—that you didn't *want* this change in our lives."

Marjorie smiled but didn't speak. Recognition? Hard to know.

"What did you say?" Molly asked.

"We went back and forth, each of us saying things that were increasingly dumb."

"Like what?"

Kathryn hadn't thought about it in years, yet the words rushed back. "She said I was denying her unconditional pride. I said she was denying me unconditional love. She said I had been careless and unthinking. I said she was old-fashioned. Stupid things, but we let it all out. Then it was done. We just sat there looking at each other, feeling a bond that we couldn't describe." There was actually more, Kathryn realized. When the dust settled, they talked reasonably about the inevitability of change, the idea that they had to let go what might have been and accept what was.

Kathryn thought about Robin and felt a knot in her belly. In the next instant, though, the knot loosened. *Let go what might have been . . . accept what is.*

She pressed Marjorie's hand to her throat. "You slept in my bed that night, just like Molly did with me last night. Do you remember that, Mom?" Marjorie's face was blank, but sweet—oh so sweet—and as familiar to Kathryn as her own. "But you don't," she mused quietly. "I have to accept that. So much to accept this week." She studied her mother's hand, fingers slender as ever. "Molly told you about Robin. How does a mother bury her child?" She looked up, pleading. "How, Mom? Please tell me. I need help."

"I . . . I . . . ," Marjorie stammered, upset and clearly not knowing why.

Molly touched her grandmother's shoulder, but far from being reassured, Marjorie looked at her worriedly. "Do I know you?"

"I'm Molly."

Marjorie's eyes flew back to Kathryn. "Who are you?"

"Kathryn. Your daughter. Molly's mother." When Marjorie didn't react, Kathryn said, "I grow plants. I used to bring carloads of them to your house. They were from Snow Hill." Peaceful again, Marjorie was listening—ample encouragement for Kathryn to continue talking. "You should see Snow Hill, Mom. It's gotten even bigger since you were there last. We're about to do a major rebuild of the main structure—it's that successful—and we've spread into some of the acreage I never thought we'd use. Rows and rows of trees and plants."

"Plants?" Marjorie asked.

"Plants are what we do. They're who we are. I'm good with plants. Molly's even better. She's my heir apparent."

"By default," Molly murmured.

Startled, Kathryn looked up. "Why do you say that?"

"Robin was your heir apparent."

"Not when it came to Snow Hill. Snow Hill was always yours." She frowned when Molly looked surprised. "You didn't know that?"

"No."

"Plants?" Marjorie asked again.

"And trees," Kathryn said gently. "We sell pine trees and maple trees. And weeping willows, cherries, Russian olives, and oaks."

"I'm a shade person," Molly argued softly. "I work behind the scenes. I couldn't run Snow Hill the way you do."

"Change is good," Kathryn said. That was the day's lesson, as fine a Sunday sermon as any.

"You said you'd never retire."

"I may have been wrong."

"What would you *do* without Snow Hill?"

"I don't know." She hadn't thought of it before now. Exhausted as she was, though, the idea held appeal. What was it Robin had written in *Who Am I?* about Marjorie urging her to just BE? Another lesson there, too.

"Nothing is imminent. But you and Chris managed just fine without me this week. If Erin took over some of what your father does, he and I could travel. We could sleep late. Maybe focus on developing a Web-based Snow Hill. Who knows."

"Willows?" Marjorie asked, bringing Kathryn back.

"They're beautiful trees, Mom. They like water. Look," she pointed, "there's one way over there by the stream. See how low the branches dip, and when they sway in a breeze . . ."

The conversation was so easy and her mother's curiosity so innocent that Kathryn felt a new calm. Born of a night at Molly's place, reinforced by the woman Marjorie was now, Kathryn couldn't fight it. Calm was good. Some battles couldn't be won.

Again, she thought of Robin. If ever there was a fight that couldn't be won, it was in that hospital room. Her Robin wasn't there anymore. Accepting it—grieving and moving on to a place where the memories were good—suddenly seemed better. Charlie knew that. So did Molly and Chris. Even Marjorie did, whether she remembered it or not. Robin had always been a ball of energy. She wouldn't want to lie in bed doing nothing.

Kathryn talked quietly with her mother for several more minutes. Without knowing, Marjorie *had* helped. But Robin was Kathryn's child, and the final decision was hers to make. Much as she had cursed that fact in the last few days, she saw it differently now. Now it was about freeing Robin. That was a gift.

She didn't speak as she left. She would be back to see Marjorie soon, very soon. Before then, she faced a challenge that she couldn't put off. She waited until they were on the road, then asked Molly to tell her everything she knew about organ donation.

chapter 21

AFTER NEARLY A WEEK OF ENDLESS WAITING, A SIN-
gle phone call got things going with unsettling speed.
Agents from the organ bank were at the hospital within
hours, and though they were every bit as compassionate as
Molly had been told, the meeting wasn't an easy one. Her
parents and Chris, and even Erin, looked stoic; she herself
felt weak.

The final decision is the family's, the agents kept saying.
We won't rush you. But how not to feel urgency? The instant the papers were signed giving these people access
to Robin's medical records, there would be no turning
back.

Molly had been the one pushing for organ donation, but

there were moments when she would have given anything to slow things down—because what no one said, but everyone in the room knew, was that once the mechanism for harvesting Robin's organs was put into place, life support had to end.

The doctors promised that death would come quickly and without pain. Once the machines keeping Robin alive were turned off, it was final. For all her new insight, Molly had trouble accepting that.

Not so Kathryn. Composed while Molly was tearful, she listened quietly to everything the agents said. She asked questions, perhaps with a tremor in her voice, but she never broke down. She nodded her understanding when the agents talked of the emotions the family might feel, but declined their offer of counseling. Having made the decision, she was committed.

Molly envied her that. Her mother had come a long way from those first horrifying hours. So had Molly, but she still had a ways to go. Her stomach was knotting and her legs were weak—classic symptoms of hitting the wall. She tried to dredge up Robin's mantra, but couldn't quite remember it. Her eyes were glued on her mother.

Kathryn held the pen, hesitating for an instant while she looked at Charlie, then at Chris and Molly, but her message was one of conviction. *We have to do this. We love Robin too much to not let go.* Her face was pale, and though her eyes reflected agony, they were clearer than they had been all week. Finally, she lowered them and signed the papers.

Moments later, the Snows were alone in the conference room. No one spoke. Molly's heart was breaking. For all her talk of accepting what couldn't be changed, she didn't want her sister to die.

Chris was the first to speak. His voice was low. "When will they do it?"

Kathryn pressed her lips together, then nodded. "Later today. When we're ready." Seeming to understand Molly's regret, she reached for her hand. Her voice was light. "So many different organs they can use. But they won't take her heart. That'll always be ours."

"I don't want this," Molly breathed.

"None of us does, but it's one of the few things we know Robin wanted. She would like knowing she was helping other people. There's a huge need. You told me that. How can we not do this?"

"But it means—"

"Robin can't come back," she said, giving Molly's hand a little shake. "She can only lie senseless in that room down the hall. I've been with her all week, Molly. I've talked and begged and demanded. I've *prayed*. But she doesn't respond. She can't. And that's unfair. It's not the way she wanted to live. And then there's us. She wouldn't want us holding an endless vigil. She would want us *doing* things. She would want us at Snow Hill." Her voice softened. "Turning off the machines is a technicality. Her mind is already gone. Her spirit lingers, but it's tied to her bed because we are. If we want it free, we have to do this for her."

Molly heard an echo of her father and saw no inconsistency. Yes, Robin's soul was in heaven. Her spirit, though, was different. It was the part of her that lived on in everyone she left behind. In that regard, what Kathryn said made sense.

Still, Molly didn't feel her mother's calm. When Kathryn rose to return to Robin's room, Molly took the elevator to the ground floor and pulled out her phone.

Fifteen minutes later, David joined her on a stone bench in the patio. "I feel responsible," she said after telling him of the papers Kathryn had signed. "I was the one who pushed for organ donation. Tell me I did the right thing."

Five days and what seemed an eon ago, David had asked her the same thing. Taking her hand, he returned the support. "You did the right thing. Besides, it was what Robin wanted. You simply passed on her wishes and gave your mother information. The final decision was hers."

"But is it the right one?" Molly asked. She would never forget that moment when the family was suddenly alone in the conference room—as if, with the signing of those papers, Robin was no longer *theirs*.

"The only issue is timing," David said, soothing and calm in his own right. "Would you have felt better waiting?"

Yes, she thought. *Anything* to keep Robin with them.

But, of course, that was wrong. David had called her practical, and when the smoke cleared, she was. "Knowing there was no hope? No. This has been hanging over our heads since they declared her brain dead." Turning off the machines. Ending her life. "Why am I having trouble now?"

"Because you love your sister," he said.

She did. She couldn't recall the envy, the resentment, even what she might have called hatred at times. Right now, there was only love.

"You aren't the only one," David said. Opening his backpack, he pulled out a sheaf of papers.

Nick. Molly knew it before she even read the front page. *The Heart of a Winner: A Biography of Robin Snow.*

"Not the most profound title," David said, "and this is only a small part of what he has, but it's beautifully written."

Molly turned to the foreword. *Fame can be cruel,* he wrote. *The world of sports is filled with stories of stars who soar one minute and fall the next. In some cases, their bodies fail them, and they limp silently into oblivion. In other cases, the burnout is mental and the legacy more tarnished.*

Then there are those like Robin Snow. She ran her first race at five, her first marathon at fifteen, and in the years between and since, she fought to do well. At times, she was so nervous before a race that she was physically sick, at others so hampered by a physical injury that the only thing keeping her going was sheer grit. She claimed she wasn't the best runner, only the most determined. History supports her in that. For nearly every marathon she won, she had been a runner-up the year before. She always came back tougher, stronger, and more focused.

*Ask about her greatest achievements, and she'll list San
Francisco, Boston, and L.A. Ask about her most satisfying ones,
and she'll tell you about the young girl in Oklahoma who had
only run alone along rural roads until Robin ran with her.
She'll tell you about jumping in to coach a running club in
New Mexico that lost its coach to breast cancer two weeks before a major race.*

Robin Snow was an inspiration . . .

Molly put down the paper and burst into tears.

Drawing her close, David let her cry until her tears
slowed, and even then he didn't speak. Sitting there with
him on the stone bench, she began to let her heartache go.
Inspiration was a positive word.

She was taking strength from it when he murmured,
"Here comes your mom."

Quickly drawing back, she wiped her eyes and glanced
across the patio. Kathryn was near enough to have seen
David holding her.

Coming closer, though, Kathryn didn't look upset.
"Scoot over," she said softly and, perching on the edge of
the bench, extended a hand across Molly to David. "I owe
you an apology."

Molly vividly recalled Tuesday morning's scene.

"I've had misgivings, Mrs. Snow," David said. "I caused
a hard week for you and your family."

Kathryn waved a hand *no*. "The week was a gift. It
gave us something we wouldn't otherwise have had. We
learned a lot—about each other, even about Robin. We

needed the time to come to terms with her death. You gave us that. Thanks are inadequate, but they're all I have right now."

For forgiving David—for *accepting* him—Molly had never loved her mother more than at that moment. With renewed confidence, she held out the papers. "You need to read these, Mom."

When Kathryn saw Nick's name, she frowned. "Is it for the paper?"

"No. He gave them to David to read. Long story," she said, seeing Kathryn's confusion, "but they say something important."

Lifting the pages, Kathryn read silently at first, then softly aloud. *"Robin Snow was an inspiration to athletes around the world. No born champion, she struggled to overcome the terror of increasingly fierce competition and the rising pressure of running among America's elite. As she approached the Olympics and what would have been a triumphant high in her career, she was the first to cite the many advantages she had. Her family was at the top of the list."* Kathryn's voice cracked. Taking a breath, she read on. *"She considered their support so crucial to her success that when she met a talented runner without the backing of family, she either found surrogates in the running community or filled in herself. She was in close contact with more than a dozen young women whom she had mentored this way."*

Kathryn looked at Molly. "Is this true?"

Molly was as surprised as her mother. "It must be," she realized. "Some of her e-mail is amazing. Robin was worshipped by those girls."

"I want to ask them to the funeral," Kathryn said, swallowing the last syllable of the word.

Molly might have started crying again if she hadn't been focused on Nick. "Could you tell how much he loved her? Is that tragic or what?"

"And those are only the first pages," David said. "He describes races and events—and the details are accurate. I checked them out. But when he writes about Robin's character, his words glow."

Kathryn was turning a page when she paused. "Why did Nick give these to you?"

"Because my family is in publishing. He's hoping I'll be a link."

"I thought you were a teacher."

"I am. But my family is well-known to people in publishing. Nick made the connection."

"In his way, he's suffering as much as we are," Molly declared. She was fascinated by the level of caring she had found in his words. "Maybe it's even worse for him. His feelings were unrequited. But they were real. All those hopes and dreams—just gone. He needed to talk about Robin, and we wouldn't listen."

"Will the rest of the world?" Kathryn asked. When she looked at David, he raised a brow.

"He knows how to write a gripping story."

"What would your family do with these?"

"Nothing at all until the whole bio is done. If they like it, they would buy excerpts—but only if you're comfortable with that."

"What say do we have?" Kathryn asked with a hint of defeat.

"Total say."

"I have no sway with your family."

David smiled reassuringly. "I do. My mother may not be on the corporate payroll, but she's a power to contend with. Anything she vetoes is out, and she'll veto anything I argue against. I'm still her baby. I'd play on that in a heartbeat if you're not given final approval of anything that makes it into print."

Molly knew it was way too early to love David. What with losing Robin and the house and even her friendship with Nick, she was probably a pathetically needy person who might fall for *anyone*. But David didn't seem like anyone she had ever known. He was a quality person who was already invested in her family, and that meant a lot to her. Family mattered. Even Robin saw that.

A SHORT TIME LATER, MOLLY AND KATHRYN WENT BACK inside. Their arms were linked. In this darkest of hours, Molly actually felt heartened. "Thank you," she told her mother. "You were good with him."

"I meant what I said. He gave us a gift. It's been a week filled with gifts."

"I'm amazed you can say that."

Kathryn squeezed her elbow. "Who kept harping on what Robin would want? She loved giving gifts. He's one himself, by the way. Not only what he did, but who he is. He's been there for you in ways I have not."

At that moment, Molly couldn't blame her mother for anything. "You've had other things on your mind."

"That's no excuse. I depend on you, Molly. I may not have said it enough, may not have *realized* it. I do now."

"You're feeling alone," Molly reasoned. And she was the only daughter left. *By default* was the phrase that came to mind, as it had that morning with Marjorie. First daughter *by default*.

"Because I'm losing Robin? No. I've taken you for granted. You've always been my backup at work. And with Nana. You were there for her when I couldn't take the pain."

"Easier for me. I'm not her daughter."

"But how selfish of me? It wasn't about Thomas. It was about me not dealing well with loss. I've grown up this week. You, too."

Molly wanted to think so. Her mother's confidence in her meant the world. She still wasn't sure about taking over Snow Hill, had never seen herself as a leader. But if Kathryn thought she could do it, maybe she could. Then again, "Perhaps it's the clothes."

"No, Molly. Don't put yourself down. It's what's inside." Quietly, Kathryn added, "So there's another gift from Robin."

"My growing up?"

"My seeing it."

"But my growing up, too. You're right. I had issues with Robin."

"All sisters have issues."

"But I always loved her."

Kathryn squeezed her arm. Glancing at her, Molly saw that though her eyes were on the elevator numbers, they were filled with tears.

Molly kept her arm through Kathryn's, giving and taking strength, even after they reached Robin's floor. Her father, Chris, and Erin were standing in the hall near her room. Just as Molly and Kathryn reached them, the door opened and Peter Santorum came out.

Molly gasped.

"I called him," Kathryn explained softly. "It was the right thing to do."

The gesture erased whatever residual guilt Molly had felt bringing him here in the first place. "Thank you," she whispered. It wasn't only Peter, but everything Kathryn had said. So much mending in the midst of a nightmare. Perhaps crises did that.

With a final squeeze, Kathryn released her arm. Crossing to Peter, she gave him a hug, and Molly was grateful for that, too. He looked devastated.

If Kathryn said anything to him, she didn't hear, because it was her turn to hug Peter, her turn to comfort. Whether they would ever see him after this was irrelevant. For now he was in their lives. Robin would be pleased.

THE ROOM WAS QUIET. THE HEART MONITOR STILL BEEPED and the respirator made its blowing sounds, but Molly no longer heard them. It was her mother's calm that she felt. *Loving . . . letting go . . .* fragments of thought—oh so valid. Still, when Kathryn smoothed Robin's hair from her brow, kissed her cheek, and said ever so softly, "We're all here, angel—you can go now—it's all right," Molly burst into tears. She wasn't the only one crying. But the sound of weeping didn't dim the click of the switch when Kathryn turned it to OFF.

As the sough of air stopped, the doctors and nurses stepped forward. Barely breathing herself, Molly watched Robin closely. They had been told she might take a residual breath, but she did not. Her heart continued to beat for a minute, drawing final waves on the monitor, before the lack of oxygen took its toll. Beeping gave way to a steady hum; the monitor line went flat.

Muffling sobs, Molly watched her mother lean forward and put her cheek to Robin's. Her shoulders shook. Charlie went to her and held her away while the doctor listened for a heartbeat, turned off monitors, gently removed the breathing tube. Then the medical team left, giving Robin to her family for a few final moments.

Without the tube taped to her mouth, she looked more

like the old Robin—but deathly still and, in that, not like Robin at all. Standing at the side of the bed, Molly took her hand. It was still warm. She didn't know how long she held it, but Charlie had to physically ease her fingers away before she finally let go. He led her out, giving Kathryn a few minutes alone. Then it was done.

chapter 22

WORD SPREAD QUICKLY. BY THE TIME KATHRYN AND Charlie reached the house, a small cortege of cars was already there. After a week of near solitude, Kathryn welcomed the company. It kept her from thinking about the procedure taking place in the operating room. Easier at that moment to share memories of her firstborn.

Robin would have loved the gathering. There was food aplenty, and more than enough help in the kitchen so that she might have partied to her heart's delight. Kathryn moved graciously from friend to neighbor to Snow Hill employee. Someone refilled her coffee, another gave her a muffin. Normally the one to serve, she let herself be helped.

Peter's presence was a comfort, rounding out Robin's family if only in Kathryn's own mind. She introduced him to others as an old friend, and his nod said he liked that. Having no stories to tell about Robin, he seemed content to listen. With so many people needing the catharsis of talk, it worked well.

Chris and Erin had stopped home for Chloe, and Kathryn held the baby for a time as she walked from one room to the other. Chloe embodied innocence and hope. She was too young to remember today; but as she grew, Kathryn would tell her about her Aunt Robin. She would retell some of the stories told today, take out pictures, even read aloud. *She ran her first race at five, her first marathon at fifteen, and in the years between and since, she fought to do well. At times, she was so nervous before a race that she was physically sick, at others so hampered by a physical injury that the only thing keeping her going was sheer grit. She claimed she wasn't the best runner, only the most determined. History supports her in that.*

Written journals, computer files, an authorized bio—there were ways to keep Robin alive. Kathryn was just starting to see that.

When the baby started to fuss, she returned her to Chris. That was when she spotted David. Molly was introducing him to a group from Snow Hill, but Kathryn had a more important introduction to make. Taking his hand, she led him to Charlie.

How to introduce him? David Harris—Good Samaritan—Molly's friend—our future son-in-law? She left off the last, though it had already taken root in her mind. Molly might have just met him, but Kathryn was as sure of David as she had been of Charlie thirty-two years before. Both had happened fast and in trying times. Moreover, with Charlie coming at the very start of Robin's life and David at the very end, there was a certain symmetry.

As Charlie talked with David, she saw Nick come in the front door looking devastated. She quickly put a hand on Charlie's arm.

Charlie followed her gaze. "Want me to deal?"

No. Kathryn had to do this. As she wove between groups to the door, she thought of how Nick had used the family. But as he stood here now, regarding her through pain-filled eyes, he didn't look as much like a user as a man who had lost someone near and dear. She let it go. Wasn't that the lesson of the week? Anger accomplished nothing. Denial was a crutch. Nick may not be the man Kathryn had wanted for Robin, nor had Robin loved him, but he had loved her.

She stood before him for only an instant, smiling sadly, before opening her arms. He was suffering. Molly was right about that. And a mother's job was to comfort.

Nick was complex, definitely ambitious. But then, hadn't Robin been, too? She might have thrown up before races, but she ran, won, and came back for more. She wanted to be the best. That didn't make her a bad person.

Same with Nick.

"I'm sorry," he said quietly.

For more than just Robin's death, Kathryn chose to believe. "I saw some of what you've written about Robin, Nick. It's very beautiful. We'll be needing an obituary. Perhaps you could work with us on that?"

He didn't have to say the words. The gratitude on his face was answer enough.

THE PHONE RANG. AT CHARLIE'S BECKONING, KATHRYN took the call in the den. It was the hospital calling to say that the harvesting was done, that organs were on their way to recipients, and that Robin was being discharged.

It was a bittersweet moment. But as she hung up the phone, the reality of the next step hit. There would be a meeting at the funeral home that evening to make plans for the next few days. Kathryn dreaded it all. She couldn't bear to think of lowering Robin into the ground. And a future without her? Hard to accept. But it had to be done.

One look at Charlie, bless him, and he read her mind. Gesturing her to the desk, he removed an envelope from the drawer. "This came Friday. It's renewal time for Robin's CD. I always call the bank to get her the best rate, so the total has grown. This holds a portion of her winnings over the last five years. Take a look."

Removing the statement, Kathryn was startled. "So much?"

"There's more in stocks and bonds."

Another reality hit Kathryn. "She'll never use any of it."

"Not directly. A track scholarship in her name might be nice. Maybe even a house."

It was a minute before Kathryn followed. Then she smiled. "Robin would *like* that."

Motioning to her to stay, Charlie left the den. He returned with Molly. Kathryn handed her the bank statement. Molly read it. She looked puzzled, which made Kathryn's words even sweeter.

"Did I not see Dorie McKay in the living room?" When Molly remained confused, Kathryn touched her face. Sweetly naïve, far too self-effacing, but steady and strong— her youngest child deserved this. "A gift from your sister," she said softly, thinking as clearly now as she ever had. "So often this week, you said you loved Robin. Well, there's something Robin couldn't say back, but something I know. I remember the first time she saw you. You and I were in the hospital, you only hours old and swaddled in a nursery blanket, but Robin wanted to *see* you, she said. When I started to unwrap you, she pushed my hand aside and insisted on doing it herself. The awe on her face was something to behold. She was opening a special present, the best one she'd ever had—her baby sister." Kathryn took her chin. "She loved you, Molly. She would want you to have your house."

Molly's eyes filled with joy, sadness, tears. Drawing her close, Kathryn smiled. Here was a glimpse of the future, a tangible gift that she would see in her daughter's pleasure every day of the week. Robin wouldn't just like this. She would *love* it.

And so would Kathryn.

MOLLY STAYED IN THE DEN FOR A TIME. SOME OF ROBIN'S friends in the other rooms were tearful, but she couldn't get a grip on her emotions. Kathryn stayed with her until Charlie returned from talking with the realtor.

"No promises," he said, "but she knows her job. She'll do the math and come up with a fair offer for Terrance Field. If anyone can make this happen, Dorie will. She's a persuasive woman."

Molly felt overwhelmed. "So much happening."

"Some say life is a roller coaster. I see it as riding a wave. You're out there on your board and everything is calm—"

"Excuse me," she broke in. "You never surfed."

"I did," he insisted, all innocence. "Well, I tried. I was never particularly good at it, but I did get the drift. You're out there in a huge ocean, straddling that board. The water is smooth, but deceptive. You know the waves are moving, and you watch and wait, and suddenly you feel that little shift underneath. You stand up. You totter, but regain your balance, then give yourself to something far bigger than you are. You have no control. You're just along for the ride, swept downwater so fast it takes your breath. Then it's done. Smooth water again."

Molly still wasn't sure he had ever surfed, but the

analogy cleared her mind. The ocean, like the earth, was soothing.

She hugged him. "I love you." His arms returned the words. When she pulled back, she took a deep breath. "I . . . am going outside," she said, hitching her chin toward the door that led from the den to the backyard.

"Want company?"

She shook her head and kissed his cheek. Then she let herself out. She didn't have to go far. Her parents owned acres here, too, but the lawn itself wasn't big. The grass had grown over scars left by the swing set; but she saw the swings now, backed by the large sugar maple they had tapped as kids. She remembered Robin stirring the pitiful little bit of sap they had collected as it boiled into syrup. Robin couldn't have been more than ten, Chris seven, Molly five. Molly was always the first to taste the sweet, thick stuff—licking it off the large wooden spoon that her sister offered to her with pride.

And the swing? Robin pushing her in the little bucket before she was old enough for the big kid swing. Robin holding her legs while she crossed the monkey bars. Robin with her arms out at the bottom of the slide, waiting to catch her.

Syrup, swings, and slides. Vases, hair clips, sweaters. Self-confidence. A house. Robin had loved her. Realizing that, Molly was humbled.

Needing to be where she felt the strongest, she took her keys from her pocket.

"Where you going?" came a quiet voice from behind.

Without turning, she smiled. David. "I need a little grounding," she said.

"Rephrase, please?"

She turned. "I haven't been to the greenhouse today. I'm sure everything's fine; other people watered. But I need my plants."

"Can I drive you there?"

She held up her keys. "Got my own car."

But he shook his head, quick and sure. "You shouldn't be alone."

She wouldn't be alone. Her plants would be there. So would her cats.

Then again, if the greenhouse was what kept her sane, David needed to see it.

ALL WAS QUIET. SUNDAY HOURS HAD ENDED, AND THE STAFF had closed up. Unlocking a side door, Molly led David inside. The air was cooler now. In another few weeks, dawn would find frost on the panes. It would melt with the sun, but return thicker as the days grew shorter and the air crisped. But the changes went well beyond fading leaves and harvested fruit. With the end of one season came the promise of another.

Like her father on his wave, Molly was along for the ride.

Slow things down, a frightened little voice cried. So she pulled a bag from the supply corner and dug her hands inside. She didn't speak, simply worked her fingers through the cool earth. No matter what the future held, whether Molly took over Snow Hill or decided to do something else entirely, there would always be this.

Finally feeling better, she looked up. "Too much, too fast. I needed this." When she pulled out her hands, every nail was lined with dirt. "If you were hoping for pretty, you're in for a disappointment."

"I'm not disappointed."

Nor was Molly. David's temperament worked here. She sensed it the minute they arrived. Nothing at all about him changed the aura of the place.

Encouraged, she brushed off her hands and showed him around. Her aphelandra was bright with yellow flowers, her catharanthus with pink and white. Moving on, she gestured to a vivid orange bloom. "Hibiscus," she said. "With controlled air and lots of love, we'll keep it blooming for another month or so." She showed him her cactus garden, positioned for the greatest sun. And, of course, her shade plants. "My babies," she said with a fond smile.

A thunk came, followed by a plaintive meow and the scurry of paws as furry bodies flew past. Returning to the corner, Molly found her bag on its side in a spray of spilled dirt. One cat remained. It was Cyrus, an arthritic Maine coon that must have figured he couldn't move fast enough to try to escape. Carrying him to a bench, Molly settled him on her lap and stroked the soft spot between his ears. An old man, he had lived at the nursery since she was a teenager. She wouldn't have him much longer. But he was a sweet thing and, suddenly, making him comfortable mattered. He could do with less space, was even docile enough in his dotage to tolerate a small, skittish cat. The cottage might work really well.

Her cottage. Once the sorrow of the next few days passed, once Robin's things were home with Kathryn— where they were meant to be—Molly would feel the excitement. She would unpack her own things, rearrange furniture, even make some of the improvements Terrance Field had planned. Knowing that memories of Robin would always be there gave her a deep sense of warmth.

A new sound interrupted her thoughts. David had found a broom and was cleaning up the spilled dirt.

Touched, she said a fast, "You don't need to do that."

He simply smiled and continued to sweep.

acknowledgments

My deepest thanks go to Eileen Wilson for sharing her knowledge of the medical issues faced by the Snow family and to Shelley Lewis for helping make Snow Hill a credible plant nursery. Instances where I've strayed from pure fact should be blamed on literary license, not on either of these two wonderful women.

I am eternally grateful to Phyllis Grann, whose editorial guidance has improved my writing immeasurably, and to my agent, Amy Berkower, for her unstinting support.

As always, I am blessed by my family, which helps me in countless untold ways.

ALSO BY BARBARA DELINSKY

FAMILY TREE

For as long as she can remember, Dana Clarke has longed for the stability of home and family. Now she has married a man she adores, and she is about to give birth to their first child. But what should be the happiest day of her life becomes the day her world falls apart. Her daughter is born beautiful and healthy, and, in addition, unmistakably African American in appearance. Dana's determination to discover the truth about her baby's heritage becomes a shocking, poignant journey.

Fiction/978-0-7679-2518-1 (trade)
978-0-307-38846-9 (mass-market)

THE SECRET BETWEEN US

Deborah Monroe and her daughter, Grace, are driving home from a party when their car hits a man running in the dark. Grace was at the wheel, but Deborah sends her home before the police arrive, determined to shoulder the blame for the accident. Her decision then turns into a deception that takes on a life of its own and threatens the special bond between mother and daughter. *The Secret Between Us* is an unforgettable story about the terrible consequences of a lie gone wrong.

Fiction/978-0-7679-2519-8 (trade)
978-0-307-38847-6 (mass-market)

ANCHOR BOOKS
Available at your local bookstore, or visit
www.randomhouse.com